The Engagement Bargain

SHERRI SHACKELFORD

HARLEQUIN® LOVE INSPIRED® HISTORICAL

Recycling programs for this product may not exist in your area.

ISBN-13: 978-0-373-28299-9

The Engagement Bargain

This edition published by arrangement with Love Inspired Books.

www.Harlequin.com

Printed in U.S.A.

"The thought of people believing we are engaged is actually quite amusing."

"Yes," Caleb replied, his voice gruff, though his expression remained hidden from her.

"There'll be no need for me to burden your sister with a houseguest."

"Likely not."

This conversation was embarrassing enough without looking him in the face. He'd echoed her sentiments. Which was perfect. Excellent. Although none of her resolute thinking explained why she became instantly tongue-tied the instant he entered a room.

"Thank you, Mr. McCoy, for everything. Truly. I hope I haven't seemed ungrateful."

It's just that you tie me in knots, and I've never been the tied-in-knots-over-a-man sort of person.

He stuck his hands into his pockets and avoided looking directly at her. "Caleb." He cleared his throat. "I saved your life. I think that puts us on a first-name basis."

"I amend my apology. Thank you, Caleb. And you must call me Anna."

She tripped a bit over the last syllable.

"You have nothing to apologize for, Anna."

Her stomach fluttered. The use of her name lent an air of intimacy to the exchange. She'd never been particularly fond of her name. She liked hearing Caleb say it. She liked hearing him say her name very much.

Sherri Shackelford is an award-winning author of inspirational books featuring ordinary people discovering extraordinary love. A reformed pessimist, Sherri has a passion for storytelling. Her books are fast-paced and heartfelt with a generous dose of humor. She loves to hear from readers at sherri@sherrishackelford.com. Visit her website at sherrishackelford.com.

Books by Sherri Shackelford

Love Inspired Historical

Winning the Widow's Heart
The Marshal's Ready-Made Family
The Cattleman Meets His Match
The Engagement Bargain

Visit the Author Profile page at Harlequin.com for more titles

Therefore if any man be in Christ
he is a new creature: old things are passed away;
behold, all things are become new.

—*2 Corinthians* 5:17

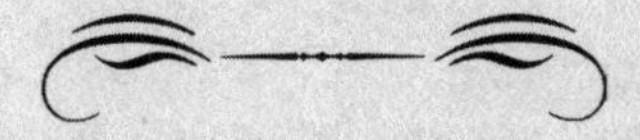

This book is dedicated to Shelley Miller-McCoy
and Renee Franklin, because some women
will always be ahead of their time.

Chapter One

Outside the Savoy Hotel, Kansas City, Kansas 1884

"Remind me again why we're here." Caleb McCoy glared at the growing mass of people jostling into his space.

He didn't like Kansas City. There were too many people in too little area. A man could hardly breathe. He'd much rather be home. Working. The sooner they were on their way home to Cimarron Springs, the better.

His sister, JoBeth, flashed a wry grin. "You're here because my husband obviously forced you."

JoBeth's husband, Garrett, had been unable to accompany his wife to the suffragist rally in support of a sixteenth amendment to the constitution, an amendment for the women's vote.

Jo had been adamant on attending.

Fearing for her safety, Garrett had strong-armed Caleb instead. The opposition to the women's movement had been disruptive on more than one occasion.

The buildings surrounding the tiny grassy square loomed over Caleb like brick-and-mortar sentinels. As the time for the suffragist speech neared, the mood of the crowd had shifted from lazy joviality into restless impatience.

His sister adjusted the gray knit shawl draped around her shoulders against the brittle fall breeze. "As you're quite well aware, *I'm* here for Anna Bishop's speech. This is the closest she's come in the year since we've been corresponding, and the best chance I have to see her in person again. If you'd met her when she traveled through Cimarron Springs last fall, you wouldn't be so surly."

"And yet she never replied to your telegram."

Jo pursed her lips. "It's possible she never received my message. She travels quite a bit."

Caleb mumbled a noncommittal response. Having been raised with five younger brothers, Jo was tougher than tanned leather. She was smart and independent, but vulnerable in the relationships in her life. Fiercely loyal, she naturally expected the same in her friends.

A good head taller than most of the women in the crowd, and several inches above the men, Caleb searched for any sign of dissention. "There's no trouble yet. That's a relief, at least. The sooner this speech is underway, the sooner it's over."

A faint, disgruntled snort sounded beside him.

While his sister had maintained an active correspondence with the prominent suffragist, the fact that Miss Bishop hadn't responded to Jo's most recent telegram had left him uneasy. "What do we know about Miss Bishop, anyway?"

"Well, she's the current darling of the suffragist movement, a sought-after speaker for the cause and an outspoken advocate for women's rights. You can't possibly find fault in any of that."

"An absolute paragon."

"She must be. You wouldn't believe the names people call her or the threats she receives. It's positively nauseating."

A grudging admiration for the suffragist's conviction filtered through his annoyance. His work as a veterinarian introduced him into people's lives during unguarded moments, and he wasn't naive to the injustices women faced. Men who were cruel to animals were just as apt to be violent toward the women and children in their lives. And yet a man who beat his horse was more likely to be censured or fined than a man who abused his wife.

Jo chucked him on the shoulder. "Even if Garrett forced you to accompany me, it's good for you to get out once in a while. You talk to animals more than people."

"That's my job," he grumbled. "Animals don't expect small talk."

Undaunted by his annoyance, she slipped her arm through the crook of his elbow. "I've been saddled with a male escort to an event celebrating the independence of women. You're lucky I'm not insulted."

"Then you should have mentioned that to your overprotective husband."

Jo sighed, her expression rueful. "And let you spend the day alone? Again? You're becoming too set in your ways. You're turning into a hermit. Everyone thinks you're still sweet on Mary Louise."

"I'm not—"

"Shush. Anna is about to speak."

Caleb lifted his eyes heavenward. He wasn't a man who sought attention. He wasn't a man who liked crowds. That didn't make him a recluse. He lived a good life. He had a thriving practice and he enjoyed his work. He'd tried his hand at romance once already. He'd been sweet on Mary Louise, but she'd chosen his younger brother instead. Since then he'd never had the desire to court anyone else.

With four brothers altogether, a confirmed bachelor in the family was hardly a great tragedy.

A smattering of applause drew his attention toward the podium. A nondescript woman in a gray dress took the stage and spoke a few words in a voice that barely carried beyond the first few rows of standing people.

Jo tugged her arm free. "I can't hear a thing. I'm moving closer."

She forged a path through the crowd, and he reluctantly followed. The scores of people pressing nearer had exhausted the oxygen from the space. Yanking on his collar, he sucked in a breath of heavy air. Bodies brushed against him, and sweat dampened the inside band of his hat. As the square had grown congested with late arrivals, the audience had abandoned their picnics and stood. He picked his way over the baskets and blankets littering the ground.

His heel landed in something squishy. Glancing down, he caught sight of the cherry pie he'd just decimated. No one cast an accusing glare in his direction, not that Jo paused long enough for him to apologize. He limped along behind her, dragging his heel through the flattened grass in a futile attempt to clean the sticky filling from his boot.

Near as he could tell, the gathering was an unequal mix of women to men. Judging from the expressions on their faces, the spectators were split between supporters and curiosity seekers. Jo charged ahead and found a spot near the barricades separating the makeshift stage from the audience. A young girl, no more than eight or nine years old in a bright yellow dress and white pinafore, scooted in beside Caleb. She rested her chin on the barricade and stared at the podium.

Caleb frowned.

While the onlookers currently appeared harmless, this wasn't the place for an unattended child. "Shouldn't you be at home? Or in school or something?"

Two dark blond braids rested on the girl's shoulders, and she blinked her solemn gray eyes. "She's the prettiest lady I ever saw." The girl's voice quivered with admiration.

"The prettiest lady *I've* ever *seen*."

"You like her, too?"

"No, that is...."

The woman on the stage announced Anna Bishop, and the girl's face lit up.

Caleb held his explanation. He'd been correcting his younger brothers' speech for years, and the habit was ingrained.

The girl in the yellow dress rose onto the balls of her feet and stared. Caleb followed her gaze and froze. He rubbed his eyes with the heels of his hands and looked again. Anna Bishop couldn't have been much older than her midtwenties or thereabouts. Her dark hair was smoothed away from her face and capped with a pert velvet hat decorated with an enormous teal plumed feather. Her skin was radiant, clear and pale, her cheeks blushed with excitement.

The cartoons he'd seen in the newspapers had depicted Miss Bishop as a dreary spinster with a pointed jaw and beady eyes. Having expected a much less flamboyant person, he fixated on the vibrant details. Her satin dress matched her feathered hat in the same deep, rich shade of turquoise. Rows of brilliant brass buttons created a chevron pattern mimicking a military style. The material at her waist was draped and pulled back into a modest bustle, the flounces lined with rope fringe.

She glanced his way, and he caught a glimpse of her eyes. Blue. Clear, brilliant blue.

His heartbeat skittered before resuming its normal rhythm. Miss Bishop marched up the stairs and exchanged a few words with the woman who'd made the introduction, then faced her audience.

"I am here as a person whose opinions, according to the laws of this nation, are of no merit to my community. I am here as a soldier in a great Civil War to amend this gross injustice," she declared, her lyrical voice pulsating with each word.

As she detailed the importance of the amendment, her eyes flashed, and the passion in her voice swelled. "We live in a country founded on the right of revolution and rebellion on the part of those suffering from intolerable injustice. We cannot fail to recognize the injustices heaped on one half of the population simply because that half is female. The Fifteenth Amendment was progress, but there is more to be done. If the question of race has been removed as a restriction, must the question of gender stand between us and the vote?"

Caleb forgot the crowds, he forgot the little girl standing beside him. He forgot everything but the woman on the stage. She was captivating. Her passion infectious, her furor beguiling.

He leaned forward, his grip on the barricade painful. Loosening his hold, he studied the rapt audience. He wasn't the only person riveted. Jo appeared equally enthralled by the charismatic speaker, as did most of the folks standing near the front. With each subsequent declaration, Miss Bishop's enthusiasm held the audience in captivated silence.

Caleb exhaled a heavy breath and shook his head.

Just his luck. The one woman who'd caught his attention in the time since his childish infatuation with Mary Louise was a suffragist. A woman who, according to the newspaper clippings Jo collected, considered men an unnecessary nuisance and marriage a legalized form of bondage. If Jo hadn't been standing beside him, he'd have hightailed it out of there. The last time he'd noticed a girl, he'd wound up with his heart broken and a whole passel of trouble besides.

"Go home to your mother," a hoarse voice near his left shouted, jarring Caleb from his glum ponderings.

"I think her mother is here!" Another jeered.

"Yeah," a third man bellowed. "How about you do something useful? Find yourself a husband."

A chorus of titters followed.

Caleb yanked upright, blinking as though he'd been awakened from a dream. The growing hostility in the crowd sent a slither of apprehension up spine.

The dissenters remained buried in the confusion of people. Anonymous in their enmity. *Cowards.*

He glanced at the little girl in the yellow dress, then leaned down. "Where are your parents?"

She pointed at the Savoy Hotel across the crowded square.

Caleb tugged on Jo's sleeves and nodded toward the girl. "She shouldn't be here."

Jo's eyes widened, clearly noticing Miss Bishop's young admirer for the first time. "Is she all alone?"

"Near as I can tell."

His sister tightened her bonnet over her dark hair,

tossed a wistful glance at the podium, then sighed. "The atmosphere here is growing hostile. We should take her home."

He stepped back and let Jo pass before him.

A gunshot sounded.

Someone screamed.

Miss Bishop's brilliant turquoise skirts disappeared behind the podium. In an instant the scene descended into chaos. A man tripped and slammed into his back, shoving Caleb forward, and he careened into Jo. They crashed over the barrier. He angled his body and took the brunt of her weight, knocking the wind from his lungs. His ears rang, and he shielded Jo with his arm, searching for the girl in yellow.

She stood in the midst of the stampede, her eyes wide, her hands covering her face. The crowd parted around her like water skirting a boulder.

Caleb pushed off and forced his way through the fleeing mob. A sharp heel dug into his foot. A shoulder knocked him off balance. With a burst of strength, he lifted the girl into his arms, turned and leaped back over the toppled barricade.

The mob pushed and shoved, scattering like buckshot away from the podium. A cacophony of deafening voices shouted as people were separated in the confusion. While disorder ruled, Caleb crouched behind the limited protection of the barricade with his sister and the girl, shielding them as best he could with his outstretched arms. He'd rather take his chances with a stray bullet than risk getting trampled beneath the fleeing spectators.

After several tense minutes that seemed to last an eternity, the ground ceased vibrating. The noise lessened. A gentle breeze stirred the hair at the nape of his neck.

He chanced lifting his head, astonished by the sudden silence. In an instant the square had cleared. Only a few people remained, looking dazed but uninjured.

Jo shoved her bonnet from her face. "Is everyone all right?"

The little girl nodded. She straightened and brushed at her yellow skirts, appearing no worse for wear.

A panicked voice shouted behind him. "We need a doctor!"

Caleb searched for the source of the frantic call. The dispersing crowd had all but emptied the grassy square, taking cover in the nearby hotels and businesses, leaving a mess of blankets and overturned baskets in their wake. Caleb pushed himself upright and reached for Jo.

She yanked her hand from his protective grasp. "Find out who needs a doctor, and I'll take care of this little sprite."

"I'm a veterinarian."

"You're better than nothing," Jo declared with her usual blunt edge. "Can you see Anna? Is she all right?"

"She took cover as soon as the pandemonium started. I'm sure she's fine."

His answer was mostly truthful. While his attention had been focused on Jo and the young girl, he'd caught a glimpse of Anna's turquoise blue dress near the podium.

"Help," the frenzied voice called. "We need help."

Though reluctant to lose sight of his sister, Caleb knew Jo better than most anyone. She wouldn't put herself in unnecessary danger. She was smart and resourceful. They had to separate.

He touched her sleeve. "Whatever happens, meet me in the lobby of the Savoy at noon. That's twenty minutes."

At his easy capitulation, Jo's expression lost its stubborn set. “Noon.” She reached for the girl’s hand. “We’re going to find your parents. What’s your name?”

The girl pressed her lips together, as though holding back her answer.

She shook her head, and her two long braids whipped around her neck. “I’m not s’posed to tell strangers.”

Jo shrugged. “That’s all right. You don’t have to tell me. My name is Jo. Can I least walk you back to the hotel?”

The girl screwed up her face in concentration. “To mama?”

“Yes, to your mother.”

The girl nodded.

Satisfied Jo had control of the situation, Caleb spun around and pushed his way through the knot of people toward the frantic voice. He broke through to the center, and his stomach dropped.

Anna Bishop lay sprawled on her back, a growing pool of blood seeping from beneath her body. Though ashen, she blinked and took a shuddering breath. The white banner across her chest was stained crimson near the point where the chevron ends met at her hip. The gray-haired woman kneeling beside her clutched Anna’s limp hand in both of hers.

Caleb swallowed around the lump in his throat. “She needs a surgeon.”

The woman’s eyes filled with tears. “The streets are clogged with carriages. The hotel is closer. She’s losing so much blood. I’m not strong enough to carry her.” Her voice caught. “Help us, please.”

“I’ll do whatever I can.”

He knelt beside Miss Bishop and took her limp wrist

in his hand, relieved by the strong pulse thumping beneath his fingers.

Anna's stunned blue eyes stood out starkly against her pale, almost translucent skin, providing the only color in her pallid face. Even her lips were white with shock. At the sight of such a bold woman struck down in such a cowardly fashion, raw emotion knifed through him.

Who had such fear in their heart that they'd fight words with bullets?

A fierce protectiveness welled in his chest. Whoever had done this might still be near.

"Miss Bishop," Caleb spoke quietly. "I'm going to take you back to the hotel. I'm going to help you."

For a dazzling moment she'd appeared invincible. The truth sent his stomach churning. She was just as fragile, just as vulnerable as any other mortal being.

She offered him the barest hint of a nod before her eyelids fluttered closed, blotting out the luminous blue color.

"Don't give up," Caleb ordered.

Seeing her on that stage, he'd recognized a woman who didn't shrink from a fight. If she needed a challenge, he'd give her one.

"Don't you dare let them win."

The words drifted over Anna. She'd already lost. She was going to die for the cause.

At least her death would not be *ordinary.*

Clenching her jaw, Anna fought toward the surface of her consciousness.

Don't you dare let them win.

The opposition would not have the satisfaction of her death. She'd traveled to Kansas City alone, an unusual occurrence. The speech had started well. There'd been hecklers. There were always hecklers. Anna had learned to ignore them.

Then she'd heard the shot.

The truth hadn't registered until searing pain had lanced through her side.

For a moment after the disruption, the world had gone silent. Disbelief had held her immobile. She'd looked in horror as a dark, growing stain had marred her turquoise day dress. The ground tilted. She'd staggered and her knees buckled.

Her mother had advised her against speaking in such a small venue. Reaching a few hundred people wasn't worth the effort when crowds of thousands awaited them back East. Grand gestures were needed for a grand cause.

Two ladies from the Kansas chapter of the movement hovered over her, shouting for help. She'd met them this morning—Miss Margaret and the widow, Mrs. Franklin.

A dark-haired man knelt at her side and pressed his palm against the wound, stemming the flow of blood. Anna winced. The stranger briefly released the pressure, and she glanced down, catching sight of a jagged hole marring the satin fabric of her favorite teal blue dress. She always wore blue when she needed extra courage.

The man gently raised her hip to peer beneath her, and she sucked in a breath.

"It's not bad." The man's forest-green eyes sparked with sympathy. "The bullet has gone through your side. Doesn't look like it struck anything vital."

Her throat worked. "Are you a doctor?"

"A veterinarian."

Perhaps her death would not be quite so ordinary after all.

The absurdity of the situation lent Anna an unexpected burst of energy. "Will you be checking me for hoof rot?"

"I'll do whatever is necessary." The man glanced at the two women hovering over them. "If the hotel is our only option, we must leave. At once. You keep fighting, Miss Bishop."

She was weary of fighting. Each day brought a new battle, a new skirmish in the war for women's rights. Each day the parlor of her mother's house in St. Louis filled with women begging her for help. Though each problem was only a single drop in the oceans of people swirling around the world, she felt as though she was drowning. She'd given all her fight to the cause, to the casualties subjugated by an unfair and biased system. She didn't have any fight left for herself.

Mrs. Franklin lifted her gaze to the nearby buildings, then jerked her head in a curt nod. "It isn't safe for her here. I've sent two others to fetch a surgeon and notify the police. Someone else may be hurt."

"I'll see to Miss Bishop," the man said, "if you want to check for additional injuries."

"Maggie will stay here and coordinate with the authorities," she said, her expression stalwart. "I'll remain with Miss Bishop."

Anna nearly wept with gratitude. Despite his reassuring words, the man kneeling at her side was a stranger, and she'd never been comfortable around men. Her encounters were rare, often tied with opposition to the cause, and those men mostly looked at her with thinly veiled contempt. Or, worse yet, speculation. As though her call for independence invited liberties they would never dream of taking with a "proper" woman.

The man ripped Anna's sash and tied it around her waist as a makeshift bandage. All thoughts of men and their rude propositions and knowing leers fled. The pain in her side was like a fire spreading through her body. It consumed her thoughts and kept her attention focused on the source of her agony.

The stranger easily lifted her into his arms, and her head spun. Her eyelids fluttered, and he tucked her more tightly against his chest.

A wave of nausea rose in the back of her throat, and her head lolled against his shoulder. What reason did she have for trusting this man? Someone wanted her dead. For all she knew, he'd fired the shot. With only the elderly Mrs. Franklin as her sentry, there was little either of them could do if his intentions were illicit. Yet she was too weak to refuse. Too weak to fight.

"Who are you?" she asked.

He picked his way over the debris left by the fleeing crowd. "I'm Caleb McCoy. I'm JoBeth Cain's brother."

Her eyes widened. "Is Jo here?"

He nodded. "We're staying at the Savoy Hotel, same as you. Jo was hoping to see you."

Over the past year, Jo's letters had been a lifeline for Anna. Her glimpse into Jo's world had been strange and fascinating. Anna had been raised with an entirely different set of values. Husbands were for women who lived a mediocre existence. As her mother so often reminded her, Anna had been groomed for the extraordinary.

The cause was her purpose for existing.

Her mother had been fighting for women's rights since before Anna was born. There were moments when Anna wondered if her birth had been just another chance for her mother to draw attention to the suffragist movement. Women didn't need men to raise children. They didn't need men to earn money. They didn't need men for much of anything, other than to prove their point. Her mother certainly hadn't been forthcoming about the details of Anna's father.

He doesn't matter to me, why should he matter to you?

Why, indeed.

The pain wasn't quite so bad anymore, and Anna felt as though she was separating from her body, floating away and looking at herself from a great distance.

Mr. McCoy adjusted his hold, and her side burned.

She must have made a noise because he glanced down, his gaze anguished. "Not much farther, Miss Bishop."

An appropriate response eluded her. She should have answered Jo's telegram. When Jo had discovered Anna was speaking in Kansas, she'd requested they meet. Anna had never replied. She couldn't afford to be distracted, and Jo's world held an undeniable fascination.

Pain slashed through her side. "Will you tell Jo that I'm sorry for not answering sooner?"

"You can tell her yourself."

Jo was intelligent and independent, and absolutely adored her husband. She had children, yet still worked several hours a week as a telegraph operator.

Anna had never considered the possibility of such a life because she'd never seen such a remarkable example. Marriages of equality were extremely rare, and if Anna let her attention stray toward such an elusive goal, she lost sight of her true purpose. Besides, for every one example of a decent husband, her mother would reply with a hundred instances of drunkenness, infidelities and cruelty. Unless women obtained a modicum of power over their own fates, they'd forever be at the mercy of their husbands.

Mr. McCoy kicked aside a crushed picnic basket, and Anna's stomach plummeted. Discarded blankets and the remnants of fried chicken and an apple pie had been crushed underfoot. "Was anyone else hurt?"

"Not that I know of."

Disjointed thoughts bobbed through her head. This was the first time her mother had trusted her with a speech alone. Always before, Victoria Bishop had picked and pecked over every last word. This was the first time Anna had been trusted on her own.

The concession was more from necessity than conviction in Anna's abilities. Her mother had been urgently needed in Boston for a critical task. The Massachusetts chapter had grossly underestimated the opposition to their most current state amendment vote, and the campaign required immediate reinforcement. More than ever, Anna must prove her usefulness.

Maybe then she'd feel worthy of her role as the daughter of the Great Victoria Bishop. The St. Louis chapter was meeting on Friday. Anna had to represent her mother. She'd arranged to leave for St. Louis tomorrow.

She'd never make the depot at this rate. "I have to change my train ticket."

Mr. McCoy frowned. "It'll wait."

"You don't waste words, do you, Mr. McCoy?"

A half grin lifted the corner of his mouth. "Nope."

The sheer helplessness of the situation threatened to overwhelm her. She wasn't used to being dependent on another person. She'd certainly never been carried by anyone in the whole of her adult life. She felt the warmth of his chest against her cheek, the strength of his arms beneath her bent knees. She was vulnerable and helpless, the sensations humbling.

Upon their arrival in the hotel lobby, Jo rushed toward them. "Oh, dear. What can I do?"

Though they'd only met in person the one time, the sight of Jo filled Anna with relief. Jo's letters were lively and personal, and she was the closest person Anna had to a friend in Kansas City.

"She's been shot." Caleb stated the obvious, keeping his voice low.

Only a few gazes flicked in their direction. The people jamming the lobby were too busy, either frantically reuniting with their missing loved ones or nursing their own bumps and bruises, to pay the three of them much notice.

Mr. McCoy brushed past his sister and crossed to the stairs. "They've sent for a surgeon, but we're running out of time. Fetch my bag and meet me in your room."

"Why not mine?" Anna replied anxiously. Moving to another room was another change, another slip away from the familiar.

"Because we still don't know who shot you," Mr. McCoy said. "Or if they'll try to finish what they started."

Jo gave her hand a quick squeeze. "Caleb will take care of you. My room isn't locked. I'll let them know where to send the doctor, and I'll be there in a tick."

Panic welled in the back of Anna's throat. All of the choices were being ripped away from her. She'd always been independent. As a child, her mother had insisted Anna take charge of her own decisions. The idea of putting her life in the hands of this stranger terrified her.

Caleb took the stairs two at a time. Though she sensed his care in ensuring she wasn't jostled, each tiny movement sent waves of agony coursing through her, silencing any protests or avowals of independence she might have made. Upon reaching Jo's room, he pushed open the door and rested her on the quilted blanket covering the bed.

The afternoon sun filtered through the windows,

showcasing a cloudless sky. The sight blurred around the edges as her vision tunneled. Her breath strangled in her throat. Her heartbeat slowed and grew sluggish.

Mr. McCoy studied her wound, keeping his expression carefully blank. A shiver wracked her body. His rigidly guarded reactions frightened her more than the dark blood staining his clothing.

"Am I going to die?" Anna asked.

And how would God react to her presence? She'd had Corinthians quoted to her enough over her lifetime that the words were an anathema.

Let your women keep silent in the churches: for it is not permitted unto them to speak.

And since women were not allowed to speak in church, they should not be allowed to speak on civic matters. Were they permitted to speak in heaven?

Mr. McCoy's lips tightened. "You're not going to die. But I have to stitch you up. We have to stop the bleeding, and I can't wait for the surgeon. It won't be easy for you."

She adjusted her position and winced. "I appreciate your candor."

He must have mistaken her words as a censure because he sighed and knelt beside the bed, then gently removed her crushed velvet hat and smoothed her damp hair from her forehead. His vivid green eyes were filled with sympathy.

A suffragist shouldn't notice such things, and this certainly wasn't the time or place for frivolous observations, but he really was quite handsome with his dark hair and warm, green eyes. Handsome in a swarthy kind of way. Anna exhaled a ragged breath. Her situation was obviously dire if that was the drift of her thoughts.

"Miss Bishop," he said. "Anna. It's your choice. I'm

not a surgeon. We can wait. But it's my educated opinion that we need to stop the bleeding."

Every living thing died eventually—every blade of prairie grass, every mosquito, every redwood tree. She'd been wrong before—death, no matter how extraordinary a life one lived on earth, was the most ordinary thing in the world.

Feeling as though she'd regained a measure of control, Anna met his steady gaze. "Are you a very good veterinarian?"

"The best."

He exuded an air of confidence that put her at ease. "Then, do what needs to be done."

She barely managed to whisper the words before blackness swirled around her. She hoped he had enough fight left for both of them.

Chapter Two

She'd trusted him. She'd trusted Caleb with her life. He prayed her trust wasn't misplaced because the coming task filled him with dread.

After tightening the bandage on Anna's wound, Caleb shrugged out of his coat and rolled up his sleeves. The door swung open, revealing Jo who clutched his bag to her chest. The suffragist from the rally appeared behind his sister. He'd lost sight of her earlier; his attention had been focused elsewhere, but she'd obviously been nearby.

The older woman glanced at the bed. "Where is the surgeon? Hasn't he arrived yet?"

"I'm afraid not." Caleb lifted a corner of the blood-soaked bandage and checked the wound before motioning for his sister. "Keep pressure on this." He searched through his bag and began arranging his equipment on the clean towel draped over the side table. "Unless the doctor arrives in the next few minutes, I'm stitching her up myself."

He'd brought along his case because that's the way he always packed. When his services were needed on an extended call, he threw a change of clothing over his instruments so he wasn't hampered by an extra bag. He'd packed for this trip the same way by rote.

Swiping the back of his hand across the perspiration beading on his forehead, he sighed. Perhaps Jo was partially right, perhaps he was growing too set in his ways.

The suffragist clenched and unclenched her hands. "You're the veterinarian, aren't you?"

Caleb straightened his instruments and set his jaw. Anna didn't have time for debate. "It appears I'm the best choice you've got right now."

"I'm Mrs. Franklin." The suffragist stuck out her hand and gave his a fierce shake. "I briefly served as a nurse in the war. I can assist you."

"Excellent." A wave of relief flooded through him. "I've got alcohol, bandages and tools in my bag. There's no ether, but I have a dose of laudanum." He met the woman's steady gaze. "I'm Caleb McCoy. This is my sister, JoBeth Cain."

Mrs. Franklin tilted her head. "I thought you must be related. Those green eyes and that dark hair are quite striking." The woman's eyes filled with tears. "Anna is tough. She'll do well." She pressed both hands against her papery cheeks. "I requested her appearance. I had no idea something like this would happen."

Jo snorted. "Of course you didn't. Assigning blame isn't going to stop a bullet. Caleb, tell us what to do." She lifted a pale green corked bottle from his bag. "And why do you have laudanum, anyway?"

"Got it from the doc when John's prize stallion kicked me last spring." Caleb rolled his shoulder, recalling the incident with a wince. John Elder raised horses for the cavalry, and his livelihood depended upon his horses' continued good health. Caleb's dedication had left him with a dislocated shoulder and a nasty scar on his thigh from the horse's sharp teeth. "I figured the laudanum might come in handy one day. I'll need the chair. You'll have to sit on the opposite side of the bed."

He uncorked the still-full bottle and measured a dose into the crystal glass he'd discovered on the nightstand. Jo rested her hip on the bed and raised Miss Bishop's shoulders. Anna moaned and pulled away.

Caleb held the glass to her lips. "This tastes foul, but you'll appreciate the benefits."

A fine sheen of sweat coated Miss Bishop's forehead. Her brilliant blue eyes had glazed over, yet he caught a hint of understanding in her disoriented expression. He tipped the glass, and she took a drink, then coughed and sputtered.

"Easy there," Caleb soothed. "Just a little more."

Jo quirked one dark eyebrow. "For a minute there, I thought you were going to say, easy there *old girl*."

Miss Bishop pushed away the glass. "This old girl has had enough."

"Don't go slandering my patients," Caleb offered with a half grin. "I've never gotten a complaint yet."

She flashed him a withering glance that let him know exactly what she thought of his assurances. "The next time you have a speaking patient, we'll compare notes."

He was heartened Miss Bishop had retained her gumption. She was going to need it.

After ensuring she'd taken the full dose, he rested the glass on the table and adjusted the pillow more comfortably behind Miss Bishop's head. "You'll be sound asleep in a minute. This will all be over soon."

"I have an uneasy feeling this is only the beginning,

Mr. McCoy." She spoke hoarsely, her eyes already dulled by the laudanum.

"You'll live to fight another day, Miss Bishop. I promise you that."

Her head lolled to one side, and she reached for Jo. "Please, let my mother know I'm fine. I don't want her to worry."

While Jo offered reassurances, Caleb checked the wound once more and discovered the bleeding had slowed, granting him a much-needed reprieve. He desperately wanted to wait until the laudanum took effect before stitching her up. This situation was uncharted territory. He understood an animal's reaction to pain. He knew how to soothe them, and he took confidence in his skills, knowing his treatments were for the ultimate benefit.

People were altogether different. He wasn't good with people in the best of situations, let alone people he didn't know well. He never missed the opportunity to remain silent in a group, letting others carry the conversation.

Miss Bishop fumbled for his hand and squeezed his fingers, sending his heartbeat into double time. He wasn't certain if her touch signified fear or gratitude. Aware of the curious perusal of the other two women, Caleb kept the comforting pressure on her delicate hand and waited until he felt the tension drain from Miss Bishop's body. Once her breathing turned shallow and even, he gently extracted his fingers from her limp hold.

Satisfied the laudanum had taken effect, he doused his hands with alcohol over a porcelain bowl, then motioned for Mrs. Franklin to do the same. Without being asked, the suffragist cleaned his tools in the same solution, her movements efficient and sure.

Caleb breathed a sigh of relief. Mrs. Franklin knew her way around medical instruments. He put her age at midsixties, though he was no expert on such matters. Her hair was the same stern gray as her eyes and her austere dress, the skin around her cheeks frail. She was tall for a woman, and wiry thin. Her fingers were swollen at the knuckles, yet her hands were steady.

Jo cleared her throat. “Caleb, I never thanked you for coming with me today. I’m thinking this is a good time to remedy that.”

They exchanged a look, and his throat tightened. A silent communication passed between them, a wealth of understanding born of a shared childhood that didn’t need words.

A sudden thought jolted him. “Did you find the little girl’s parents? Was anyone else injured?”

“One question at a time.” Jo admonished. “Anna’s youngest follower discovered her mother in the lobby, frantic with worry. As you’d expect, there was much scolding and a few tears of relief. I asked around, and, as far as anyone can tell, Anna was the only person hurt.”

Relieved to set one worry aside, Caleb focused on his patient. “Most likely we’d know by now if someone else was injured.”

Or shot.

The enormity of Miss Bishop’s condition weighed on him. She’d placed her trust in him, and he wouldn’t fail her. “If Anna comes around, you’ll need to keep her calm. I’ve enough laudanum for another dose, but it’s potent, and I’d like to finish before the first measure wears off.”

He’d never been a great admirer of the concoction, and the less she ingested, the better.

Jo pressed the back of her hand against Miss Bishop’s

forehead. “Don’t forget, I helped Ma for years with her midwife duties. I know what to do.”

The irony hadn’t escaped him. Of the three of them, Caleb was the least experienced with human patients, yet he had the most experience with stitching up wounds. After modestly draping Miss Bishop’s upper body, he slid his scissors between the turquoise fabric and her skin and easily sliced the soaked material away from her wound.

He held out the scissors, and they were instantly replaced with a cloth.

His admiration for the suffragist grew. “How long did you serve in the war, Mrs. Franklin?”

“It was only a few months in ’65. I’d lost both of my sons and my husband by then. Our farm was burned. There really wasn’t anything left for me to do. Nothing to do but help others.”

Caleb briefly closed his eyes before carefully tucking the draping around the bullet wound. “I’m sorry for your losses.”

Mrs. Franklin lifted her chin. “It was a long time ago. I’ve been a widow longer than I was ever married. Would you like the instruments handed to you from the right or the left?”

“The right.”

Her brisk efficiency brought them all on task. Caleb exchanged another quick look with his sister, and she flashed a smile of encouragement. Caleb offered a brief prayer for guidance and set about his work.

From that moment forward, he focused his attention on the process, certain the surgeon’s arrival was imminent. While Caleb might be the best option at the moment, he was perfectly willing to cede the process to a *better* option. He wasn't a man to let false pride cloud his judgment.

Taking a deep breath, he studied the rift marring the right side of Miss Bishop's body. He'd seen his fair share of gunshot wounds over the years. It wasn't unheard of for careless hunters or drunken ranchers to miss their mark and strike livestock. Often the animal was put down, but depending on the location of the wound, he'd been able to save a few. His stomach clenched. Had the bullet gone a few inches to the left...

He set his jaw and accepted the needle and thread, his hands rock steady. While he worked, his pocket watch ticked the minutes away, resounding in the heavy silence. Though Miss Bishop wasn't anything like his normal patients, the concept remained the same. He watched for signs of shock, stemmed the bleeding, cleaned the area to inhibit infection, and ensured Jo kept his patient calm.

Once he was satisfied with his stitches on the entrance wound, he swiped at his forehead with the back of his hand. "We'll need to turn her to the side."

Jo grasped Miss Bishop's shoulder, and Caleb carefully tilted her onto her hip. Anna groaned, and her arm flipped onto the bed, her hand palm up, her fingers curled, the sight unbearably vulnerable.

Not even an hour earlier she'd held an entire audience enthralled with her bounding energy, and now her life's blood drained from her body, vibrant against the cheerful tulip pattern sewn into the quilted coverlet. Impotent rage at whoever had caused this destruction flared in his chest.

He shook off the distraction with a force of will and resumed his stitching. With any luck they'd already apprehended the shooter.

Miss Bishop drifted in and out of consciousness during the procedure, but remained mostly numbed throughout his ministrations. For that he was unaccountably grateful.

Jo dabbed at Anna's brow and murmured calming words when she grew agitated, keeping her still while Caleb worked. Mrs. Franklin maintained charge of the instruments with practiced efficiency. Despite having only met the widow moments before, their impromptu team worked well together.

Caleb tied off the last stitch and clipped the thread, then touched the pulse at Miss Bishop's wrist, buoyed by the strong, steady heartbeat beneath his fingertips. He collapsed back in his chair and surveyed his work.

He'd kept his stitches precise and small. While he couldn't order his usual patients to remain in bed after an injury, he'd ensure Miss Bishop rested until she healed.

With the worst of the crises behind him, the muscles along his shoulders grew taut. Mrs. Franklin sneaked a surreptitious glance at the door.

When she caught his interest, a bloom of color appeared on her cheeks. "You've done a fine job. But I thought… I assumed…"

"You assumed the surgeon would be here by now." Caleb pushed forward in his chair and reached for the final bandage. "As did I."

He'd made his choice. Instead of walking away, he'd stayed. That choice had unwittingly linked him to Miss Bishop, and he'd sever that tie as soon as the surgeon arrived. The two of them were worlds apart, and the sooner they each returned home, the better.

He sponged away the last of the blood and sanitized the wound. The instant the alcohol touched her skin, Miss Bishop groaned and arched her back.

Caleb held a restraining hand against her shoulder. "Don't undo all of my careful work."

She murmured something unintelligible and reached for him again. Painfully aware of his sister's curious stare, he cradled Miss Bishop's hand and rubbed her palm with the pad of his thumb. His touch seemed to soothe her, and he kept up the gentle movement until she calmed. The differences between them were striking. His hands were work-roughened and weather-darkened, Anna's were pale and frighteningly delicate. A callous on the middle finger of her right hand, along with the faded ink stains where she rested her hand against the paper, indicated she wrote often.

The ease with which she trusted him tightened something in his chest. He never doubted his ability with animals. For as long as he could remember, he'd had an affinity with most anything that walked on all fours…or slithered, for that matter. Yet that skill had never translated with people. An affliction that wasn't visited on anyone else in his family. The McCoys were a boisterous lot, gregarious and friendly. Caleb was the odd man in the bunch.

Once her chest rose and fell with even breaths, he reluctantly released his hold and sat back in his chair, then rubbed his damp fingers against his pant legs.

Her instinctive need for human touch reminded him of the thread that held them all together. All of God's creatures sought comfort when suffering.

Voices sounded from the corridor, and Jo stood. "If that's the surgeon, I'm going to give him a piece of my mind."

Mrs. Franklin tucked the blankets around Miss Bishop's shoulders. "We should tidy the room and change the bedding. Perhaps Mr. McCoy should deal with any visitors we have."

Caleb took the hint. "If I'm unable to locate the surgeon, I'll check on Miss Bishop in half an hour."

He snatched his coat and stepped into the corridor, then glanced around the now-empty space. He caught sight of the blood staining his vest and shirt and blew out a breath. The voices they'd heard had not been the surgeon's, and he couldn't visit the lobby with such a grisly appearance. The telling evidence discoloring his shirt also placed him at the rally, and he wasn't ready to answer questions.

Or make himself a target.

He crossed to his room and quickly changed. Now that the immediacy of the situation had passed, exhaustion overtook him, and he collapsed onto the bed, clutching his head.

Of all the things that he'd dreaded when Jo had invited him to accompany her to Kansas City, he hadn't anticipated this dramatic turn of events.

He took a few deep breaths and raked his hands through his hair, letting the emotion flow out of him. This happened sometimes. Once the emergency had been dealt with, he often experienced a wave of overwhelming exhaustion. The greater the emergency, the greater his fatigue. He scrubbed his hands down his face and stood, then stepped into the corridor and made his way to the lobby. There'd be time for resting later.

A man in a loose-fitting overcoat brushed past him on the staircase.

"Say, fellow," the man said. "Were you at the rally this afternoon?"

"Yes. And you?"

Perhaps this gentleman knew if there had been any further injuries as a result of the shooting.

"Nope. I was supposed to be covering Miss Bishop's speech for *The Star* paper. Figured I'd slip in for the last few minutes. Who wants to listen to them ladies whine? Now I gotta figure out what happened or the boss will have my hide. There was some kind of commotion, right?"

Caleb measured his words carefully. "There was a disturbance. The crowd scattered."

"What kind of disturbance?"

Great. Now he'd gone and cornered himself into telling the whole of it. "A gunshot."

The man's eyes widened, and he gleefully rubbed his hands together, then splayed them. "I can see the headline now, Shot Fired Across the Bow of Suffragist Battle."

The man's elation turned Caleb's stomach. Brushing past the reporter before he said anything more revealing, Caleb loped down the stairs and paused on the balcony overlooking the lobby. A discordance of noise hit him like a wall.

Having survived the encounter at the rally, scores of people from the audience had obviously congregated at the hotel to share their dramatic stories. Voices were raised in excitement, and more than one gentleman clutched a strong drink.

Caleb sucked in a breath and made his way across the room. He couldn't have designed a better nightmare for himself. Twice in one day, he'd been forced into a crush of people.

Upon reaching the concierge desk, he waved over the gentleman in the bottle-green uniform he'd seen his sister approach earlier. "Did the surgeon arrive?"

The man lifted his hands. "Not that I know of. It's been like this since the rally. It's all we can do to keep the crowd contained in the lobby." The concierge glanced left and right and ducked his head. "I caught a reporter upstairs, and there are several policemen waiting to speak with Miss Bishop. I'll hold them off as long as I can."

Caleb rubbed his forehead. "That would be best."

The man cleared his throat. "I also took the liberty of removing Miss Bishop's name from the guest register." The man cleared his throat again. "I have your party listed in the register book as yourself, your sister and your fiancée."

Caleb's head shot up. "Say again?"

"I have a large staff. I can handpick the workers on the fourth floor. I cannot guarantee the characters of all my employees."

"But fiancée?"

The man lifted his hands as though in surrender. "The title seemed the least likely one for Miss Bishop to take. Since she's a, you know, she's a..."

"She's a suffragist. It's not a profanity."

"My apologies, sir. I can change the register."

Caleb pictured Anna, her turquoise dress ruined, her bold speech silenced. Why would anyone want to live in the public eye? And yet he couldn't deny her obvious appeal, the way her vivacious speech had captivated the crowd. He couldn't imagine a better figurehead for the cause.

"No, you've done well," Caleb said. "Keeping her identity hidden is best."

As he surveyed the scene, voices ebbed and flowed around him. All of these people had come to hear her speak. He fisted his hands. Not all of them. For all he knew, the man who'd pulled the trigger was here. Waiting. Watching.

Caleb searched the faces of the spectators milling around the lobby. There was no way of knowing, no way of telling who held violence in their heart.

He raked his hands through his hair. Until they discovered the shooter, the less said, the better. What did it matter how Anna was registered? No one would know but the hotel staff.

After a few more words with the concierge about the new room arrangement, he returned upstairs and met Jo as she exited Miss Bishop's room.

Caleb checked the corridor, ensuring the space was empty of curiosity seekers before pulling Jo aside. "It's not safe for Miss Bishop. She needs a guard at her door. I've arranged for another room for you. Simply switching with Miss Bishop is out of the question. There are reporters and policemen. Not to mention whoever fired the shot is still out there."

His sister propped her hands on her hips. "She should come home with us."

Caleb had briefly thought the same thing, and had come up with a thousand reasons why the plan was not sound. "This isn't our concern. Surely she has family, friends."

A sweetheart, perhaps. The thought brought him up short. He shook his head. Nothing in the papers had ever indicated that Miss Bishop was linked with a gentleman—and that would certainly be newsworthy.

"I've corresponded with her for months. She doesn't have anyone close. Her mother lives in St. Louis, but she's in Boston for an extended stay. Besides, it's too far for Anna to travel in her condition."

Caleb sensed a losing battle ahead of him. This was the Jo he knew and admired. Given a problem, she immediately grasped for a solution and charged ahead.

He held out his arms in supplication and assumed his most placating tone. "Slow down. We don't have any influence here."

Jo slapped his hands away. "I'm not one of your animals. Stop speaking to me as though I'm a goat. Anna is my friend. She'll need a place to rest, a quiet place to recuperate. People who care for her."

"Jo, listen to me, even if you invited her back to Cimarron Springs, do you really think she'd accept your offer? She's not a country girl. She'd be bored in an instant." He indicated the elaborate appointed hallway with its hand-knotted rug and brass fixtures. "This is her world."

Though he knew the idea was ludicrous, he couldn't shake an impending sense of despair. He didn't want their paths to cross any more than necessary. Anna Bishop was beautiful and witty and captivating. In the brief time he'd seen her on that stage, he'd known she was different from anyone else he'd ever met. He was drawn to her, and those feelings were disastrous.

He was a veterinarian from a small town who loathed big cities. She was a nationally renowned speaker with a following. She had a calling. There was clearly no room in her life for someone like him. He'd grown emotional over someone who hadn't returned his affection once before. Only a fool made the same mistake twice.

His sister approached him and crowded into his space until they stood toe to toe. "She needs us."

"Why us?" Caleb stood his ground. "Why does she need us?"

Jo glared. "Until they discover who tried to kill her, Anna is going to need a place to hide. And you're good at hiding, aren't you?"

With that, she pivoted on her heel and stomped down the corridor.

His burst of fury quickly died, replaced by a bone-deep weariness. He wasn't hiding, he was simply a loner who should have stayed in Cimarron Springs where he belonged. And yet if he'd stayed at home, what would have happened to Anna? Who would have cared for her?

The answer troubled him more than he would have cared to admit. Which was why he needed as much space between them as possible, as soon as possible. Becoming embroiled in Anna's life was out of the question.

Chapter Three

A week following the shooting, Anna staggered from bed and took a few lurching steps, determined to reestablish her independence. Winded, she collapsed onto a chair before the window. She'd considered dressing, but even the simple task of standing had become a tiring battle in her weakened condition.

From this moment on she was taking charge of her life. No more depending on others, no more sleeping the days and nights away. Except her body had refused the call to action.

The bandage wrapped around her side restricted her movements, and the slightest agitation sent a shock of pain through her side. Near tears, she rested her forehead against the chilled windowpane.

A soft knock sounded at the door. She smoothed the front of her dressing gown and tucked a lock of hair behind one ear, relieved they'd had her trunk delivered to the room when she and Jo had switched.

"It's Mrs. Franklin," a voice called.

Anna sat up as straight as her wound allowed. "Please, come in."

As the door swung open, she recalled her embroidery and quickly shoved the evidence beneath her pillow. For reasons she couldn't explain, she kept the feminine hobby to herself.

The older woman took one look at Anna and tsked. "Why didn't you call for me? I would have helped."

The past week was a blur of disjointed memories. Between sleeping and waking, she recalled the visits from other suffragists. The room had erupted with flowers like a meadow after a spring rain. They crowded every available surface, perfuming the air.

"I managed well enough," Anna said. "I didn't want to inconvenience you."

"It's no trouble." Mrs. Franklin's gray eyes clouded over. "It's the least I can do."

As she crossed before her, Anna caught her hand. "This wasn't your fault."

"You can't blame me for feeling guilty." The older woman paused. "Will you at least let me help you dress this morning?"

"That would be lovely. I'm tired of lazing around in my nightclothes."

While Anna was eager to press her independence, she sensed the other woman's need to be useful, and remained docile beneath her ministrations. The widow was the opposite of everything Anna had been taught to hold dear. Mrs. Franklin seemed to revel in her role as protector and nurturer—character traits her mother abhorred. Victoria Bishop took great pains to surround herself with the like-minded. No action was ever taken without a purpose. Independence was prized in the Bishop household. Tutors and nannies who had coddled Anna as a child were quickly corrected or dismissed.

You are not here to care for the child, Anna recalled her mother's oft-repeated order, *you are to teach the child how to care for herself.*

After Anna donned her simplest outfit, a white cotton shirtwaist and brown plaid skirt, Mrs. Franklin spent several minutes fussing with her hair.

The older woman stood back and surveyed her work. "I'm no lady's maid, but you're presentable."

Having done her own hair for many years, the sensation was odd. Being pampered and cared for was not nearly as repellent as it should have been. In fact, Anna quite liked the relaxing sensation. Unbidden, her mother's fierce countenance popped into her head. Victoria Bishop had not raised her only daughter to be spoiled.

Anna took the brush from Mrs. Franklin and ran the bristles away from her temple, smoothing the wave created by her impossible curls. "It's lovely, really. I don't usually wear it this way."

The widow had pinned her loose hair in a cascade atop her head. When Anna perched her hat over the arrangements, the curls framed her face. The effect softened her countenance and made her look younger, more approachable.

Mrs. Franklin tugged one of the ringlets free and let it fall against Anna's cheek. "Oh, yes, I quite like that. You have lovely hair, my dear. If I'd had that hair back in '45, oh the trouble I could have caused."

Judging from the twinkle in Mrs. Franklin's eye, Anna guessed she'd broken more than one heart. "I have a feeling you caused plenty of trouble, no matter your hair."

"True, my dear. Quite true," the widow answered with unabashed pride.

Anna couldn't help but laugh with Mrs. Franklin's

reflection in the mirror. When she turned away, Anna's smile faded.

Why was accepting assistance such a shameful weakness? If the situations were reversed, if Mrs. Franklin had needed help, Anna would have happily aided her. And yet each time she relinquished even the tiniest bit of her independence, she heard her mother's stern disapproval. Why was the desire to look attractive such an appalling offense?

If a woman's sole purpose in life was to attract a mate, then nature would not have given us the superior brain.

Anna patted her hair and recalled her manners. "Thank you, Mrs. Franklin, for your assistance. You've been absolutely indispensable. I don't know what I would have done without you this week."

"You must call me Izetta."

Mrs. Franklin—Izetta—straightened the horsehair brush on the dressing table. "There's a gentleman here to see you, if you're up for it."

"Mr. McCoy?" Anna's heartbeat tripped. "He's here?"

"No. A detective. A Pinkerton detective at that. Can you imagine?"

"Well, of course Mr. McCoy will have gone." Anna held out her hands and studied her blunt fingernails. She mustn't let her emotions turn at the mere thought of him. "I was only hoping for the chance to thank him properly."

"Oh, no, Mr. McCoy hasn't gone. He and his sister have been keeping the vultures at bay." Mrs. Franklin folded Anna's discarded nightgown and laid it on her trunk. "It's been a circus, let me tell you. I don't know what we would have done without those two."

Anna's memories of the past week were hazy at best. The police had questioned her briefly, but she had nothing to offer. She hadn't seen anything, and despite the ubiquitous protestors from the opposition, she'd never been threatened with bodily harm. Or shot at, for that matter. The police had pressed her for information until Mr. McCoy had ordered them away, but not before demanding they leave a guard at her door.

Mr. McCoy's soothing voice had been the one constant in a sea of confusion. She'd caught Jo teasing him, ribbing him for treating them all as though they were his four-legged patients, and yet she'd found the deep timbre of his reassuring voice a lifeline in the darkness. She'd been injured and out of sorts, that was all. Surely this curious fascination with the man would fade soon enough. Her fellow suffragists would not approve.

Love will ruin a woman faster than rain will ruin a parade.

Mrs. Franklin paused with her hand on the doorknob. "We kept your room number secret until that reporter grew weary of trying. After you speak with the detective, you'll have to make some decisions."

The door swung open, and Anna's breath caught in her throat. "Mr. McCoy! I was expecting the Pinkerton detective."

She desperately hoped he attributed the breathless quality of her voice to her recent injury. And surprise. Yes, she was simply surprised.

He jerked his thumb over his shoulder. "That'd be him."

Her eyes widened. If she didn't know better, she'd have thought the other man was derelict. The detective appeared to be in his late forties with a curiously rounded middle and stick limbs. As though all of his weight had congregated in his belly, starving the fat from his arms and legs. He wore an ill-fitting coat in a nondescript shade of brown which matched the shock of disordered, thinning hair covering his head.

Anna swept her arm in an arc. "I'm afraid I don't have enough seats for all of you. I wasn't expecting company."

Mr. McCoy propped his shoulder against the door frame. "I'll stand."

How did he manage to pack such a wealth of meaning into so few words?

The detective huffed.

Annoyance radiated from Mr. McCoy's stiff demeanor. There was obviously no love lost between the two men.

The detective straddled a chair and rested his arms on the back. "The name is Reinhart. I'm here on another case."

A sharp ache throbbed in her temple, and Anna pressed two fingers against the pain. "I don't follow."

"When I'm working on a case, I pay attention to things. To everything. You never know what you might hear."

"I see," Anna replied vaguely, though she didn't see at all.

Reinhart shrugged. "Anyway, I'm from St. Louis. Moved to this office last May."

Caleb pushed off from the wall. "Just get to the point. Tell her what you told me this morning."

The detective rubbed the salt-and-pepper stubble on his chin. "I've been doing some digging and I've heard a few things. Mind you, if you want to find the shooter, that's a separate job. Like I said this morning, that'll cost you extra."

Mr. McCoy cleared his throat.

The man glared over his shoulder, his movements twitchy and nervous as a rat. “Anyway, I’ve been doing some digging, and I ain’t found nothing.”

Oddly deflated by his vague speech, Anna tilted her head. “That’s what you came here to tell me?”

“Don’t you get it? No one has claimed responsibility. No one seen nothing. Nothing.”

“I still don’t follow.”

“This is personal. Someone with a grudge against women voting wants his voice heard. He wants attention. Someone with a personal vendetta is going underground. He doesn’t want to get caught. Leastways not until the job is done right.”

While the man’s clothing and grooming might lead one to believe he was not educated, his speech let slip his intellect. Clearly playing the bumbling fool suited his work.

He glanced meaningfully at her side and Anna pressed her hand against the bandages beneath her clothing.

She sat up and winced. “Someone wants me dead. Just me?”

“That’s the way I see it.”

Blood roared in her ears. Somehow she’d pictured the act as random. A lone, crazed shooter with a grudge against women who was bent on causing an uproar. Someone determined to halt the rally.

In the back of her mind, she’d even wondered if the whole thing had been an accident. Years ago, their neighbor in St. Louis had inadvertently discharged a firearm while attempting to clean the weapon. He’d shattered the parlor window and taken a chunk out of the porch railing.

This was no accident.

This was more focused. This was *personal.*

As the realization sank in, her heart thumped painfully in her chest, leaving her light-headed.

The twitchy man shrugged. "That's the problem. That's *your* problem. My guess is, he's going to try again."

Anna searched the expectant faces staring at her. What was she supposed to do? What was she supposed to say? She glanced at Izetta who remained at her vigil near the window.

"I've asked the others." The widow offered an apologetic grimace. "There's been no great trouble with our local chapter. We've gotten the usual threats, of course. The occasional brick through the front window and painted slurs. But no one has taken responsibility for the shooting. Perhaps they wanted the notoriety of targeting a suffragist with a large following."

Though no hint of censure showed in Izetta's voice, Anna's ears buzzed. "I'm only well-known because of my mother. I'm hardly worthy of notice otherwise."

She thought she heard mutterings from Mr. McCoy's direction, but when she caught his gaze, his face remained impassive.

Jo sidled through the doorway and exchanged a glance with her brother.

Anna welcomed the interruption. "Have you heard anything new?" she asked Jo.

With any luck the criminal had been found and all this conjecture was pointless.

"Nothing. But there's a telegram from your mother. I've been keeping her informed of your progress. I did as you requested, I brushed over the details so she wouldn't worry. Perhaps I blunted them too much." Jo glanced at the curious face of the detective and cleared her throat. "Never mind. We can discuss that later. Alone."

Anna exhaled slowly, gathering her thoughts, following Mr. McCoy's lead by keeping her face bland. Perhaps they *had* kept the details too blunted. Thus far her mother had been sympathetic, but impersonal. As though she was commiserating with a distant acquaintance instead of her only daughter. Not that Anna expected her to come charging to Kansas City. Victoria Bishop had never been one for nursing the sick. She considered any weakness, even ill health, an inconvenience.

There was no need to involve anyone else in this mess, especially if the shooting was targeted at her. Anna might have been injured, but she was no victim.

Bracing her left hand on the seat, she suppressed a grimace. "Then I shall return home. To St. Louis."

She'd been sitting upright too long, and the injury in her side had turned from a dull ache into a painful throbbing.

"Nah." The Pinkerton detective grunted. "I don't think that's a good idea either. You're known. You're not hard to find. I ain't that smart. Other people could do the same."

He was plenty smart, Anna had no doubt of that. Studying the faces turned toward her, she had the distinct sensation they wanted something from her.

That she was the only person in the room who hadn't been apprised of the predetermined plan. "What do you propose I do?"

Caleb held up his hand, silencing Reinhart. "Come to Cimarron Springs. Stay with Jo."

A thread of anxiety coiled in her stomach. She wasn't helpless. She wasn't a victim. She wouldn't be delivered onto someone's doorstep like an unwanted package.

"And how will that attract any less attention?" Anna gritted her teeth against her clouding vision. "I do not mean to sound arrogant, Mr. McCoy, but my name is not unknown. I have dealt with reporters before. They are far wilier than one supposes. It won't take long for them to discover where I am."

Jo stepped forward. "Not if we give you a new name. You can be Anna Smith or something. Caleb and I will keep in touch with the detective. Cimarron Springs is quiet. You'll have a chance to recuperate."

A chilly perspiration beaded on her forehead. Anna couldn't shake the sensation she was missing something in the exchange. "It's very kind of you, but I am not unfamiliar with small towns either. Gossip is rampant, and curiosity is lethal to your plan. We're bound to slip up sooner or later."

The excuse sounded weak even to her own ears. She'd been a controversial figure since before she was born—the illegitimate daughter of heiress Victoria Bishop. Her mother had been singularly remorseless in her infamy. Senior ladies in their chapter had regaled Anna with stories of her mother's brazen disregard for convention.

Anna had eventually grown old enough to hear the harsher opinions of her mother's behavior, and suffer for them. For a time she'd ignored her notoriety. Then the parents with children attending Miss Spence's Boarding and Day School for Girls had demanded her removal. They didn't want their daughters' reputations sullied by association.

Victoria Bishop had marched into the school, her heels click-clacking along the marble floors. Anna had waited outside the office, her buttoned leather boots swinging to and fro, while her mother told Miss Spence exactly what she thought of Anna's expulsion.

A succession of tutors proficient in various subjects

had followed. A more focused education, if a touch lonely. Training for solitude had served her well. Despite all the women she met in her travels, most of her time was spent alone. Traveling. Writing letters. Organizing the many separate chapters into a united front.

Proving herself worthy of her mother's legacy.

"You'll be there as my friend," Jo said. "A friend who had an accident and needs some quiet."

"It could work." The detective spoke. "Remember, though, if you show up out of the blue with someone they ain't never heard of before, people will talk. You gotta give them something to talk about or else they'll make up the missing pieces on their own."

Anna's side was on fire, and she wasn't opposed to resting. After her near-failed attempt at dressing herself this morning, she'd admitted the gravity of her wound. She was exhausted. Mentally and physically. Though she'd never admit her weakness, she was still grappling with the realization that someone wanted her dead.

Dead.

Jo planted one hand on her hip and drummed her fingers on the dressing table. "The last page of the *Crofton County Gazette* has a listing of visitors with each edition. You know the stuff, 'Mrs. Bertrand's two grandchildren are visiting from St. Louis. The Millers have gone to Wichita for the wedding of their niece.' That sort of thing. How would we print Anna's visit in the paper? That should give us some ideas."

Caleb reached into the side pocket of his bag. "You're brilliant, Jo. I've got a copy right here."

Anna surveyed their enthusiasm with a jaded eye. A small town was simply Miss Spence's School for Girls all over again. She'd be a pariah once the townspeople uncovered her true identity. Already, too many people knew their secret, and the McCoys didn't strike her as proficient in subterfuge. Sooner or later someone was bound to discover the truth.

While she didn't think the townspeople would stalk her with pitchforks and torches like the beast in Mary Shelley's *Frankenstein*, there was bound to be awkwardness. Most small communities she'd frequented had narrower rules of propriety than larger cities.

Flipping over the paper, Caleb frowned at the last page, his eyes scanning the columns. "It's all family visits. We're too well known. If we dig up another McCoy cousin, they'll figure out we're lying soon enough. What about Garrett? Could she pretend to be a relative of his?"

"No," Jo spoke emphatically. "Garrett's family is quite off-limits."

The sorrow in her voice gave Anna pause.

Caleb didn't seem to notice. "All right then, let's see what else." A half grin lifted the corner of his mouth. "Here's something interesting. 'JoBeth Cain and her brother, Caleb McCoy, will attend the suffragist rally in Kansas City calling for an additional amendment to the constitution allowing for the women's vote. Daughter of the renowned suffragist, Victoria Bishop, is set to give the keynote speech. Garrett Cain is escorting a prisoner to Wichita.'" Caleb shook his head. "I guess we did make the news."

"It's a small town." Jo shrugged. "Everyone makes the newspaper."

Mr. McCoy folded the paper and squinted. "Well, I'll be, here's something I didn't know. 'Mr. Frank Lancaster has brought his fiancée, Miss Vera Nelson, for an extended visit with his family. A mail-order bride advertisement was recently listed in *The Kansas Post* by a woman with the name of Miss Vera Nelson. Mr. Lancaster declined to comment on the happenstance.'" Caleb rubbed his chin. "I spoke with him two weeks ago when his dog had the mange. I had no idea he was considering taking a wife."

"I suppose if you sent away for a bride like a pair of shoes from the Montgomery Ward wish book," Jo said, "you wouldn't want that to be common knowledge."

Mrs. Franklin crossed her arms. "There's nothing wrong with doing what needs to be done. I'm sure the girl had her reasons. For a woman, sometimes marriage is the only answer."

"Wait," Jo snapped her fingers. "That's perfect. Marriage is our answer, as well. Anna can come to visit as your fiancée."

"My fiancée." Caleb's eyes widened.

Anna started. "What?"

"You two can pretend to be engaged."

Shocked silence filled the room. Anna recalled the scores of letters her mother had received over the years from desperate women. All of them had one thing in common—they had pinned their hopes on a man.

"No!" Anna and Caleb replied in unison.

Chapter Four

Anna leaned more heavily on her left arm. "Absolutely not. I mean no disrespect, Mr. McCoy, but I will not hide. I'm not going to change my name or pretend to be something I'm not. That goes against everything I stand for."

She wasn't relinquishing her independence. Killer or no killer. If the shooting had been caused by the opposition, then such a concession meant they'd won.

Jo's arms flopped to her sides. "We can say you had a whirlwind romance."

Caleb laughed harshly. "No one would believe it."

"You're right." Jo appeared crestfallen. "Of course you're right."

"You're missing the point," Caleb said. "No one would ever look for anyone in Cimarron Springs. She might as well wear a banner and parade down Main Street."

"True enough. Remember Elizabeth Elder's first husband? The bank robber? He hid all his loot in a cave by Hackberry Creek. No one ever suspected a thing. You didn't suspect him, did you, Caleb?"

"He didn't treat his livestock very well."

"Or his wife." Jo's voice strangled. "This may have

escaped your notice, but people are just as important as animals." She pinched the bridge of her nose. "People are *more* important than livestock."

"I was making a point. There were obvious signs of bad character."

Caught up in the tale of the loot hidden by the creek, Anna made a noise of frustration at the sudden change of subject. "What happened to the bank robber and his poor wife?"

"He's dead now, God rest his soul." Jo's voice was stripped of remorse. "Elizabeth remarried and she's doing fine. She's living in Paris now."

"France?"

"Texas."

"I see," Anna said. "At least I think I understand."

A little dazed by the turn of the conversation, Anna considered Mr. McCoy's earlier denial. Why would no one believe they were engaged? The idea didn't seem far-fetched enough to incite laughter. Disbelief, certainly. Skepticism, perhaps. But outright mocking laughter?

She studied the fidgety detective and knitted her forehead. "All we have are rumors and speculation. For all we know, they've captured the man responsible, and this conversation is all for naught."

Reinhart's continued presence, especially considering his fierce demand for payment if he provided information, struck her as suspect. What had he said before? Something about cataloguing everything he saw and heard. Why the sudden interest in an injured suffragist if no one had offered him compensation? She had the distinct impression the detective never made a move without an ulterior motive. He certainly hadn't moved from his chair during the entire conversation.

"This isn't your case, Mr. Reinhart," she prompted. "You indicated that a moment before. Why are you here?"

"Because it suits me."

He shot her a look of such naked disgust that Anna inhaled a sharp breath. The sudden effort sent a shaft of agony tearing through her side.

She'd seen that reaction before, a curious mixture of disdain and resentment. "You're not an admirer of the women's movement, are you?"

"A woman's place is in the home. Not squawking out in public and making a spectacle of herself. Women are too emotional for politics."

Izetta gasped. "How dare you!"

Mr. McCoy pushed away from the door frame, plumping up like a gathering thundercloud. Anna gave an almost imperceptible shake of her head. The Bishop women were not victims.

They did not need to be saved like milquetoast princesses from a Grimm's fairy tale. "A woman's place is wherever she chooses."

The detective made a great show of rolling his eyes. "If the woman wears the pants, what's the man supposed to wear?"

"Short pants," Izetta declared. "Especially if they insist on acting like children."

"Say now!"

"That's enough," Caleb growled. "You're not here for your opinion."

"I don't work for you." The detective rested his fisted knuckles on his thighs, elbows out, one bony protrusion jutting through a hole in his sleeve. "Either way, you got a problem, Miss Bishop. A big one. This wasn't a warning. Whoever took that shot meant to leave you dead."

Stomach churning, Anna shifted to the edge of her seat. She'd underestimated the limits of her endurance, but she wasn't about to let that infuriating little man witness her frailty.

Mr. McCoy's sharp gaze rested on her ashen face. He motioned toward the detective. "You've had your say. If you hear anything else, let us know."

"For a price."

Widening his stance, Mr. McCoy fisted his hands beneath his biceps. The posture was uniquely male, a declaration of his authority.

He might be a quiet man, but she doubted anyone who knew Mr. McCoy well would readily cross him.

He leaned toward Reinhart. "For a fellow who says he's not very smart, you seem to do all right."

Mr. McCoy was far too perceptive by half. Hadn't Anna thought the same thing only moments before?

Reinhart stood and tugged his ill-fitting jacket over his rounded stomach. He tipped back his head since Mr. McCoy was a good foot taller, and waved his bowed and skeletal index finger. "You know my rate. Pay or don't. Don't make me no never mind."

Once he'd exited the room, Anna's flagging reserve of strength finally deserted her. Desperate to alleviate her discomfort, she pushed off from the chair and stumbled. Mr. McCoy was at her side in an instant. He hooked his arm beneath her shoulder, carefully avoiding her injury.

"I'm quite well," she said, and yet she found herself leaning into the bolstering support he offered.

Her stomach fluttered. This was what her mother had warned her about. Victoria Bishop had declared men the ruin of women, turning perfectly sensible ladies into churning masses of emotions—robbing them of the ability to make sensible decisions. Sheltered from even the most banal interactions with gentlemen her own age, Anna had inwardly scoffed at the exaggerated tales.

Occasionally older men had flirted with her over the years. Once in a while, a stray husband of one of their acquaintances decided that charming a suffragist was a sign of virility. She'd been singularly unmoved by the obvious ploy. Their honeyed words had sluiced off her like raindrops off a slicker.

With Mr. McCoy near, a whole new understanding dawned. This wasn't the forced regard she usually deflected. His touch made her restless for more. There was an unexpected tenderness within him, a compassion that drew her nearer, tugging at the edges of her resolve.

"You're not well at all." He gingerly assisted her to the bed. "You're exhausted. We've overdone it. I'll fetch the doctor."

"No," Anna said, crumpling onto the mattress, too tired to care about detectives and gunshots and unassuming veterinarians who surprised her with their fierce protectiveness. "I simply need to rest."

To her immense relief, no one argued. Instead, in a flurry of pitying looks and murmured orders to repose, Izetta and Jo reluctantly exited the room.

Only Mr. McCoy lingered, one hand braced on the doorknob, the other on the wall, as though propelling himself from the room.

Was he that eager to be free of her?

He briefly glanced over his shoulder. "Rest. We can discuss what needs to be done later."

At least the change in position had temporarily alleviated the worst of her pain. If only her troubled thoughts were calmed as easily.

She desperately searched her memory for the events preceding the rally. A little girl had handed her a bouquet of flowers. Yellow flowers. Anna had recalled the color matched the child's dress.

My mama says you're a hero.

Anna was no hero. She was hiding in her room. Once she stepped out the door, she'd have to face reality. Just the idea sent a wave of fatigue shuddering through her.

You two can pretend to be engaged.

How did one simple sentence cast her emotions spinning? Disparate feelings pummeled her senses faster than she could sort them all out. She should have been more outraged by the suggestion. Her injury had obviously sapped her strength. For all her uncharacteristically mild response, she knew she *should* have felt as horrified as Mr. McCoy had appeared.

A lowering realization. She might be a suffragist, but she was also a woman. Not a bad-looking woman either. Anyone would have believed they were engaged. He could do worse. Anna wrinkled her nose. His opinion was of absolutely no concern.

Or was she reading him all wrong? Was he uncertain of his own appeal? No. That couldn't possibly be the case. Certainly there were plenty of ladies in Cimarron Springs eager for the attentions of the handsome veterinarian. While she may have been relatively isolated from the normal courting and machinations of men and women, she was not completely ignorant. If she trailed him through the crowded lobby, no doubt she'd observe more than one lady casting him a second glance. Which meant he couldn't possibly believe the problem rested with him.

Why on earth was she debating with herself?

She was wasting all sorts of time and energy on an absolutely worthless endeavor. None of her speculations mattered. The only way to navigate this mess was with facts—identify the difficulty and solve the problem. Mr. McCoy wasn't a problem. He was simply a diversion.

A diversion who'd soon be out of her life.

Another thought sent her stomach lurching. "How did he find me, anyway? The detective. Could someone else do the same?"

"He saw me. The day of the rally, carrying you. You're listed in the hotel register as my…as my guest."

Long after he was gone, Anna stared at the closed door. Something about how he'd said *guest* piqued her curiosity.

Mr. McCoy was hiding something.

Caleb caught up with his sister and blocked her exit. "What were you thinking?"

"I don't know what you're talking about."

"Yes. You do."

"Fine." She sniffed. "I saw the register. You're already listed as her fiancée. The engagement seemed like an excellent idea."

"No. It's not."

What if Anna discovered his deception in the guest registry, as well? With Jo spouting off about fiancées and his own collusion with the hotel, she'd never believe the two occurrences were not connected.

What would she think? He didn't even want to contemplate the answer.

"At least everyone would quit assuming you're mooning over Mary Louise," Jo said.

While that idea did hold some appeal, he wasn't letting her off the hook that easily. "Stop pushing, Jo. This is Anna's decision."

"Anna?"

"Miss Bishop is an intelligent, independent woman. She will make her own decisions regarding her life. If she wants help, she'll ask."

He kept thinking about her trunk. The week before, when they'd switched rooms, he'd carried the trunk himself. While he trusted the hotel staff, the fewer people who knew her whereabouts, the better.

The trunk had been expensive. A sturdy wooden affair with brass buckles and leather straps. Even the stack of books she'd plunked on her side table were leather bound. Her clothes were exquisitely tailored, there was nothing ready-made about Anna Bishop. Nothing at all. He'd traveled far enough away from Cimarron Springs, and he understood that even in the United States, a land built on equality, a class system prevailed. The McCoys had always been a hardworking lot who eked out a humble existence.

Judging from her wardrobe and her luggage, Anna had probably never cooked a meal for herself. He'd read the newspaper clippings Jo collected. Anna's mother was not just Victoria Bishop; she'd been nicknamed "the heiress." He might not know much about women, but he didn't figure an heiress would cotton to the kind of living in Cimarron Springs.

She was above his touch, both in wealth and in her ideology. And while his brain understood the implications, he feared his heart was not as wise.

Jo rubbed her thumbnail along her lower teeth, a sure sign she was worried about something. "Did you think Anna looked pale?"

He'd thought she was stunning. His heart picked up its rhythm, and he absently rubbed his chest. The first few days he'd corralled his wayward thoughts. When he caught himself staring at her lips, he closed his eyes and pictured the day of the rally. He pictured the blood staining his shirt and his hands. Anything that prevented him from thinking of her in a romantic fashion.

With her sitting up and dressed, her hair swept up in a tumble of curls, smelling like cherry blossoms, her lips rosy, he'd found himself staring at those lips once more. Wondering if she'd ever been kissed. While the detective had been talking, he'd been aching to run his hand over the soft skin at the nape of her exposed neck.

Jo pinched him back to attention. "I said, didn't you think she looked a little pale?"

Come to think of it, he'd noticed the lines around her mouth had deepened and the skin beneath her eyes had taken on the bruised look of fatigue.

"I noticed." He dragged the words from his throat. "It's my fault. I shouldn't have brought the detective."

Jo's expression softened, and she touched his arm. "No, you were right."

When the hotel staff had let him know the detective wanted to speak to Anna, he'd vetted the man first. "I'll ask Anna if she wants me to fetch the doctor."

"She'll say no," Jo said. "You know she will. She doesn't want to be a bother. I can tell."

"Then I won't give her a choice."

Jo didn't hide her triumphant expression fast enough.

"It won't make a lick of difference," he said. "If she refuses our help, we can't force her."

"We can show her we care."

Some of the steam went out of him. "Sure."

"I'll check the train station for times. We can give her the information. She can make her own decision after that. We're doing the right thing." Jo insisted.

Were they? Were they truly? Anna was in danger, and he was a country veterinarian. Were they really the best choice for her protection? He did know one thing—after seeing her that first day, the blood pooling beneath her, something primal inside him had broken free. He'd do anything to protect her, he knew that much for certain.

Jo rubbed her thumbnail on her bottom teeth once more. "I'll try and be back by the time the doctor comes. No promises, though."

"I'm sure Mrs. Franklin will be available if you're not."

At least fetching the doctor gave him something to do, something besides thinking of how Anna had looked at him when Jo had suggested the engagement. The look was the same one Mary Louise had given him when he'd asked to court her.

She'd looked at him with shock and derision.

At least this time his heart hadn't been involved. Not yet, anyway. He didn't plan on staying around long enough for any more damage to be done.

He'd go to the grave before he let anyone know he'd been playing her fiancé behind her back.

After a fitful nap that left her no more rested and no closer to a solution, Anna awoke more determined than ever. Her path ahead was clear. Her best hope at ending this turmoil was finding the person who wanted her dead or proving the whole thing was a mistake. Then she could go home.

There was every chance the police would discover that

someone had accidentally shot out their parlor window like her inept neighbor, nearly killing Anna in the process. Either way, she'd go back home. Back to traveling during the week and corresponding with other suffragists over the weekends. Back to a future that looked remarkably like her past.

There was nothing unsatisfying about her life, was there? And yet her mind rebelled at the notion. The nagging feeling lingered. A sense that something was missing.

A knock sounded at the door and Anna groaned.

Was it really too much to ask for a moment's peace? The guard at her door announced Mr. McCoy, and her agitation intensified. She wasn't ready to see him again. Her thoughts and feelings were too jumbled, too confusing.

She considered refusing him entrance, then dismissed the idea as churlish. "Come in."

The door swung open, and Mr. McCoy entered with another, shorter, gentleman in his later years with a smooth-shaven face, a bulbous nose and prominent ears.

The second man tipped his hat. "I'm Dr. Smith. You probably don't remember me, but I checked in on you a few days ago."

Anna glared at Mr. McCoy. "As I stated earlier, I'm fine. I simply need rest."

"I'm quite sure you do," Dr. Smith said. "I recommend several weeks of light activity. A visit to the country would do you good."

Anna huffed. She was usually quite reasonable, but this constant interference was unacceptable. "Did Mr. McCoy put you up to this?"

The doctor washed his hands in the basin. "No. Can't say that he did. It's simply a treatment course recommended for my gunshot victims. I must say, my gunshot victims are usually men, but the convalescence procedure is the same. These are modern times, I suppose. Not sure I like all the change. Let's have a look, shall we?"

Deciding it was easier to concede than argue, Anna lifted her arm and tugged her shirt loose, exposing her bandaged side.

She glanced across the room to where Mr. McCoy had suddenly discovered an intense fascination for the flocked wallpaper. Staying annoyed with the man was impossible. Which annoyed her even more.

Dr. Smith perched on a chair near the bed, peeled away the bandage and squinted. "You're excellent with a needle, Mr. McCoy. Your talents are wasted on livestock. Sorry I missed the excitement firsthand but I was paying a house call on another patient when they came to fetch me after the accident." He reached for his bag. "While I hate to unravel all your fine work, it's time we take out the stitches. Might hurt a bit. Can I send for someone?"

Caleb glanced around as though searching for help. "Jo had an errand. Can I fetch Izetta to sit with you?"

"No. She's home. She's been running herself ragged."

"I should leave," he said brusquely.

"Stay," she blurted, immediately regretting her outburst. "Talk with me," she added quickly, covering her embarrassment. "Tell me a story. I've read Jo's letters, the McCoys must be excellent storytellers."

What on earth was she blubbering about? A little pain was nothing. She didn't need her hand held like a child.

"I'll stay," he said, a wealth of reluctance in his voice.

Though she'd had plenty of visitors, she'd also had too much time alone. She clung to him because he was the one constant in all her confusion, which was understandable.

That wasn't exactly true. He and Jo and Izetta had become her salvation.

All the logic in the world failed to ease her fear. She didn't want her independence right then. She wanted someone to hold her hand and tell her everything was going to be all right.

The doctor clipped the first stitch, and Anna hissed a breath, closing her eyes. Caleb's hesitation said everything. She'd pushed their relationship beyond the boundaries he'd established. A forgivable mistake.

The situation had forced them into a false intimacy, and that state was temporary. She'd do well to remember the distinction. Except she'd lost all of her usual soft landing places. Normally when she was feeling alone or out of sorts, her work filled in the desolate spots. Here there were only four walls decorated with that abysmal olive-colored flocked wallpaper. She much preferred looking at a pair of kind, forest-green eyes. That was her downfall. Those infernal eyes.

Once she was home, certainly she'd forget all about him. Here there was too much time for thinking, too much temptation to read more into a kind gesture or a caring word.

Too much time for realizing that she'd almost died.

Chapter Five

She'd asked the wrong McCoy for a story, but he'd do his best. She'd been through a rough time, and Caleb wanted to infuse her with some of his own strength.

The bed depressed beneath his weight. "I'll tell you about the time my cousin nearly got himself killed at the husking bee."

He watched as the doctor lifted the first stitch free, then adjusted his position on the edge of the bed. The doctor studied the wound, humming softly, ignoring their exchange. With the doctor claiming the only chair, Caleb was left with a sliver of the bed for sitting on the opposite side. He plumped one pillow against the headboard and pushed up straighter, his right leg stretched out on the coverlet, his left knee bent and his foot braced against the floor so that he didn't take up too much room.

"What's a husking bee?" Anna asked, her head turned toward him, her expression curious and devoid of the fright he'd seen earlier.

Despite the pain and the forced confinement, she'd not complained, not once that he'd heard. She'd soldiered on through the worst of conditions. Caught in her trusting gaze, the last of his reluctance melted away.

He might not be the storyteller in the family, but for Anna, he'd give his best effort. "Back in the day, a farmer put up his corn in the barn before winter came and husked it at his leisure during the cold months. But old farmer Bainum had a better idea. He figured if all the ladies gathered every Saturday for a quilting bee, then all the fellows could hold a husking bee. He figured if he disguised the work as a party, he'd get a lot of help. That first year, he rolled out a barrel of his best hard apple cider, and every able-bodied man in the county showed up. Except Bainum cider is strong stuff. Only half the husking was finished before the boys decided they were having more fun drinking than husking."

The doctor muttered something unintelligible.

The groan that came from Anna's lips died in a hiss. His heart clenched at the sight of her distress. He'd never felt so helpless, so utterly inadequate.

Her grimace eased and she said, "Liquor has never been conducive to work."

"Not even in the country," Caleb babbled, desperate to keep her mind off her hurts. "Old Mr. Bainum was stuck husking the rest of the corn himself, and he'd given up a whole barrel of apple cider for his trouble. The next year he had an even better idea. He'd invite the ladies. Even though he'd been widowed longer than he'd been married, he knew enough from family gatherings and church picnics to realize a thing or two about ladies. A wife never showed up at an event without a covered dish, and they always kept an eye on how much cider the men drank."

"Sounds like more work for the women." Anna hoisted a disapproving eyebrow.

"He thought of that, as well. Once all the corn was husked, old farmer Bainum decided to throw a barn dance. Around Cimarron Springs, the ladies always like a good dance. Mr. Bainum made a game of the husking, too. He threw in a couple of ears of red corn. When a young man discovered an ear of red corn, he was allowed one kiss with the lady of his choice."

The doctor lifted another stitch free.

For a brief moment, Anna's face contorted in pain. "What if a lady found the red ear?"

"Then she made certain that red ear made its way into the stack of the fellow she was sweet on."

"Did you ever find the red ear?" she asked, then winced.

The doctor murmured an apology.

Maintaining his perch on the opposite side of Anna, Caleb touched her shoulder. "Don't get ahead of the story." Though she was clearly uncomfortable, his tale was distracting her, and for that he was grateful. "This is about my cousin Gus. You see, one particularly memorable husking bee, we were all sitting around on stools, shucking the corn and throwing the ears onto the floor in the center, when my cousin Gus found the first red ear and asked Becky Bainum for a kiss."

"Mr. Bainum's daughter?"

"The one and only."

"How outrageous. What did Mr. Bainum think?"

"Old farmer Bainum was not happy about Gus's selection. You see, the Bainums fought for the Confederate Army during the War Between the States. The McCoys, being of good, strong Irish stock and having arrived at the Castle Garden Depot as fast as the County Cork could send them, lived in the North and fought for the North.

Sometimes voluntarily, sometimes by order of President Lincoln. One thing you have to know around these parts, the war never really ended for some folks, especially old farmer Bainum."

"Poor Gus."

"Don't feel bad for him just yet. Gus found three more red ears in less than an hour."

Anna grimaced. "How did Becky feel about all those kisses? Could she refuse if she wanted?"

"She didn't mind a bit." Caleb grinned. "Old Mr. Bainum was another story. A man who'd gotten his neighbors to husk his corn and bring all the food for the party afterward is no fool. He knew well enough the McCoys didn't have that kind of luck. No Irishman does. That's when Mr. Bainum decided to fire up the pot-bellied stove."

The doctor blotted the wound with an alcohol soaked pad, and Anna sucked in a breath. Her skin grew ashen. "Isn't a fire in the barn, even in a stove, dangerous with all those dry husks lying around?"

"Old farmer Bainum took the risk." Though he kept his voice even, Caleb battled the guilt swamping him. Seeing her in pain invoked a fury he'd never experienced before, along with a deep sense of tenderness. The two disparate emotions raged a battle within him. "Mr. Bainum stoked that stove until it burned hot. Soon enough, everybody took off their coats and rolled up their shirtsleeves. Everyone except Gus."

A knowing smile stretched across her strained and pale face. "How long did he last with his coat on?"

Caleb's stomach dipped. He shouldn't be staring at her lips while talking about kisses. This was hardly the time or place for amorous thoughts. "Through two more kisses. Finally got too hot. Gus pulled off his coat, and six more red ears of corn fell out."

Anna chuckled. The movement didn't seem to bother her, an excellent sign for her continued healing. While he preferred leaving the stitches in for longer, the doctor was right, Anna was young and healthy and healing fast.

She brushed the hair from her forehead. "The McCoys don't need any luck. They make their own."

"That they do."

Caleb sneaked a discreet glance at her side. The doctor had finished removing the row of stitches from the front of the wound. The skin was healthy, the scar puckered, with no sign of infection. He breathed a sigh of relief. A septic wound was often worse than the original injury.

The doctor motioned with one hand. "On your side and I'll take a look at the exit site."

Anna reached out her arm, and Caleb grasped her fingers; together they carefully rolled her toward him onto her left side, her left hand tucked beneath her cheek. Her fingers were icy cold, and he longed to infuse them with his own warmth. All too quickly she was settled, and he reluctantly released his hold.

The color deserted her cheeks, and her lips pinched together, a sure sign of pain. He touched her shoulder. "Should I stop?"

"No. I'm fine," she said, although they both knew she was lying. "I want to hear how the story ends. What happened with Gus and Becky?"

"Gus borrowed a Confederate coat and a Union Jack from a fellow in town. He marched right up to Mr. Bainum's door and told him he was there to enlist in the Confederate army."

"He did not."

"He might have." Caleb shrugged. "A fellow will do odd things when he's in love."

"You almost had me fooled. What really happened?"

The exit wound was larger than the entrance wound, meaning Caleb better stretch out the ending of his story. A difficult task since his concentration kept slipping. He loathed the marring of her beautiful skin. He hated her suffering.

"Mr. Bainum kept them apart, even though everyone told him that he was a crotchety old fool for doing so. My uncle, Gus's dad, even tried reasoning with him, but he wouldn't listen. All the while Becky kept those six ears of red corn wrapped in an old flour sack. She didn't hum when she gathered eggs in the morning, she didn't whistle while she churned the butter. She didn't take the long path around the pond and cut lilacs for the table."

Sorrow darkened Anna's brilliant blue eyes. "My mother always said love ruined a woman faster than rain ruined a parade."

A deep tenderness welled within him. "Your mother is wrong."

He'd seen the redeeming power of love lift even the most shattered soul from the darkness.

"Victoria Bishop is never wrong," Anna stated matter-of-factly.

"Of course she is. Nobody is right all the time."

"Don't let her hear you say that."

Another tick mark against the elder Miss Bishop. While Anna's expression held no rancor, his own feelings were clear. How had such a rigid woman raised such a compassionate child? Did the elder Miss Bishop scorn all love or merely the love between a man and a woman? She'd certainly poisoned her daughter with her attitude.

What of Anna's father? From what Caleb had read in the papers, Anna's mother had never revealed his name. Had the man taken advantage of her? Was that what had shaped her attitude? He doubted Anna even knew. Her convictions were too innocently stated. Was her mother hiding something? Victoria Bishop didn't seem the sort to protect a man, but what did he know? Seeds of hate were just like any other seeds; they started small and, with careful tending, grew into massive things.

Anna stared at him expectantly, and he forced his attention back on the story. "It wasn't love that took the skip out of Becky's step. It was keeping that love hidden away. Mr. Bainum had already lost his wife, and he realized soon enough that he was losing his daughter, as well. He could remain a stubborn old coot, or he could put the song back in his daughter's heart."

"I suppose they lived happily ever after?" Anna asked, her voice dripping with sarcasm. "Isn't that always the way?"

"You've read too many fairy tales. This is real life."

"You're wrong on that account. Fairy tales were strictly forbidden and considered frivolous except for educational purposes. I was allowed to read Peter Parley, but only because his adventures were deemed educational. Although I did smuggle a copy of *Little Women*. I still have the book."

"What's wrong with *Little Women*?"

Not that he'd read the book, he was simply curious of the reasoning behind the ban. Jo had a copy dog-eared from multiple readings.

Anna's expression turned wistful. "Miss Alcott considered true love a necessary facet of a woman's identity.

My mother disagreed. Vehemently. Fairy tales and love were frivolous and unnecessary."

He opened his mouth, a scalding retort for the elder Miss Bishop on the tip of his tongue, but he couldn't say the words. What did he know of raising children? He pictured Anna as a child, her wide blue eyes alight with curiosity. What other activities had been deemed frivolous? Why was something as innocuous as true love vilified?

Clamping shut his lips, he sucked in a breath through his nose. He wasn't here for debate. He was here to take Anna's mind off the pain. "Nobody lives happily ever after, near as I can tell. My ma and pa love each other, but I've seen them go at each other like a couple of raccoons fighting over the same bone." He grinned at her shocked expression. "They're married, Becky and Gus. Most days are good, some days are bad. Same as everyone else."

"What happened to old farmer Bainum? Did he die a lonely death after his daughter left?"

"You can't jump the ending." He brushed the stray lock of hair from her forehead once more. "Mr. Bainum got used to the idea of having a Yank for a son-in-law, especially after he saw his first grandbaby. Gus and Becky have four boys, and he's got his hands full teaching them all to fish and farm."

Anna tucked both hands beneath her cheek. "Does he still host the husking bee?"

"Every year. And since he only has one daughter, he doesn't care how many red husks the other fellows smuggle in."

"I knew it!" She scowled. "You're just as bad as Gus."

"I didn't say I snuck a red ear into the batch."

"But you did."

"I did. I just didn't say it."

"It's the same thing and you know it. Shame on you." She rubbed her cheek against the back of her fingers. "Who did you kiss?"

The years rushed away, and he was a green youth again, all of his tender hopes pinned on a girl who didn't love him. "I didn't kiss anyone. My brother David got the girl before I did."

She touched his hand, and he started. "I shouldn't have teased you."

"Nah. It's all right. That's the thing about being young. You think if you love someone enough, you can love them enough for both of you. But that's a selfish love."

He'd never thought about Mary Louise's feelings, only his own. He'd been young and self-centered, too wrapped up in his own feelings to think about her, to notice she was only using him to make David jealous. He'd forgiven her by and by. They'd all been little more than children.

The doctor removed the last stitch. The area around the wound was pink, and the edges holding together nicely. Caleb might have waited a few more days, considering the placement of the stitching, but the skin had already healed over some of the sutures, causing her discomfort as they were removed. There were no signs of infection on this side either, and for that he was grateful.

Anna tugged on his hand for his attention. "I bet there were plenty of other young ladies who wanted your attention."

"Too many to count. There's not a stalk of red corn in the county before a husking bee. By the end of the night, I have a whole pile at my feet."

"That's the only part of the story I believe." Her eyes shimmered with laughter.

There was no use telling the truth. He'd never kissed a girl. The desire had been long dormant.

Until now. He feared she was his undoing.

Anna kept her attention on Caleb's bent knee, finding his eyes far too distracting.

The doctor pulled up the blanket and sat back. "All finished. No strenuous activity for the next few weeks. Don't lift anything heavy. No horseback riding or bronco busting."

"I'll pull my name from the rodeo lineup."

Mr. McCoy stood and took a few steps away, his attention focused on the olive-green flocked wallpaper she'd grown heartily sick of staring at from morning till night.

She'd embarrassed him with her request, though she'd enjoyed his story. Whether or not the tale was entirely true was suspect. In any event, the distraction had worked, she'd hardly noticed the doctor's painful poking and prodding. Her glum mood had also lifted.

The interlude was over, and she'd best place their relationship back on normal footing. Show him that he needn't fear another lapse. She wasn't a clingy helpless female hoping for a boy to kiss her.

Well, she wasn't a clingy, helpless female, at any rate. The thought of Caleb kissing someone else hit her in the chest like a cannon ball. She did not like the idea one bit.

"I'd recommend staying put for the next several days," Dr. Smith said.

The delicate start of her lighthearted mood fled. The walls closed in on her, and the air in the room thickened. She'd been resting because of the stitches. She hadn't thought much past the future. She'd harbored the naive belief that once the stitches were removed, she'd skip out of her room, down the corridor and out the front door to freedom once more.

She'd never been confined to bed. Not even when she'd had the chicken pox as a child. The rest of the household, including her mother, had been too busy with their own chores and affairs to pay her any mind. After the few first days she'd been up and about. Until the spots went away, she'd had the run of the house. She was used to being independent and spontaneous, not lolling about in her room.

Being ordered to stay put sparked a burst of restless energy and an immediate urge to escape. The guard outside her door had her feeling more like a prisoner than protected.

Mr. McCoy continued his study of the raised pattern on the wall covering, tracing his fingers along the edges. "How soon can she travel by train?"

"Yes. I'd like to travel as soon as possible."

There'd be no more talk of Cimarron Springs. She wouldn't be foisted on Jo's family like an impoverished relative. The detective was obviously mistaken, and after a day or two of quiet, they'd all realize his error. There was absolutely no reason for someone to want her dead. She had few friends in her solitary life, let alone enemies. The bullet had been meant as a warning to the suffragists. Or an accident. No one had considered that likelihood. They still hadn't ruled out the possibility that this was all some horrible mistake.

"Hmm, travel by train." The doctor smoothed his thumb and forefinger along the edges of his mouth. "Anytime, really, if she's up to it. As long as the trip isn't too lengthy." The doctor snapped shut his bag and stood. "Try and sleep. Rest will do you the best good. If you have any problems, send for me."

As the doctor exited with a tip of his hat, Mr. McCoy cleared his throat, then stared at the floor. "I'm sorry about what Jo said earlier. I don't know what she was thinking. I'm sure they'll find the shooter and this will all be over soon. Jo and I are in the two rooms across the way. If you need anything, just holler."

The tips of his ears had reddened. Obviously he'd regretted his sister's impulsive suggestion.

He kept edging toward the door. Most likely he was frightened she'd insist he tell her another story.

Anna plucked at the stitching of her coverlet. "We have the word of one man. There's no need for everyone to descend into a dither. We should have taken Jo's suggestion for what it was—a light moment during a tense situation. The thought of people believing we are engaged is actually quite amusing."

"Yes," he replied, his voice gruff, though his expression remained hidden from her.

He took another step toward the door.

She fixed her gaze on the coverlet. "They'll be no need for me to burden your sister with a houseguest."

Another step.

"Likely not."

Yet another step.

This conversation was embarrassing enough without looking him in the face. He'd echoed her sentiments. Which was perfect. Excellent. Although none of her resolute thinking explained why she became tongue-tied the instant he entered a room.

That was a problem best solved at another time. In another place. Perhaps safely ensconced at home in St. Louis.

Her mother's home, more accurately. Perhaps it was

time she sought living arrangements of her own. A spinster's residence. Anna nearly gagged on the word. Unmarried men were "confirmed bachelors," treated with mild admiration by other men, as though they'd achieved some sort of higher standing by remaining unattached. Women were spinsters.

Yet another distinction she abhorred. No matter how they referred to her, she was looking into moving out of her mother's home once she recovered. She had a modest trust from her grandfather—a man who'd died before she was born. Anna was never quite certain why he'd provided for her since he didn't seem the sort of man who would have approved of his daughter bearing an out-of-wedlock child. Whatever his thoughts, the money was there and she was a fool not to make use of it.

Having a goal strengthened her flagging reserves of energy. "Thank you, Mr. McCoy, for everything. Truly. I hope I haven't seemed ungrateful."

It's just that you tie me in knots, and I've never been the tied-in-knots-over-a-man sort of person.

He stuck his hands in his pockets and avoided looking directly at her. "Caleb." He cleared his throat. "I saved your life. I think that puts us on a first-name basis."

"I amend my apology. Thank you, Caleb. And you must call me Anna."

She tripped a bit over the last syllable.

"You have nothing to apologize for, Anna."

Her stomach fluttered. The use of her name lent an air of intimacy to the exchange. She'd never been particularly fond of her name. She liked hearing Caleb say it. She liked hearing him say her name very much.

He straightened and smoothed his jacket. "Rest. We don't need to decide anything right now."

She opened her mouth with a protest, then quickly changed her mind.

Later she'd tell him that all of her decisions had been made. She'd go home as soon as the train schedule allowed. Most likely they'd never see one another again. She'd only hear of him through Jo's letters.

The vague headache she'd been fighting all morning throbbed into life. "I'm certain we'll discover this is all some mad mistake. I'm hardly important enough to have attracted an enemy."

"I think you're quite attractive." Caleb's face flamed. "That is, you gave a very impassioned speech. I was quite moved. The crowd was quite moved. In any case," he rushed on, "I'm certain this will all be resolved soon."

He spun out of the room so quickly she half expected a plume of smoke in his wake.

He'd called her attractive.

The frantic beating of her heart didn't signify anything. Reacting positively to a compliment, whether deliberate or accidental, was human nature. Though the admission had been a slip of the tongue, his mortification had lent the unintentional admission truth. Not that a woman's looks defined her worth. Quite the opposite.

She studied the bright sunlight streaming into her room. Soon he'd be part of her past, a diverting memory mixed in with the pain and fear of this past week.

The sense of relief she expected never came.

Feeling beneath her pillow, she located her embroidery and finished stitching the edges of a red poppy. Truth be told, she'd been intrigued by the idea of concealing her true identity. Assuming a new identity meant she'd be invisible. There would be no expectations. No comparisons to the Great Victoria Bishop.

How liberating, to be anonymous. There would be no living up to her mother's reputation.

An envelope on the table caught Anna's attention, and she reached for the forgotten telegram. Her mother's familiar clipped speech greeted her in bold capital letters. Her worry was evident, the concern apparent. It was the last line that gave Anna pause. She read and reread the words.

BEST YOU RECUPERATE IN KANSAS CITY STOP YOU MUSTNT RISK THE JOURNEY STOP

For some inexplicable reason, tears sprang in her eyes. Despite all the solitude she'd endured during her life, she couldn't recall a time when she felt more utterly or completely alone.

Chapter Six

Upon returning to the hotel after a brief walk the following day, Caleb took the steps two at a time. He didn't know why, the closer he got to Anna, the greater his sense of urgency. He'd been fighting an inexplicable sense of anxiety all day.

A woman blocked his path on the landing, and he nearly toppled over her, stopping short just in time. The other hotel guest was in her midtwenties, dressed in an expensive burgundy brocade jacket with a fur muff, even though it was only early fall.

"Pardon me," he said.

"No need for pardon." She patted the side of her brassy blond hair, her eyes glittery blue chips against her powdered cheeks. "Are you staying at the hotel long?"

"Checking out soon," he answered, his voice clipped.

He wasn't in the mood for polite small talk. Occasionally people mistook his silence for interest, and the woman standing before him appeared the sort who'd have plenty to say.

She shrugged and continued on her way, glancing once over her shoulder.

After nearly a week cooped up at the Savoy Hotel, it was time he returned home. He'd left his younger brother, Maxwell, in charge of his animals while he was gone, but there was no one available to take over his practice. Truth be told, he wanted some space between him and Miss Bishop. She held an undeniable draw, and he was going to make a fool of himself if he didn't leave soon.

His face flushed. He'd gone and called her attractive. He'd always been reticent around women, and Anna exacerbated his condition. His first instincts had been correct—the longer he was around her, the likelier he was to make a fool of himself. A bigger fool, he silently amended.

His purpose here had been served. Miss Bishop—Anna—had a guard outside her door. The suffragist women had kept up a steady stream of visitors. They'd brought enough flowers to blanket a meadow. Even now the scent of roses perfumed the corridor.

He didn't consider himself an intuitive man; more often than not he missed the signs other people assured him came from women. With Anna he felt a definite sense of distance, as though she kept a protective space between them, like a wounded animal, skittish of contact. A part of him longed to challenge that distance.

Which was precisely why he needed to find Jo and arrange their departure. Certainly Garrett, Jo's husband, was growing impatient by now. She must miss her children.

Upon arriving at Jo's room, she waved him in. "Where have you been?"

Her obvious annoyance took him aback. "I'm sorry, was I supposed to leave a note?"

"You might have told me where you'd gone. I was worried."

"I didn't mean to worry you. I was looking at some plumbing fixtures."

"Plumbing fixtures?" She paused, then planted her hands on her hips. "You were looking at plumbing fixtures with all that's going on?"

"There have been some amazing improvements in indoor plumbing. Kansas City is the closest place to find the modern equipment."

"If you weren't my own brother, I'd think you were being deliberately obtuse."

"Why are you so cranky? We're sitting around the hotel waiting for Miss Bishop to be well enough to travel. I'm going crazy. Besides, yesterday you bought taffy for the kids, and I didn't lecture you."

She'd gone and left him alone with Anna. Every encounter had him craving more. If he was staying away from the hotel, avoiding more encounters with Anna, his decision was none of Jo's concern.

"When I said I was going for taffy, you rolled your eyes."

"That is not a lecture." Best he changed the subject. They were all on edge. Torn between oppressive fear and crushing tedium. "Have you heard anything from Anna's mother?"

"No. And I'm tempted to give the woman a piece of my mind. Anna's never said a cross word, but what kind of mother leaves her daughter all alone, in a strange town? Injured. I've been away from Jocelyn for a week, and I'm already crawling up the walls with worry. And she's fit as a fiddle. If she were hurt…" Jo grimaced. "If she were hurt, I'd be by her side in an instant."

His thoughts had run along a similar vein. "Anna's an adult. I have a feeling her mother values independence. I have a feeling they both value independence."

Yet another reason he needed space between them. He didn't hold her background against her, though he recognized plenty of others did. He knew enough about himself to realize he was more traditional. Back when he'd been interested in courting, he'd always pictured a marriage similar to the one his parents shared. A wife and children, a quiet life in Cimarron Springs. Another reason he and Anna didn't suit.

"The Bishops are a unique pair," Jo said. "From what I've read, Victoria is one of those rare individuals who seems larger than life in any setting, no matter how mundane."

"Like mother, like daughter on that account."

Anna certainly had the ability to draw in a crowd. He'd been singularly transfixed the moment she stepped behind the podium. While he might have chalked up the experience to his own attraction, he'd seen Jo respond the same way.

"They are similar in that way, I suppose," Jo said thoughtfully. "Anna possesses much the same appeal, but there's a gentler, more compassionate aura surrounding her."

Caleb's gaze sharpened. "Don't let Anna's mother hear you say that. I have a feeling that *soft* is a word she abhors."

Life with Victoria Bishop must surely have been anything but conventional. Their own upbringing had been completely ordinary. What must childhood have been like for Anna, living with such a forceful personality? What expectations had been laid at her feet? Did she ever feel the weight of responsibility crushing her?

Judging from her dedication to the cause, most likely not. She already had her own legacy in the making. Probably why she kept her distance. Anna had a calling.

Anna.

Her name whispered at his conscience. He should have kept their relationship on a more formal footing. Calling her Miss Bishop kept him detached. First, Jo had gone and said they should pretend to be an engaged couple. Then, he'd blurted out that he found her attractive. Anna must have thought their whole family was daft.

No doubt she was ready to see the last of them both. The longer they stayed in Kansas City, the more he worried about their deception, of Anna discovering she'd been hiding out as his fiancée. He and Jo had offered their assistance, and she'd refused. There was nothing more to be done.

Another knock sounded, and Jo scooted past him to admit a young, uniformed maid clutching a handful of bedding.

The girl bobbed her head. "Fresh linens, miss."

"Thank you," Jo replied distractedly, then turned toward Caleb. "We should talk with Anna. Make some decisions about what to do next. I don't want to abandon her, but I can't be away from the children any longer."

Her obvious longing for her children reinforced his own plans. "If Miss Bishop refuses our help, there's not much else we can do. This was never our responsibility in the first place."

The maid straightened from her crouch beside the bed. "You know Miss Bishop? Did her relatives find her? Her uncle seemed quite concerned."

Caleb and Jo exchanged a confused glance.

Jo touched the girl's arm, halting her exit. "Are you certain the man was looking for Miss Bishop?"

"Oh, quite certain."

His sister frowned slightly. "I don't recall Anna ever mentioning an uncle."

Caleb sprinted into the corridor, relieved to see the guard stationed before Miss Bishop's door. Taking a slow deep breath, he stilled his racing thoughts. For all any of them knew, she had a whole bevy of aunts and uncles and cousins. No need for panic. He'd speak with Anna before charging off in a frenzy. Then he'd alert the hotel staff as an additional precaution.

A commotion snapped him upright. A shrill scream sounded from Anna's room. Glass shattered. A male voice shouted.

The guard whipped around and kicked open the door. In a blaze, Caleb raced after him and tripped over the maid's linen basket. He cracked his knee on the floor. A flurry of movement caught his attention. From his awkward crouched position, he managed to grasp the man's leg as he raced by. The assailant went down hard. Caleb scrambled upright and the man kicked out with his free leg. The blow glanced off the side of Caleb's head. An explosion of pain burst behind his eyes.

He lost his hold and his vision blurred. Staggering upright, he braced one hand against the wall. Someone shrieked. Squinting, Caleb made out the hazy form of the maid. He blinked a few times, unable to clear his vision.

The man shoved the maid forward and she careened into Caleb. The collision tipped him backward and they slammed into the wall.

Bracing his hands against the maid's shoulders, he

caught only the blurred image of her pale face in a halo of blond hair because of his impaired vision. "Are you all right?"

"Shaken, that's all."

He set the woman aside and staggered toward the stairs. Feeling along the banister, he managed his way to the lobby. By the time he reached the front doors, his vision had mostly cleared, but the improvement was too late.

The assailant had disappeared. He spun around and searched the surrounding streets. People hustled to and fro. There was no sign of the intruder.

He turned back to the hotel and nicked something with his foot. Bending, he caught sight of a knife, blood still visible on the blade. His heart seized.

He took the stairs two at a time and burst into Anna's room a moment later.

Miss Bishop leaned over the guard who lay writhing beneath the broken window, his hands clenching his face as blood seeped through his fingers.

Caleb's pulse thundered in his ears, adrenaline still coursing through his body. "Are you hurt?"

He knelt beside Anna and grasped her shoulders, turning her toward him. He kept his arms rigid, resisting the urge to crush her against his chest. Her scream had taken a decade off his life. The vision of the bloody knife was still forefront in his thoughts.

Seconds before, he'd been making plans to leave her. Now he couldn't let her go. His fingers remained clenched on her upper arms, his arms shaking. She was safe and nothing else mattered. Nothing else mattered except finding the man responsible.

"I'm fine," she replied, a tremor in her voice. "This

poor man took the brunt of it. The intruder had a knife. He must have thought I was sleeping."

Caleb released her, tearing his fingers away, hoping she didn't notice his reluctance. Jo caught his stricken gaze, and he quickly looked away, afraid she might read the raw emotion behind his actions.

After quickly ensuring the guard's wound was superficial, he stood and crossed the room.

While Anna and Jo plucked glass from the floor, Caleb leaned out the broken window and briefly searched the roofline and the ground three stories below. A flash of silver pipe caught his attention. No other movement flickered in either direction. The intruder had obviously swung in from the fire escape attached to the adjoining room, a dangerous endeavor, but obviously not impossible. Even if Caleb made the jump as well, the man already had a head start, he was no better off than before. He'd never find him.

With a muttered curse, he snatched a towel from the washstand and pressed it against the guard's face. "This isn't as bad as it looks. Facial wounds, well, they tend to bleed more."

He should have been with her. He should have alerted the guard instead of lingering in the corridor like an inept fool. He should have done a lot of things differently. Anna might have lost her life because of his hesitation.

From that moment on, he wasn't letting her out of his sight. "What happened? Did you see who did this?"

Anna swiped the hair from her face, inadvertently smearing the guard's blood across her forehead. "I was resting and I heard a noise. A man broke through the window."

A desperate act. Though the room faced the much-less traveled alleyway, it was broad daylight. The man had climbed the fire escape three stories and navigated a narrow ledge, probably holding the pipe Caleb had eyed below in order to break the window. The guard outside the door had thwarted any attempts of gaining entrance through the hotel, forcing the ill-fated break-in attempt.

Reality slammed into him. The man had been mere feet from Anna. Shooting someone from a distance was impersonal. Stabbing or bludgeoning someone at close range was far more heinous.

Jo turned toward the stricken maid cowering near the door. “Fetch the doctor. He should know the way by now.”

Anna’s jaw tightened. “This has gone too far. I’m going to hire that fidgety Pinkerton detective and find out who’s responsible before someone gets killed.”

“The offer still stands.” Jo crouched beside them. “You can come to Cimarron Springs with us. Whatever you decide, we’ll support you. Won’t we, Caleb?”

“Of course.”

Anna didn’t answer immediately, and neither of them pushed her for answer. Not that her reply mattered. He’d talk her into coming back with them, no matter how long it took.

Caleb caught his shirt cuff over his wrist and anchored the material with his fingers, then lifted his arm, gently wiping the blood from her face with his sleeve. The events of the previous week came rushing back. How close they’d come to losing her. Not once but twice.

When the last evidence of the blood had been wiped away, he realized his hands were shaking. He’d let Anna say her piece, but he planned on arguing their case until she saw reason.

She lifted her lashes and met his steady gaze. His

breath caught in the back of his throat. She had the most fascinating, expressive eyes. A blue so deep and pure, he was drawn into the exquisite pool of color.

She tugged her lower lip between her teeth. "I'm wondering… That is…"

Her rare hesitation had his attention. He edged closer.

Close enough that if he leaned just a little farther, he might touch his lips to the curve of her ear. "You were saying."

His breath whispered against her cheek.

Curiosity overcame him. Her unspoken words became paramount.

"I'm wondering if we should…"

The guard sat up between them with a grunt, bumping them apart, the reddened towel pressed against his face. "Hey, now, what's wrong with you people? I'm bleeding to death here."

Caleb bristled at the interruption. "It's only a scratch."

The guard lurched upright, and Caleb hooked his arm beneath the man's elbow, pulling them both into a standing position.

He reached for Anna, but she'd turned away. Disappointment knotted in his stomach. The moment was gone. She'd lost her courage. Whatever she'd been about to say was lost to him forever.

With a startled gasp, Mrs. Franklin appeared in the doorway. "For goodness' sake. I only left for a moment and it's chaos."

Guiding the injured man toward a chair, Caleb motioned for the widow. "Can you see to him? He's been cut on the cheek. It's not deep. It looks bad, though. You know how these facial wounds are."

She studied the wound with an expert eye. "I saw plenty of those from my boys growing up."

A sorrowful shadow passed over her eyes. She cleared her throat and dusted her hands, as though brushing away the troubled memories of her lost sons. "Let's see what's to be done."

Caleb held out his hand and reached for Anna. Her fingers clasped his, trembling.

His momentary annoyance at the interruption fled. "You've had a fright. Would you like to lie down?"

A delicate shudder swept through her. "I've had enough of lying about to last a lifetime. Besides, I believe the bed is otherwise occupied."

The guard had slumped from the chair onto the bed. Flat on his back, he clutched his face and stared at the ceiling, moaning.

Mrs. Franklin reached between Anna and Caleb. "Just amongst us," she spoke in a harsh whisper, "I've tended children with stronger constitutions than this one."

In a scene eerily reminiscent of the one that had played out only a week before, the room descended into a flurry of controlled pandemonium. The doctor arrived, his chest puffing with exertion, and the guard was stitched up with much groaning and complaining before he was hustled away.

Once the four of them were alone again, Anna perched on the edge of the bed. Jo continued gingerly plucking the shards of glass from the floor, and Caleb took the only chair.

Mrs. Franklin paced the room, her hands behind her back. "Mr. McCoy, you're a far better surgeon than Dr. Smith, and Anna is a far better patient."

Jo paused in her work and scrunched up her nose.

"You'd have thought he'd been cleaved in half with all that whining."

"Let's not be so quick to judge." Anna hid a grin. "We all experience pain differently."

Mrs. Franklin straightened the plain white collar adorning her serviceable gray dress. "It is becoming increasingly clear that the detective was correct. This is the second attempt on Miss Bishop's life. She cannot possibly stay in Kansas City, and St. Louis is equally unsafe. There is an obvious solution to our problem."

When Mrs. Franklin failed to complete her thought, Caleb rolled his hand forward. "And what solution is that?"

"I shall accompany Miss Bishop to this town of yours. What was the name?"

"Cimarron Springs," the three other occupants of the room spoke in unison.

"I shall accompany you to Cimarron Springs. While one person might raise a few eyebrows, the two of us will attract less attention."

"Sounds good to me," Jo offered cheerfully.

Anna shook her head. "I couldn't possibly ask that of you."

"You're not asking. I'm offering. This is the best solution. You need care. Jo has her own family."

Caleb's sister, normally eager to add her opinion to any conversation, remained oddly silent.

"I took the liberty of making a few inquiries while the three of you were foiling murder attempts," Mrs. Franklin continued brusquely. "There is a property owned by a Mr. Stuart for rent."

Caleb slanted a glance at Jo. "Surely you don't mean that shack at the end of Main Street. It's hardly habitable."

"Idle hands make the devil's work." The widow paused once more in her pacing. "I shall enjoy the challenge."

"It's very kind of you," Anna sputtered. "But why would you do such a thing? I don't know how long I'll be staying. Won't you be missed here?"

"I'm a widow. I go where I please. And I want to help. Isn't that enough?"

Jo broke in before Anna voiced another objection. "I think it's a good idea. The Stuart house is on the same side of town as ours. And it's right across the way from Caleb. You'll practically be neighbors.

"Neighbors," Anna said weakly. "This all seems a little too neat and tidy. I sense collusion."

Jo had the decency to look abashed. "I might have mentioned the availability of the house and its convenient location over breakfast with Mrs. Franklin."

"The location is fine." Caleb made a mental note to strangle his sister once they were alone. "It's the condition of the place."

Not to mention Anna would be a stone's throw away. Every day. Even if he wanted to ignore his longing for her, how could he? The more time they spent together, the harder it would be to forget her.

She looked at him then, and for the first time he realized she'd done something different with her hair. Her appearance was softer somehow. She'd donned a blue dress this morning, almost identical to the color she'd worn that first day. The shade suited her. One silky, dark curl rested against her flushed cheek. His fingers ached to touch the loose strands.

"Caleb." She spoke his name softly. "What do you think?"

If she'd called him Mr. McCoy, his answer might have been different. He might have been stronger.

But she hadn't.

She'd called him Caleb. He knew at that moment he'd do just about anything to hear her speak his name again. He'd do just about anything to see her like she was that first day—shaking her fist at the crowd, bullying them all into action.

He'd give her the answer he dreaded most, because even if her presence scraped at his resolve, he'd rather have her near. For an hour, for a day, for a week. For whatever amount of time God deemed fit.

He'd rather spend this little time with her than never see her again.

"I think it's an excellent idea."

All he had to do was avoid her for the next few weeks. She'd be living a stone's throw away from him. In Cimarron Springs. A town with more cows than people.

Avoiding her shouldn't be a problem at all.

As long as he never left his house.

Chapter Seven

"If you're certain." Anna exhaled her pent-up breath.

For reasons she didn't want to explore, his opinion mattered. If he'd offered any dissent, any sign of reluctance, she'd never agree.

He'd spoken without hesitation. Her fate was decided.

"I still have absolutely no idea who would want me dead. This all seems a little ridiculous," she said.

She was not the Great Victoria Bishop. She was only the *daughter* of the Great Victoria Bishop. There was no reason for anyone to want her dead.

Caleb remained pensive. He'd moved from the chair and stood with his shoulder propped against the door, his arms crossed. The pose was already familiar. Comforting.

"There's something else." Anna stared at her folded hands. "The guard was hurt today because he was protecting me. You must consider the safety of your families. Mrs. Franklin, you have your own well-being to consider."

"I survived the War Between the States," Izetta said. "Nothing can frighten me off after that horror."

"My husband is the town marshal," Jo said in exasperation. "You can't get much safer than that."

Caleb spoke last. "I can take care of myself."

They'd offered their friendship and protection, though she had nothing to give in return. The realization humbled her even as a nagging sense of unease lingered. This was not the sort of arrangement her mother would approve of. Quite the opposite. Victoria Bishop would stand fast. Face the problem dead to rights. She'd never scuttle to the countryside like a startled crab cowering beneath a dark ledge.

The three impersonal telegrams her mother had sent rested on the night table. Boston was a world away. If Victoria Bishop didn't like her daughter's choices, then she could tear herself away from the cause and help Anna instead.

For once Anna didn't want to be the new rising star in the suffragist's movement. She didn't want to be the illegitimate daughter of Victoria Bishop. She wanted to be herself, not a figurehead or, worse yet, a legacy. Mostly, though, she didn't want to see the censure in the townspeople's eyes.

And there was always censure. The women's movement brought change, and change frightened people. Men and women alike. They'd thrown eggs and rotten tomatoes at her. Often before a picketing, her knees quaked and her heart pounded. The trick wasn't gathering courage like seashells along the beach; the trick was trusting that courage would come when one needed it most. This time she wasn't waiting on nerve.

She was hiding.

Every fiber of her being rejected the notion of running; every lesson taught during her rigid upbringing rebelled.

She might have been raised for daring, but the lessons hadn't taken. Nothing silenced the terror of that man bursting through the window. She was a coward through and through.

"I'll come," she said. "On one condition."

"What's that?"

"I should definitely have a new name. My middle name is Ryan. Anna Ryan should do quite nicely. It's not far from the truth."

She wasn't taking a chance that someone might recognize the name Bishop. Not only for her safety and the safety of those around her, but because the idea of having a name separate from her mother's had taken root. For reasons she refused to examine, the idea was exhilarating—and terrifying. If she was taking the coward's way out, she might as well see the game through.

Caleb stuffed his hands in his pockets. "What were you going to say earlier? You know, when the guard was injured, you started to say...*we should*."

Oh, dear. Must he recall that moment of weakness? She'd been scared. In shock. Not quite herself. "It's the silliest thing." She laughed. The sound hollow and false even to her own ears. "I was going to say that we should consider Jo's idea. Since Mrs. Franklin is accompanying me, there's no need to go to such extreme lengths."

"Which idea?" Caleb straightened. "The pretend engagement?"

Jo pushed off from the window seat and slapped her palms against thighs. "If we're leaving, I'll inform the hotel staff."

Izetta crossed to the door. "I had better start packing. I'll be back around six for suppertime in the dining room."

After they'd exited the room, Anna raised an eyebrow. "Was it something I said?"

A wry grin spread across Caleb's face. "They're not very subtle, are they?"

"No." Anna shared in his amusement. "As I was trying to explain before, with Mrs. Franklin coming along, there's no need to go to such desperate lengths."

"I wouldn't say *desperate*."

"Although, if we did pretend an attachment," she continued thoughtfully, "once this business is resolved, you'd be the jilted suitor. You could turn that to your favor. I'm sure you'd cut quite a romantic figure as the injured party. No doubt you'd find plenty of ladies to comfort you."

"Being the jilted suitor isn't nearly as romantic as you'd suppose."

The tone of his voice wiped the teasing smile from her lips. "Oh, dear, I've done it now, haven't I? I've said the wrong thing."

"I'm embarrassed to admit this," he said, heaving a breath, "but I've already played the part. I won't bore you with the particulars. Let's just say, a few years ago, I had a crush on a certain young lady named Mary Louise Stuart."

"Forget what I said." Embarrassment heated her cheeks. "I was trying to lighten the moment and doing a poor job of it."

"Her name is Mary Louise McCoy now."

The realization took a moment to sink in. "Oh."

"Yes. Oh."

"She's married to one of your brothers?"

"David."

Anna searched her memory for mention of David in Jo's letters.

"Mary Louise is having a baby," Anna blurted.

"Yep."

"Oh."

"Everyone thinks I'm still sweet on her."

"Are you?"

The question was rude. She didn't care. She needed his answer. A few days ago she'd nearly died. A lapse in polite conversation hardly seemed noteworthy after that event. Since the accident, she'd been living in a constant state of worry. Now she was running off to the country. She needed to recapture a modicum of her courage.

"No. And the worst part is, I don't know that I ever was." He raked his hand through his hair. "She was pretty."

"Pretty?"

"I liked her because she was the prettiest girl in town."

Something twisted in Anna's chest. "I see."

All of her mother's warnings came rushing back. Men only sought out women because of their looks or their station. They wanted either a trophy or a business arrangement, a way to unite dynasties or a prize. She'd thought Caleb was different.

"I was young," he said. "I wasn't thinking about much of anything else. David and I fought. Words were said. I went away for a while after that. I trained as a veterinarian. I've always been better with animals than people."

"I think you do quite well."

"You won't find many folks who agree. You were right about one thing. People felt sorry for me after David and Mary Louise were married. I even got an extra slice of pie at the Harvest Festival that year. And some ice cream, as well."

"You're incorrigible."

"Yep."

"How are things between you now? Between you and David and Mary Louise?"

The question was too personal, and she was rude for asking. None of that stopped her. She'd come this far, there was no going back.

"Things between us are good. Real good. I mean, here's the thing. Every time I see Mary Louise, I'm glad she didn't choose me."

At the look of astonished joy on his face, Anna stifled a burst of nervous laughter.

Caleb dropped his head, his shoulders shaking. "That wasn't what I meant." He fisted a hand against his own amusement. "I only mean that we wouldn't have suited."

"I think I understand." Anna wrestled with uncharacteristic jealously. She'd never met Mary Louise, and already she'd had enough of the woman. "Isn't it strange, the ideas we have about ourselves? I wanted to be a nurse when I was young. It all seemed very exciting and adventurous. Then I realized that what I really loved were the uniforms."

"The uniforms?"

"They looked so neat and tidy and efficient."

"I can see how that would appeal to a young girl."

Anna palmed her cheek and shook her head. "It does seem a little silly now that I'm admitting it to someone."

"Don't worry. I wanted to be the town sheriff because he had a tin star. I thought it must be the bravest thing to wear a tin star and carry a gun."

"Did you ever have your own tin star as a child?"

"I cut one from card stock."

"It sounds quite impressive."

"Not when it rains. Card stock melts in the rain."

"Then you must have made a very good sheriff on sunny days."

"David is a deputy sheriff now."

An unexpected sorrow tugged at her heart. "He got your job and your girl."

What a pair they made, and yet they were no different from everyone else. The world was filled with lost dreams and missed opportunities. Why should the two of them escape unscathed? He wasn't upset by the losses. Instead he appeared relieved. Though he didn't have a shiny tin star, he'd discovered something better. He'd found his calling.

Had he found another sweetheart, as well? A shaft of pain pierced her somewhere near the region of her heart. But, no, his sister never would have suggested the engagement charade if he was courting someone else.

Sensing the shift in mood, he offered a sad smile. "Maybe I should have asked for two free slices of pie at the Harvest Festival." He idly checked his watch, then flipped shut the lid. "Don't go painting me as some tortured hero. I'm happy with the way things turned out for me. Sometimes we have to wait for God's plan and not our own."

There was something she'd never understood: God's plan. If there was a benevolent being plotting out their lives, He was doing an awfully poor job of things. Not to mention the statement stripped all responsibility from those helpless souls on earth, providing a convenient excuse for setbacks and failures. A convenient excuse for quitting. *I suppose it wasn't God's plan.*

Responsibility and faith were far too tangled in organized religion. The contradiction had been an oft-debated topic amongst the more ardent suffragists.

She recalled something she'd read not long before. "Susan Anthony once said, 'I distrust those people who know so well what God wants them to do because I notice it always coincides with their own desires.'"

He didn't blink at her contrary rejoinder. "Would faith in a higher power be more acceptable if God were to want the opposite of our desires?"

A thousand heated words balanced on the tip of her tongue. If God had a plan for her, He should have left some instructions. A rudimentary map. At the very least, an arrow pointing in the right direction. Often in her own life she felt as though she was swimming upstream against her desires. What she truly wanted didn't always match what she had been groomed for, what she had a talent for, what was expected of her.

She was a good speaker. She recognized her own power over a crowd. She acknowledged the responsibility that accompanied such an influential talent. Yet she'd never felt as though she belonged on the stage. The only time she sensed a calling was when she wrote the words on paper. Planning and writing the speeches enthralled her with passion and purpose. Giving those speeches filled her with trepidation.

"It must be a comfort," she said. "Believing in something outside of yourself. Believing in a higher power."

There was no mollycoddling in the Bishop household. Personal responsibility was paramount. One did not place one's destiny in the hands of deities created by men for the continued subjugation of women. While even Victoria Bishop acknowledged there were other, more beneficial aspects of religion, she was quite clear on what she considered the most egregious offences.

Anna braced for Caleb's subsequent shock and disappointment. She'd noticed an almost identical sequence of actions when someone of faith encountered someone of doubt. First came shock, then came disappointment, then came proselytizing. She was adept at deflecting the arguments.

No condemnation appeared in his thoughtful expression. After a long moment he said simply, "What do you believe in?"

"I've never been asked that before."

"Then it's high time someone did."

Most people were eager to spout their own beliefs, bullying one into submission. No one had ever asked her about her own thoughts. The question was candid, sincere.

Since she'd quizzed him about his relationships, she supposed she owed him some honesty in return. "I don't know what I believe. I've seen the words in the Bible used for great good and great evil. I have seen the words used to justify a multitude of charity, as well as a multitude of offences."

She readied herself for a barrage of reproach. If his overzealous response caused him to sink lower in her estimation, all the better. This strange fascination she was developing for the man must stop. No good could ever come of it. They were from two different worlds. Their paths led in opposite directions.

He'd no doubt marry a nice girl from the neighboring farm who would never dream of questioning the veracity of a supreme being. Which suited her just fine. To each his own.

Annoyed by his continued silence and determined to goad him into revealing himself, she spoke more sharply than she'd intended. "How do you justify the evil men do? Is that God's plan, that we should fight amongst ourselves? Is it God's plan that a woman be beaten by her husband with no recourse? Does God condone the subjection of women and children?"

He remained infuriatingly impassive beneath her barrage. Exhausted by her uncharacteristic temper, Anna fell silent.

"We are, all of us," he said thoughtfully, his voice quiet, "capable of both good and evil. It's too easy to slip into indulgence, assuming that because one man is capable of great evil, his actions refute all the light in the world. If the limits of evil are endless, then so must be the limits of good. God may have a plan, but He has also given us free will. We have a choice. We struggle toward the light or we drift toward the darkness. The secret is ensuring we're always moving in the right direction. That we stay on the side of righteousness."

Suddenly exhausted, Anna abandoned her argument. "It sounds like a great deal of work."

"Every relationship in our lives requires work. Even our relationship with God."

He replaced his hat and ran his fingertips along the brim. A habit, she supposed, judging by the wear marks in the felt.

He was a man of faith, and she was a woman consumed by doubts. Together they made a poor match.

A poor match indeed.

Chapter Eight

Caleb dreaded the task ahead of him. This time he'd keep his resolve. He'd keep his emotions in check.

A thread of cigar smoke led Caleb toward the cramped parlor horseshoed into the end of a corridor. Reinhart glanced up from the sheaf of papers he'd been studying. "Can't say I'm surprised to see you, Mr. McCoy."

Caleb touched his breast pocket. "I have the first payment. The amount you requested. We'll see how things progress from there."

Anna had insisted on paying, but she wasn't able to visit the bank herself. He'd tell her the truth one day, that he'd paid the fee himself, if the question ever came up. He doubted she'd appreciate his interference. Independence was one thing, bullheadedness was another.

"Fair enough." Mr. Reinhart smoothed a palm over his dark, thinning hair. "Found something."

They'd chosen to meet the detective at the hotel before their train departed. They'd moved Anna's room yet again, a location with an undamaged window far from the fire escape.

Caleb straightened. "Already?"

"Miss Bishop's name was familiar. It stuck with me. That's what got me thinking about this case in the first place. Asking questions. Then I realized why. Somebody was looking for Miss Bishop before."

"Who?" Caleb asked, then shook his head. "No. We'd best wait for Miss Bishop. This concerns her most of all."

"She's late."

"She's not late. There's still five minutes until nine o'clock."

The detective seemed to take great satisfaction whenever he thought Anna had failed in some regard. As though lack of punctuality might somehow justify the lack of vote. As though if Reinhart put enough ticks in one column he justified his prejudices.

Caleb grunted. As if anything in life was that simple.

Anna appeared at the end of the corridor and Caleb automatically stood, his pulse quickening. Reinhart remained stubbornly ensconced in his seat. She glided toward them with her inherent grace, her feet barely whispering over the carpet runner. Only a slight hitch in her step indicated her injury.

She wore an elegant dress in a deep shade of green, the trim black. She carried herself with instinctive elegance and an economy of movement. There was nothing clumsy or rushed about Anna Bishop, and her natural confidence drew him forward.

Even Reinhart started to rise before thumping back down on his seat again. "Don't s'pose these ladies appreciate civility."

"Civility is the whole point."

Reinhart grunted and rolled his eyes.

Caleb held a chair for Anna. She swept her skirts aside

and sat. "You said in your note that you'd discovered something. I hadn't expected news quite this soon."

"This is old news," Reinhart said. "That's what's been bothering me. I was telling Mr. McCoy here, your name was familiar. I figured it was because I'd heard about you from the papers. Then I remembered something. Months ago, in St. Louis, a solicitor was looking for you."

"A lawyer? What was his name?"

"Don't remember the name." Reinhart punctuated his sentence with one of his quick, tight-lipped smiles. "It wasn't my case. I sent a message back to St. Louis. The telegrams are costing me a pretty penny already, I can tell you that. Telegrams ain't cheap."

"The cost is included in your fee." Anna smoothed her gloved hands down the armrest. The only sign of nerves Caleb had seen thus far. "Can you at least tell me why this lawyer was looking for me?"

"Your father hired him."

Anna blanched, half stood, then caught herself and sat back down. "You must be mistaken. The man must have used that as an excuse."

"Mebbe. But I don't think so."

"If the inquiry was a hoax—" Caleb placed his hand on the back of Anna's chair "—do you think the shooting was planned that far in advance?"

His suspicions had finally been validated, though he took no satisfaction in the victory. Anna clearly didn't think the threat was personal. This information proved her wrong.

Reinhart leaned forward. "The shooter might have been planning something, but not what happened at the rally. How could he? They only arranged the speech three weeks ago."

As much as it galled him to admit, the unkempt detective had a point.

Anna's booted foot beat a steady tattoo on the carpet near his own foot, the tufted covering on the armrest compressed beneath her fingers.

Caleb pressed against his forehead with a thumb and index finger. "How can you be sure the man wasn't lying? How can we know he was really Anna's father?"

"I figured he was on the up and up because Miss Bishop's mother agreed to meet with the fellow last April," Reinhart said. "The solicitor met with Victoria Bishop."

Anna rose from her chair and faced away from them. "No, that can't be. Surely she'd have said something to me."

Her distress cut him to the quick. Caleb approached her, keeping his body between her and the detective, then spoke low in her ear. "There's no easy way to ask this, but do you know your father's identity? We'll be able to tell easily enough if Reinhart is lying."

He'd rather risk alienating her than be led astray by falsehoods.

She pressed both hands against her pale cheeks. "I don't know. I asked my mother. Of course I asked. She'd only ever say, 'He doesn't matter to me, why should he matter to you?'"

An instant dislike for a woman he'd never met took root. What kind of answer was that for a child? The vague reply smacked of the self-indulgent excuse of a spoiled heiress accustomed to having her way.

A cold rage settled low in his belly for both the detective and Anna's mother, stripping away at his vow to remain impartial. Caleb faced the detective.

Reinhart drummed his fingers on the table. "When

the Pinkertons sent me out here, they said I'd starve for lack of work. I knew they were wrong. People come out West for a reason. Most times that reason ain't too savory, if you get my meaning. Makes for plenty of work for a man like me. Had to get me an assistant to help out."

Caleb remained silent. He wasn't revealing any information Anna wasn't sharing first. "Last spring a solicitor talked with Victoria Bishop, but she never said anything to her only daughter. Perhaps it was a mistake."

Anna resumed her chair and smoothed her skirts over her knees, wrestling back her control. The revelation had been a shock. He'd known there was a scandal connected with Anna's mother. The paper clippings Jo had saved took great delight in splashing Victoria Bishop's unmarried status across the headlines.

He'd assumed Anna knew more about her parentage. She hadn't appeared beneath a cabbage leaf, after all.

Either way the declaration by the detective had been deliberately provoking. Had Reinhart been studying her reaction? Caleb had been too focused on Anna, and he hadn't been watching the detective.

Caleb rested his hand on the armrest of her chair, and she covered his fingers with her own. Her touch was cautious, whisper light, and he kept his attention rigidly forward. He sensed her conflict with these lapses, these moments when she needed the bolstering support of another person.

She sat up straighter, her back stiff, her face so impassive her profile might have been carved from marble. "If this man was my father, why didn't he come for me himself?"

"Because he was sick. Dying."

Anna hid her distress well. Only the tightening of her

fingers on his hand and the two spots of color appearing high on her cheeks revealed her true state. "Where is my father now? Do you have a name?"

"His name was Drexel Ryan."

Anna leaned forward. "Where is he? Give me that much at least."

The detective looked away, and Caleb sagged back into his seat. The detective had spoken the name in the past tense, a telling slip. A dying man had sent his solicitor searching for Anna last April, five months ago. Anna clearly hadn't made the connection, and his heart ached for her.

Her eyes flashing, Anna gripped the arms of her chair. "I am in no mood for games. Where is my father?"

"In Omaha," Reinhart grumbled. "Buried in the Forest Lawn Cemetery."

"That can't be." Anna reared back. "It's not true. None of this is true."

Caleb reached for her and she flinched away. Her rejection cut him to the quick. She adjusted in her seat and winced, unconsciously touching her side.

With no place to vent his rage, he turned his anger on the detective. Furious, he faced Reinhart. "You might have softened the blow."

"She didn't even know the man. What does she care if he's alive or dead? He's nothing to her."

"That's not for you to say."

"Enough," Anna spoke. "This is all a game for you, isn't it? Have you humiliated me quite enough? Are you satisfied I'm not worthy of the vote or your time?"

"You don't pay me to play nursemaid. You pay me for information. I gave it to you."

This time when Caleb covered her trembling fingers with his own, she didn't pull away. "Let's hear him out."

At that moment, he loathed the detective. He loathed him for his clumsy handling of the situation and his obvious disdain. They were trapped. The realization kicked his anger from a slow simmer into a full boil. Reinhart had information they needed.

Right then he had the overwhelming desire to punch something. The detective wasn't a bad choice, but he was off-limits until they had all the information. Which left Caleb ensnared. He was entirely inadequate. Surely there was something more he should say, something more he should do. In less than a week she'd had two attempts on her life. She'd discovered her father had been looking for her, and now he was dead. Buried in a cemetery in Nebraska.

Anna reached out and with her right hand fingered the edges of the lace curtains, keeping her left hand motionless beneath his. The shades had been drawn for safety, and privacy, blanketing the parlor in perpetual gloom.

When was the last time she'd stepped outside? Seen the sun? A week at least. The confinement must have been maddening.

She drew in a breath, keeping her face averted. "Last spring my mother received a large envelope. I normally take care of all her correspondence. She wouldn't let me touch the envelope. I believe she took it to the bank. I know she keeps a safe deposit box. Do you think the envelope had something to do with the man looking for me?"

"Mebbe. If your father was dying, he may have left you something. People get sentimental that way." Reinhart shrugged. "I'll ask around. See if I can find the lawyer.

He's probably from Omaha. Can't be that hard to find. Only your mother can answer that question."

Her expression hardened. "I see."

Caleb's heart ached for her. "You told us about Anna's father. Did you discover anything about the shooter?"

At least they finally knew what had sparked the detective's interest in the beginning, though they were no closer to finding the shooter.

"That's the thing about this job. Things ain't always the way you think. You gotta be ready. You can't force the pieces to fit. A puzzle doesn't work that way."

Reinhart reached for his cigar and pinched it between his teeth, then took a long draw. He kicked back in his chair and blew the smoke toward the ceiling.

What had the detective said before…if you give people a puzzle, they'll fill in the blanks by themselves? Reinhart could fill in his own puzzle.

"Strange thing, families," the detective said. "They can be the making of a man, or they can be his destruction. Loyalty is just a step away from delusion."

"That's an odd thing to say."

"Just something I've been thinking about lately. See, all of my cases are about finding someone. Most of my cases are about finding someone who doesn't want to be found. That's the thing, see, everybody is hiding from something. From the past, from the future, from themselves. Everybody is hiding something."

The detective leaned forward and replaced his cigar in the tray, then tipped back in his chair and threaded his hands behind his head. "You're leaving Kansas City. That's good. When Miss Bishop disappears, he'll move. That's when I'll catch him."

"Then I guess you've got some work ahead of you."

Though it galled him, Caleb needed the detective. He couldn't stay in Kansas City any longer, and he couldn't leave without ensuring someone was looking for the shooter. The police had already lost interest, and his dependence on the man rankled. Needing someone's help and liking it were two different things. Reinhart already knew more about Anna than Caleb did.

"I'll find him. Mark my words." Reinhart tapped the ashes from the end of his cigar onto the mountainous pile, spilling some on the marble surface.

Anna stood and touched her temple, her gaze distracted. "Catch him. I'll be in my room if you need me."

Caleb stood and reached for her, then let his hand fall. She'd revealed something very personal. He doubted she wanted more of her past aired out before the detective. Pride held her back straight. If she felt humiliation or sorrow, she didn't show it either. A week together and he was no closer to reading her than that first, eventful day.

Sometimes he thought he knew her, then she surprised him. He was always guessing around. The feeling left him edgy and off balance. Lamps flickered along the corridor, throwing her shadow into relief. Her steps never faltered, her back never stooped. She was a proud woman. Proud and independent.

Having grown up around a large and boisterous family, he was finally catching a glimpse into Anna's world. How lonely her life must have been. Nothing in the memories she'd shared hinted at lightness or frivolity.

She was skittish of affection, reaching out and pulling back at the same time, confused by her own needs. There was nothing weak about seeking comfort. He doubted Anna shared his thoughts. Especially considering her past had been exposed before the detective. Perhaps his blunt attitude had been for the best. He'd inadvertently given her the upper hand. She had taken the news with grace and dignity, denying Reinhart a reaction.

As she reached her door, the guard stationed beside it stood and let her into her room.

Behind him, Reinhart grunted. "You be careful with that Miss Bishop. She ain't for the likes of us."

Caleb set his jaw. "Take the job or don't."

Anna hadn't given the man a reaction; neither would Caleb.

"Women like that. Getting ideas in their heads." Reinhart puffed the tip of his cigar into a cherry-red flame. "Next thing you know they'll be slugging whiskey and swearing. No good can come of that. It's men that should be in charge."

"Your ignorance has me doubting your ability." Caleb fisted his hands and rested his knuckles on the back of the tufted chair. "You want me to take my money and leave? Or do you want to keep your opinions to yourself?"

Reinhart's remarks came from a place of fear. The man's argument didn't fit the fight the suffragists had undertaken. How did the desire to vote and control one's destiny translate into trousers and swearing? What did any of that matter, anyway? How did one suffragist threaten Reinhart?

The detective chuckled, but the fine shine of sweat visible beneath his thinning hair belied his good humor. With a sudden burst of insight Caleb realized he wanted the case. Mr. Reinhart enjoyed a puzzle. He also liked money.

Reinhart mopped his brow with a dingy handkerchief. "Fair enough. But never say I didn't warn you."

His assistance, along with whatever meager inquiries the police made, were the best options Caleb had without remaining in Kansas City, and he'd already been gone from home too long. Reinhart might be a confirmed woman-hater, but according to the inquiries Caleb had made, he was one of Pinkerton's best detectives. He'd gotten his teeth sunk into a puzzle, and he wouldn't quit until it was solved. Of that Caleb was certain.

"You know where to find me," he said. "Send word if you have news."

Reinhart was right about one thing. Anna wasn't for the likes of him. With each day that passed she grew stronger, and as she regained her strength, she pulled further away from him. There'd be no more storytelling, of that he was certain.

Which left him wrenched in two separate directions. He'd prayed for her life, for her continued health. His prayers had been answered.

He'd lectured Anna on trusting in God's plan, and no part of their separate lives meshed. There was no common ground to build on. They were opposite people moving in opposite directions.

No outcome he envisioned ended with them together. Turned out swallowing his own advice was a bitter pill. Worse yet, he doubted the medicine would help. With each day that passed, he feared he was growing too far gone.

He'd double his resolution from here on out. He wasn't letting his heart take the upper hand. Even if she did have the most beautiful blue eyes he'd ever seen. All those years ago he'd thought Mary Louise the prettiest girl in the county. She was a pale comparison to Anna.

With sudden insight he realized the difference wasn't in their features, the difference was in their hearts. When

Mary Louise smiled all those years ago, she'd done it for a calculated response. A flirt or a giggle. When Anna smiled, her whole heart shone through her eyes.

From here on out, he was tripling his effort. Especially since he couldn't rest until he checked on her.

This time he'd keep his resolve.

He'd keep his resolve after he took care of one last little problem.

With Anna gone, he decided on a less diplomatic way of dealing with the detective.

Reinhart stood, and Caleb shoved him against the wall, his elbow holding the man's shoulder, his forearm pressing against the detective's throat. "I don't like the way you do business."

His pupils dilated, Reinhart smacked his lips.

Caleb pressed in slightly, his jaw set. "The next time we meet, I'll expect you to use your manners."

"S-sure," the detective stuttered.

"Then we understand each other?"

His bluster gone, the detective raised his hands in supplication. "Y-yes."

Caleb released his hold and turned away. He strode down the corridor, tugging his sleeves over his wrists. "Good."

Chapter Nine

Anna took the seat by the window and waited. He'd come. Of course he'd come. Caleb had seen through her façade. He'd seen her distress. She'd only known him a week, and she knew he'd check on her.

At least he hadn't looked at her as Miss Spence had looked at her all those years ago, with a curious mixture of pity and disgust. Her parentage wasn't her fault, why should she be blamed? More often than not, she was. As though she had any choice in the matter.

Much to her disgust, there was a very provincial side to her. A side that envied regular families who did regular things and had children that were only expected to be ordinary. Families that were building a life together instead of a legacy for the ages.

A knock sounded not fifteen minutes later. She didn't even ask, only stood and opened the door.

He glanced toward the empty chair. "Is Mrs. Franklin here?"

"She's home, packing her things."

There was another relationship she'd grown far too dependent upon. Why hadn't she refused Izetta's offer?

What was she thinking, retiring to the country with someone she'd only known a week? Once again she blamed the false intimacy of the situation. They'd all been through something harrowing. They'd been thrown together under traumatic circumstances, stripping away all the polite maneuverings taken over time in normal friendships. She'd only known the widow a short time, and yet their days together had been a lifetime.

"Would you like me to stay?" Caleb asked. "To call for her? I'll sit with you. I know the detective's revelations came as a shock to you."

"There's no need." Anna glanced toward the curtained windows of her room. She'd grown heartily tired of pulled shades and perpetual twilight.

Her days had lost their rhythm, and she desperately craved something normal. A change in the routine. Anything but the endless monotony of sitting around and waiting for another attempt on her life. "It's not as though I knew the man. I suppose I always assumed he was dead. Life was easier that way."

What must Caleb think of her? A woman who didn't even know the name of her own father. She might have passed him on the street a thousand times and never known the difference. The idea was odd, unsettling. She'd pushed it to the back of her mind and piled a thousand excuses on the mere idea of him.

He didn't matter. She was fine without him. Thousands of girls had lost their fathers during the war. All of the lectures her mother had given came rushing back. But she was different from those other girls. They knew the names of their fathers, they had stories, they had love. Without even a name to attach to her father, she'd kept even the idea of him distant.

Finally hearing his name had thrust him back into her life, into her thoughts. He might be dead, but the feelings lingered. All the thoughts she'd shoved aside and buried rose once more to the surface. There'd been too much upheaval in her life recently. Old memories broke through all the walls she'd erected.

Her mind drifted back over the years. "When I was a little girl, I thought of him all the time. Children are not always kind to one another, and everyone knew my parents were never married. They knew I didn't have a father. Not a father who was in my life, anyway. I imagined he was a ship's captain. Sometimes I pictured him as a pirate. Not very original, I know, but those professions seemed very romantic, and they explained all the questions a child knows to ask."

"His absence must have been difficult for you."

"It's odd. I never thought he mattered much to me. I'd been told often enough he didn't. He didn't matter until that one brief moment when I realized he was looking for me. At that moment he mattered very much."

"Reinhart is an idiot." Caleb spoke harshly.

She was grateful for his defense of her, but there was no need.

"I'm glad he was tactless. It's easier to be angry than sad. I've been one or the other for quite some time. I suppose as children there's always a part of us that believes we've done something, that it's our fault they're gone. I thought if I'd been a boy, he might have stayed. We might have been a family."

"You don't believe that now?" His green eyes shimmered with sympathy.

She didn't need his pity. "Of course not. I'm all grown-up now."

She'd shoved her father into a darkened corner of her soul, and someone had kicked open the door. There was no shutting out the pain, and somehow that realization was worse. She'd kicked open the door of an empty room.

"We'll find out what we can about him," Caleb said. "Find out why he was looking for you."

"She knew he was looking for me." Anna's words were barely a whisper. "Why didn't my mother say anything?"

Her thoughts should not have been voiced. She had a few theories, although none of them were suitable for sharing quite yet. The news was too raw, too immediate. She needed time. She needed distance.

Caleb kept his vigil near the door. Seeking a chance for escape, no doubt. She smothered a sigh. Even if he wanted to, he wouldn't leave her alone. He'd stay even if remaining made him uncomfortable. Because staying was the right thing to do, and Mr. McCoy always did the right thing. She mustn't read anything deeper into his actions.

"Perhaps she was protecting you," he said.

Anna scoffed. "If you knew Victoria Bishop, you'd know what a preposterous suggestion that is. She manages both her personal and professional life by rigid standards. She had a reason. She always has a reason. My middle name is Ryan. At least she left me a clue."

"Your mother must be quite an imposing woman," he said, then held up his hands. "I'm sorry. I shouldn't have said that."

"No, you're right." He'd hit upon the truth. The man was far too insightful "There is no one quite like Victoria. I remember sitting on the footstool in her room, watching her dress for meetings. I never saw her hurry. Not ever. And she didn't tolerate people who were tardy.

Once, I had a nanny who was always late. It was such a shock, all that running around and panic. The nanny did not last long."

Dr. Smith was correct, Caleb's talents were wasted on animals. He inspired her confidence, and she sensed he'd never betray her trust. He'd have made an excellent country doctor, moving from household to household, listening to his patient's woes with that steady, compassionate gaze. Keeping their secrets and sharing their sorrows.

"That must have been difficult," he said.

"I grew accustomed to the changes. Life was very busy for my mother. She was always needed. There were so many people who wanted her time. Looking back, I've often thought I was raised by everybody and nobody at the same time." He must think her a melancholy fool. She forced a smile. "I make my childhood sound very lonely. It wasn't. Not at all. There were always people around."

"Any children?"

There he went again, asking the simplest questions and invoking the most complicated answers.

"Sometimes, yes. Despite what the newspapers would have you believe, many suffragists are married women. I had plenty of children to play with. I told you, there was nothing solitary about my upbringing."

"A person can feel most isolated in a crowd."

Her eyes burned and she blinked rapidly. "I'm tired lately. Healing is much more exhausting than I expected." She rubbed a hand over her forehead. "I think I overestimated my stamina."

Life had suddenly lost its sense of urgency. Away from the cause, away from the correspondence and the meetings and the demands, life had slowed. Without the bustle of activity, she'd lost track of her routine. Her days had lost their meaning. Who was she, if she wasn't Victoria Bishop's daughter?

She'd built a pedestal of activities and proudly stood at the top. Her support had crumbled, leaving her vulnerable and exposed. In St. Louis, fighting for the vote was immediate and crucial. Away from the cause, women and girls went about their daily business, singularly unaware of the battle being waged in their honor.

"You've had a busy few days," Caleb said. "Rest. I'll make all the arrangements."

Despite her exhaustion, annoyance flared. "If someone orders me to rest once more I'm afraid I might scream. I'm quite able to take care of myself."

She didn't want rest. She wanted her energy back for fighting. She wanted to do something. She wanted to be something. Someone besides a victim.

"A strong person takes care of herself. A stronger person asks for help."

"Who said that? Some wise philosopher?"

"I did. Just now."

Anna laughed in spite of herself. "Then by all means, purchase my train tickets and make all of the arrangements. I'll finally prove to you what a strong person I am."

"You don't have to prove anything to anybody."

Anna reached for a rose dangling from a vase of flowers. The fragile petals broke free the instant she touched the stem, fluttering onto the floor. She'd been proving herself for as long as she could remember; there was no stopping now. Her mother was building a dynasty, and Anna was an integral part of that heritage. If she wasn't fighting for the greater good, then what was the point of her existence? No one raised outside the Bishop household understood the expectations heaped upon her, and there was no use explaining.

Little girls with fathers and mothers were ordinary. Anna was different, and that difference was extraordinary. Or so she'd been told. The childish explanation no longer soothed her adult heart.

She glanced at her packed trunk. "The wonders of transportation by train. We'll be in Cimarron Springs by suppertime. You must be relieved."

He must have been chafing at the bit to run as fast and as far as he could from her and the problems she dragged behind her like leaded weights.

"There is no feeling quite like the joy of coming home," he said. "You stopped there once when you met Jo. I know our little town is only a jumping-off place, a lunch rest on the way to somewhere better, but what do you remember about Cimarron Springs?"

Once he was home, she'd never see him again. There'd be no reason. A perfectly sensible outcome. Except lately she wasn't feeling quite as sensible as she used to.

"I don't remember anything. Not really." She caught herself and smiled. "That must sound insulting, but I travel through so many towns, they all blend together. My stay in Cimarron Springs was brief. I sent a telegram, and Jo was working that day. We've been friends since that moment."

"I hope—" he paused, as though struggling for words "—I hope when you see Cimarron Springs again, you like our town."

She plucked the now bare-stemmed rose from the vase. Whether or not she liked the town hardly mattered. She wasn't staying long, and both of them knew that. His words were only polite conversation, a way of passing an awkward moment.

"I'm sure I'll find your town quite lovely," she said.

Actually she hoped it was dreadful and smelly and filled with insufferable people. She didn't want to be drawn into his world any more than she already had.

Her life was in St. Louis. Everything she knew, everything she stood for was a lifetime away from Cimarron Springs. Gaining the vote for women was vital. Someone had to struggle for those who couldn't defend themselves.

Someone had to fight, and Anna had been chosen the moment she was born. Her mother lived as though victory was around the corner, a vote away, a state away, an amendment away. Anna had her doubts.

She often wondered if any one of them would live long enough to see the day when men and women were treated equally under the law. They'd made great strides, but there were more and bigger challenges ahead.

She never doubted her importance to the cause. In one afternoon in Kansas City, she'd spoken before hundreds of people. How many people could she influence in Cimarron Springs? A handful at best.

Susan Anthony, Elizabeth Stanton and so many others had given much of their lives already, and Anna was privileged to have known them. She needed grand gestures for a grand cause.

Caleb cleared his throat, and Anna realized he'd been trying to gain her attention. "What were you thinking about so intently?" he asked.

"I was wondering how history will remember any of us, or if we'll even be remembered at all."

"That is a question for the ages."

She was changing, losing track of herself, and she desperately wanted her purpose back. Only one thing was certain, her purpose was not in Cimarron Springs, and they both knew it.

Chapter Ten

Cimarron Springs was love at first sight. Well, love at *second* sight, she hastily amended. She'd made that brief stop before.

Leaning heavily on the railing, Anna exited the train and glanced around the crowded platform. Clouds had covered the afternoon sun, chilling the air. The depot sat at the far end of town, framed between the rows of buildings lining either side of Main Street.

False fronts advertised the mercantile, the haberdashery, a blacksmith shop. All of the usual trappings of a small town. Picturesque covered boardwalks, the railings and eves painted a crisp white, contained the hustle of shoppers taking advantage of the temperate fall weather.

She'd stopped here a year ago and hadn't spared a glance at Main Street. She'd been in a hurry, her head down. She'd sent her telegram, and Jo had struck up a conversation. All too soon the train whistle had blown, and she'd boarded once again, never looking back.

This time she drank in the scene, inhaling the scent of baking bread and admiring the yellowed leaves of the cottonwood trees.

She'd been living with a vague sense of unease and fear for the past week, holed up in her guarded room. Having her first taste of freedom in a week was delightful.

Izetta surveyed the platform and touched Anna's arm. "I'm going to freshen up. Every time I travel by train I feel as though I'm covered in soot by the end of the journey."

"I'll wait here," Anna said, dreading another step. "Looks as though the porters are already unloading the baggage car."

She'd thought her wound mostly healed. The constant sway of the train had exacerbated her injury, and the incessant ache had become a frustrating nuisance.

A tall man separated from the crowd, and Jo dashed around her. She launched herself at the man, and he caught her easily. Her husband, Anna hoped.

Jo stood on her tiptoes and bussed his cheek, flipping off his hat in the process. The gentleman returned her enthusiastic embrace. Unused to such boisterous displays of affection, Anna's cheeks warmed, and she glanced away. Jo pulled back and led her husband toward Anna. Without pausing in his stride, he reached down and snatched his missing hat.

"I've brought us a visitor," Jo said. "This is Miss Anna. Anna, this is my husband, Garrett Cain. Most folks around here just call him Marshal Cain."

The marshal offered a warm smile. "I realize this is the first time we've met in person, but I feel as though I know you from Jo's description."

Anna held out her hand, and he clasped it, his palm calloused, his handshake firm but not brutal. "A pleasure to meet you, Marshal."

Mr. Cain reminded her a bit of Caleb. They were both tall and dark-haired, but that's where the similarities ended. Jo's husband appeared older, more jaded by time. His features were more angular and his eyes dark and guarded, not nearly as striking as Caleb's green eyes.

He wore a silver star stamped with the word *Marshal*.

Caleb followed her gaze and winked, both of them remembering his childhood love of tin stars. Another gentleman tugged on Caleb's sleeve, and Anna turned her attention back to the marshal.

Though Jo's husband was talking with her, Anna sensed that his focus remained on his wife. He held his arm wrapped around her waist, his fingers resting on her hip. The gesture was protective and sweet. If he resented Anna's appearance in his life, he hadn't let on, though she sensed a hint of wariness in his gaze.

Anna pressed her hand against her bandaged side. "I hope you don't mind a bit of upheaval on such short notice."

"Not at all. There's always room for one more in Cimarron Springs," the marshal said.

"Where are the children?" Jo demanded. "Where are Jocelyn and Shawn? Where's Cora?"

"Coming along shortly. David is showing them his new horse."

"JoBeth!" a voice called. "There you are."

A stout woman charged ahead and elbowed the marshal aside, grasping Jo's shoulders. "You had me worried sick."

"I'm fine, Ma." Jo lifted her eyes heavenward. "You didn't have to meet me at the train station."

"Of course I did. I had to make certain you were well with my own two eyes. You can never trust the menfolk with details. The newspapers aren't much better either. *The Kansas Post* only said there'd been a disturbance at the rally. As though shooting someone was a disturbance. What's wrong with the newspapers these days, do you suppose?"

"Ma." Jo leaned closer. "Remember what Garrett told you?"

"Oh, right. Yes. Well. All's well that ends well. I'm only glad you weren't injured in the *disturbance.* Your Pa thinks they didn't have more details because they were worried there'd be too much sympathy for the cause." She huffed. "They certainly gave enough space for the editorials opposed to the woman's vote."

"As you can see, I'm no worse for wear." Jo splayed her arms as proof. "I'm fit as a fiddle."

Jo's mother looked her up and down, a deep wrinkle between her brows, presumably deciding for herself whether or not her daughter was the worse for wear.

Jo pulled away and indicated Anna. "This is Anna. Miss Ryan."

Mrs. McCoy started. "We've left the poor thing standing while you and I chatter." She hooked her arm through Anna's and tugged her toward a narrow bench. "Have a seat. I can't tell you how exciting it is having a celebrity in town."

"Ma," Jo pitched her voice in a warning. "I just reminded you."

"Yes, but your other poor…friend. That poor Miss Bishop person." Mrs. McCoy widened her eyes at Anna, demonstrating how well she was holding to the deception. "A single injury was reported. That's all the newspapers said. As though a woman nearly dying was no more important than the weather."

Anna touched her side. She'd been curious about the lack of interest in her injury, and yet she'd never considered the paper had failed to report more extensively on the shooting. Of all the outcomes she'd anticipated, she hadn't expected this one. They'd trivialized her. They'd relegated her to the last page alongside the news of robberies and quilt patterns.

A single injury was reported.

She'd been shot, for goodness' sake. There was a murderer on the loose. Well, an attempted murderer. Certainly that was cause for concern. While she'd never enjoyed the notoriety of her cause, the incident warranted more than a few lines. Without a single mention of the violence she'd experienced, they'd marginalized the cause, they'd marginalized her injury. They'd marginalized *her.*

"At least everyone is safe." Mrs. McCoy plunked down beside Anna and patted her hand. "After such an experience, are you certain you want to stay in that tiny little cottage Mr. Stuart calls a house? He hasn't done a lick of work on it since his mother-in-law passed away." She lowered her voice. "His mother-in-law lived there alone until she died. Not that Mr. Stuart didn't like his mother-in-law, he just liked her better when they weren't living beneath the same roof."

Anna searched for the question in Mrs. McCoy's rapid-fire speech. "We'll be fine. Mrs. Franklin and I are quite looking forward to fixing up the place."

Her suspicions were correct. Her secret was as good as out. How many more "slips" from Mrs. McCoy before the whole town knew she was staying here? Though she'd been shocked by the lack of newspaper coverage at first, the lack of interest worked in her favor. At least the papers hadn't picked up the news, and for that Anna was grateful. If the reporters would rather suppress her shooting than risk sympathy for the Right to Vote movement, all the better for her.

"Let's hope your enthusiasm doesn't wane after you've seen the place," Mrs. McCoy said. "It's quite a job. I wish I'd known sooner. I'd have gotten the ladies together and cleaned the house for you."

"No, no. You mustn't put yourself out. We're quite capable of caring for ourselves."

"Of course you are! We simply want to leave you with a good impression of our little town. What do you think so far?"

"Ma?" Jo planted her hands on her hips. "How can she think anything? She's only seen the train depot."

"She's had her first impression. Didn't you, dear? First impressions are important."

"Your town is absolutely lovely."

The exact opposite of what she'd been hoping for when she'd decided on her stay in Cimarron Springs.

Mrs. McCoy flashed a triumphant smile at her daughter. "*Lovely* is an excellent first impression. You'll be coming for supper tonight, won't you?"

"Well, I, uh, I hadn't thought that far ahead."

Although the idea of meeting more of Caleb's family intrigued her. There was Jo and three other brothers. She was interested in how such a large family worked.

"Then it's settled. You're a guest. Don't bring anything. We sit for dinner at six."

"All right," Anna replied.

She hadn't realized she'd accepted the invitation, but it was too late now.

Mrs. McCoy stood and glanced around. "Jo, have you seen your father?"

"Not in the last five minutes since I stepped off the train," Jo said, clearly exasperated.

"If you do, tell him I've stopped by the mercantile. Picking up a housewarming gift. We want you to feel welcome."

"That's very kind of you."

Caleb had finished his conversation and faced his mother. She grabbed him in a quick, fierce hug. "I'm so glad the three of you are home and safe." She glanced over her shoulder. "Anna, if I can call you Anna, don't forget to invite your friend for supper, as well."

"I'll tell Mrs. Franklin."

"Mrs. Franklin. That's an easy name for remembering." Mrs. McCoy released her son and patted the marshal's cheek. "I won't expect you and Jo. You two need some time alone after being apart. I will see you on Sunday, though, right?"

"Wouldn't miss your fried chicken for the world," the marshal said.

Mrs. McCoy waved over her shoulder and set off down the street, her pace clipped.

Caleb tossed Anna an apologetic smile. "I hope you don't mind. She won't be satisfied until she knows we're well fed."

"Her concern is quite endearing."

"Don't worry. You get used to it after a while."

Anna stifled any comparisons. Her own mother had never been affectionate, and she had never picked up Anna at the train station. A waste of time when there was important work to be done. Victoria Bishop had far more vital tasks than meeting her daughter at a train station. Anna was far too independent to care. She was a grown woman, for goodness' sake.

Her mother simply had a different way of showing her love.

Jo caught sight of something in the distance and clapped her hands. “There they are!”

She knelt and held open her arms, and two toddlers and her oldest child rushed into them. Jo made a great show of collapsing beneath the weight of the three squirming children and smothered them with kisses. Anna’s heart ached a bit. This was exactly the sort of scene she’d pictured reading Jo’s letters. The yearnings in her chest were exactly what she’d been avoiding.

No, that wasn’t right. She enjoyed her life. She relished fighting for something larger than herself. She knew her place in the scheme of things. She had the honor of working with women who’d carved a place in history for themselves. She had the luxury of joining a legacy already in process. Small gestures were wasted when Anna had no doubt Susan and Elizabeth would be heralded long after they were gone.

After much giggling, Jo rose and clasped hands in a row and towed them toward Anna.

“I have someone very special I’d like you to meet,” Jo said. “This is Miss Anna.”

A lovely little girl, no more than four years old, offered a quick bob of her dark head. “Hello, Miss Anna. I’m four. My name is Jocelyn.”

“That’s a very pretty name.”

Though young, Jocelyn enunciated each word slowly and carefully. She was a petite version of her mother with two dark braids slung over her shoulders and expressive green eyes.

Instantly charmed, Anna smiled. “It’s nice to meet you, Jocelyn. That’s a very unusual name.”

"It was my great-grandpa's name."

"Well I think it's a very bold name for a girl."

The younger child, a blue-eyed boy with a shock of dark hair, stuck his pudgy fist in his mouth.

Jo patted his head. "This is Shawn. He's two. He doesn't talk very much."

"Horse!" Shawn pointed a dimpled finger toward the street. "Horse."

Jo hooked him beneath the arms and hoisted him onto her hip. "He's mad about horses these days."

The oldest girl, who appeared to be about ten or twelve, was the last to speak. She had blond hair and blue eyes, and she was definitely not the natural child of the dark-haired parents standing before her. Though Garrett's niece, Jo spoke warmly of Cora as her "oldest child." More recently Jo had fretted that Cora was taking on too much responsibility for the younger two children, and Jo worried Cora was missing out on her own childhood. Seeing the obvious affection surrounding the family, Anna didn't think there was much to fret about in that regard.

Cora was simply mature for her age, a product of losing her parents young, no doubt. Grief had a way of aging people, even children.

"I'm Cora," the girl said.

"I'm pleased to meet you, Cora."

The marshal took his niece's hand. She smiled up at him, her face adoring. "Can we have ice cream?" she asked.

Jocelyn circled around to his opposite side and took his free hand. "I want ice cream, as well."

"First we have to find your mother's trunk," he said. "Then we'll have lunch. Then ice cream."

Jocelyn resisted her father's change in direction, digging in her heels. "Are you eating with us, Miss Anna?"

"That would be nice," she said, unable to recall the last time she'd eaten. The whole day was a blur. "I'm famished."

"Me, too," Jo said. "We'll find the trunks and stow them in the telegraph office while we eat. I'll sit with you while Garrett gets the trunks," Jo continued, though she gazed longingly at her husband. "I can't leave you alone, and Caleb can't escape his conversation. It's Mr. Patterson. He can talk the ears off a whole field of corn."

"You two go," Anna replied. Clearly husband and wife had missed each other, and Anna didn't need tending. "I'll wait here. I could use the rest."

A lie. Since her initial discomfort from traveling had passed, she'd rather do anything but rest. She wanted a hot meal and brisk walk after her time on the train, but she also sensed the couple needed time together.

Marshal Cain linked his free hand with his wife's, and together they meandered toward the pile of luggage the porter had retrieved from the train. Jo pressed her forehead against his shoulder, and Anna turned away. The gesture was too personal, too heartfelt.

She caught Caleb's gaze and he leaned away from Mr. Patterson. His inattention didn't appear to bother the man as he continued speaking.

Caleb rolled his eyes, clearly unmoved by the tender moment. "Nearly four years they've been married and you'd think it was yesterday."

The wistful tone of his voice was at odds with his exasperated expression.

He shook hands with Mr. Patterson and tipped his hat. "I'll get back to you on that."

The man looked as though he wanted to prolong the conversation, but Caleb didn't give him the chance, smoothly turning away without being outright rude.

"Stay here," he said, facing Anna. "I'll help Garrett with the luggage while Mrs. Franklin is freshening up."

Anna sagged. "I miss my good health. Only a moment ago I was ready for a long walk after sitting for so long." She collapsed back onto the bench with a weary grin. "But I've changed my mind. I don't know how sitting on a train doing nothing could have exhausted me so."

These swings in her health were annoying at best, debilitating at worst.

"You're healing. It takes time."

"I'd argue with you, but I'm far too drained."

He flashed another of his grins. The kind that curled her toes and sent a flutter through her belly. She rubbed a hand over her eyes. Exhaustion was taking its toll.

She took the opportunity to study the crowd. People raised their voices to be heard over each other. Someone brushed against her skirts. Sitting up, she caught the gaze of a gentleman standing near the train. He was plainly dressed in a dark suit and hat, with nothing to distinguish him from the other men milling about. Like any other banker or businessman, he naturally blended into the crowd. He surveyed the people around him, his gaze intense, as though he was searching for someone.

A shiver of apprehension raised gooseflesh on her arms. She might be anonymous, but so was the person who'd made an attempt on her life. Anybody could have shot her. Any one of these people jamming onto the platform.

Anna glanced around, searching for either Jo or Caleb. Two men hoisted an enormous steamer trunk between them and blocked her view of the spot where Caleb was giving instructions to the porter. Jo and her family had disappeared into the cramped shop attached to the depot. The telegraph office, she presumed.

The man near the train kept his steady vigil of the crowd. He lifted his pocket watch and checked the time. A young woman in a smart burgundy dress, her hair a shade of blond that defied nature, approached him and touched his sleeve. The man grinned and stuck out his elbow. Smiling in greeting, the woman hooked her hand over his bent arm.

Anna blinked.

Good gracious. The gentleman was simply waiting for his companion, and yet she'd read something sinister into his innocent actions.

Chagrined, she realized he'd been looking behind her, and yet she'd been certain he was looking *at* her. Studying her.

Her heart thudded against her ribs, and she rubbed her damp palms against her skirts. As the passengers departed for the extended break, the platform grew crowded. Footsteps shuffled, vibrating the bench, dozens of conversations melded together in boisterous confusion.

A woman in a violet dress stomped on her foot and muttered an apology. Anna's breath came in short gasps, and her head spun. Tears sprang behind her eyes, and she pressed a fist against her mouth. There were people everywhere. Closing in, brushing against her, looking at her. She wanted to run, but her legs remained paralyzed.

She'd been shot in a public square during a speech. Why was a crowded platform any different? What if the killer fired into the crowd? With her side stitched and her stamina gone, she'd never survive another stampede like the one on the day of the rally. And where would she run? A hysterical giggle bubbled in the back of her throat. Her gaze darted toward the train and then toward the street. She couldn't breathe.

A violent shudder traveled all the way down the length of her body. Clamping shut her jaw, she fought to regain control of her shaking. Despite her efforts, the shivering continued. She wrapped her arms around her middle, her teeth chattering. Nothing helped.

She had to escape.

Leaping from her seat, she clawed at the ribbons of her bonnet, desperate to escape the tunneled vision. She lurched away from the squeeze of bodies. A hand touched her shoulder, and she jerked away.

"Anna," a familiar, soothing voice said close to her ear. "It's all right. Just take a deep breath and hold on to my arm."

Her vision swimming, Anna clutched his sleeve and stared into Caleb's vivid green eyes. "I can't breathe."

She was suffocating. The edges of her vision turned hazy. In another moment she feared she'd faint dead away before the crowd of people. Her heart would hammer right out of her chest.

"You can breathe. You can. Relax."

His fingers worked the ribbons of her bonnet, brushing against her neck. He flipped back the brim, and the hat fell down her back, anchored by the loose ties at her neck.

"You're not trying." He sucked in a breath, and she automatically mimicked his movements.

"That's it," he said. "Just keep breathing."

As the air filled her lungs, her vision focused and her heartbeat calmed. He kept his fingers wrapped around her forearm for support. The voices swirling near her came into focus. She wasn't suffocating. She wasn't dying. The odd interlude had left her disoriented and exhausted.

With a muffled sniff she pressed her free hand against her forehead, unable to meet his eyes.

What must he think of her? "I don't know what's happening to me."

"It's anxiety." His deep timbered voice was soothing and free of censure. "To be expected, considering what happened to you."

Anna tipped back her head and chanced a peek at his face. "I don't know what's wrong with me. All at once I felt as though everyone was looking at me, talking about me. I knew it was silly, but I couldn't stop the panic."

"It's a common reaction," Caleb said after a long pause. A certain hesitancy in his voice sharpened her attention. "Did you feel as though your heart was about to leap out of your chest?"

"That's exactly right," she said, blinking in astonishment. "How did you know?"

Caleb considered the consequences of admitting the truth and tossed his pride aside. "It's happened to me before."

"Really?"

"I don't like cities." He sighed. "I avoid closed-in spaces. When I was growing up, everyone else was fascinated by the caves along Hackberry Creek. Especially after it turned out we had a real live outlaw hiding his loot in those caves. My brothers sold tours for years after that. I never went along."

"It's a good thing you became a veterinarian instead

of a bank robber. You'd have no place to hide your ill-gotten gains."

"I'm not much good at giving cave tours either."

"I'm glad you found your calling."

A bittersweet note crept into her voice.

He tilted his head. "As have you. We both found our place."

Her expression turned wistful. "Yes."

There was no conviction behind the word. He'd seen her fire, though. He'd seen her on the stage. From Jo's letters and the stories he'd read in the newspapers, he knew the power she wielded in the suffragist movement. She had a natural presence that drew people toward her. She reminded him of the fireflies he'd captured as a child, beguiled by their light. Fireflies died in captivity.

That's what they'd done by bringing her out here, they'd placed her in a jar for safekeeping. He knew well enough that safety didn't last long before it became smothering. She'd been pacing her hotel like a caged animal. He had no doubt she'd soon find the town oppressive.

"Caleb McCoy," a voice called. "Glad to see you're back in town."

The interruption was like a frigid dunk in the rain barrel. Caleb and Anna sprang apart. Hiding his annoyance, Caleb spun around and discovered the mercantile owner's wife from Cimarron Springs.

"Mrs. Stuart." Caleb hid his scowl. "How are you?"

Probably filled with gossip. The woman delighted in spreading the "news" of the town.

He'd much rather finish his conversation with Anna. There were things about her that none of them understood. Even Jo, who probably knew Anna better than anyone, didn't have all the pieces. Had they been making false assumptions, making the mistake Reinhart had warned them about, filling in the missing pieces of the puzzle? Forcing the edges together to make a whole?

"Good to see you, Caleb," Mrs. Stuart said coyly. "I hear congratulations are in order."

"Congratulations?"

"Well, of course you know my sister and her husband live in Kansas City. When I heard what happened at the rally, and then your stay was extended, well, I simply had to ask her to check on you." She leaned closer. "All this time I thought you were still sweet on Mary Louise when you'd transferred your affections elsewhere."

Anna was staring at him as though he'd grown a second head.

"I'm sorry," Caleb said. "I don't follow."

What was the woman blabbering about?"

"You know." She gave an exaggerated wink.

Anna had taken the opportunity to replace her bonnet, securing the ribbons beneath her ear with a large bow. He found the bonnet as annoying as she did, especially since the rounded brim blocked his view of her expression. He'd sensed her panic even before he'd seen her face. He was attuned to her, though he didn't know quite how or why.

After everything she'd been through in the past week, he was surprised she hadn't had a lapse sooner. She'd been injured in a city far from home, far from everything and everyone she knew. They were no closer to catching the man who'd shot her than they were the day of the rally. Even with the Pinkerton detective, Caleb was skeptical of finding the man before he tried again.

He moved nearer to Anna. They'd brought her back here for her safety.

A duty he took seriously. "What were you saying?"

Mrs. Stuart elbowed him. "You know."

"No, I do not know."

The day had started too early and gone on too long. He was grateful to be home at last. While he wanted Anna settled, he also wanted to check on his house and make his rounds. There'd be other needs, as well. Anything anyone had put off in his absence would gain a new urgency now that he'd returned.

Mrs. Stuart crossed her arms over her chest and opened her mouth to speak. The two men carrying the trunk grimaced and walked between them. Whatever had been packed must have been heavy. The two burly men had unloaded an entire stack of baggage without incident.

One of the men muttered. "Biscuits and beans, what's she got in this thing—rocks?"

"Bricks more like it," the second man replied.

The first man caught his toe on an uneven footing. He lurched forward, and his hand slipped. The trunk toppled to one side. The second man's arms twisted beneath the teetering weight. He released his hold and sprang away. The trunk crashed to the ground, and the top flipped open.

Two things happened at once.

Mrs. Stuart said, "Your engagement, of course. I know all about it."

And a limp, pale hand flopped out of the overturned trunk.

Chapter Eleven

Anna blinked and looked again. Caleb knelt before her, blocking her from the grizzly sight.

He chafed her cold fingers between his. “It’s all right,” he said. “Don’t look.”

“I couldn’t look if I wanted.”

A crowd of people had quickly circled the trunk, pointing and gesturing.

Caleb glanced over his shoulder and recognition lit up his face. “Here comes Tony. You’ll like her. She must be going on seventeen or eighteen now. She reminds me of Jo. You’ll see why once you meet her. Smart as a whip and unshakable. She’s good with animals, too.”

A young girl marched across the platform toward them. The resemblance to Jo was uncanny, although Tony was much taller and more angular. She wore trousers and suspenders over a button-up chambray shirt. As she approached, Anna noted her eyes were blue, another difference between her and Jo. And yet her carriage, the way she cut a path through the crowd without saying a word, reminded Anna of Jo’s forthright manner.

The girl’s hands were stuffed in her pockets, and

she bypassed them on her way toward the commotion. The crowd parted in her wake. Clearly Tony was a well-known character around town.

Upon reaching the trunk, Tony bent at the waist and tilted her head. “There’s a dead fellow in there.”

Marshal Cain jogged the distance from the telegraph office and gently moved the girl aside. “Thank you for the assessment, Tony. I’ll take care of things from here on out.”

Caleb waved the girl over. “Tony, this is Miss Anna. Can you sit with her a moment?”

“Sure. ’Cept she looks like she can sit alone fine enough.”

Anna immediately liked the young girl. “You don’t have to stay with me.”

“Oh, I’m staying. I can see and hear everything from this spot. We’ve got the best view of the hullabaloo. Not much goes on around here. When something does happen, it’s best to stay put and take in the show.”

Well, at least Tony wasn’t being forced on Anna as a companion. That thought had her feeling positively ancient.

Caleb chucked Tony on the shoulder. “Told you she was like Jo.”

“It’s a pleasure to meet you, Tony. I’m Anna.”

Tony plunked down beside her, stretched out her legs, and crossed her ankles. “How do you suppose a dead man winds up in a trunk? Someone must have put him there.”

Anna shivered. “Who would do such a thing?”

“The marshal will figure it out. He’s smart.”

Caleb surveyed the growing circle of curious spectators. “I’d best see if he needs any help.”

"We'll be fine," Anna said, knowing he'd be concerned about leaving her alone.

If nothing else, the marshal needed help controlling the crowd.

Caleb crouched before her and tilted his head. "That is absolutely the most atrocious bonnet I've ever seen. I feel as though I'm talking with the brim and not you."

"Once I unpack my things, I promise I'll burn it." Anna loosened the strings and flipped back the brim.

"That's better."

The wind whistled through the trees overhead, sending leaves drifting over them. Anna shivered. Caleb shrugged out of his coat and draped the heavy material over her shoulders.

"Do you want to sit inside?" he said. "You'll catch a chill on top of everything else."

Anna glanced up and realized the dead body wasn't the only spectacle attracting attention. More than one person stared at her and Caleb with open curiosity. Surely a town this large saw more than its fair share of strangers. Judging by the rapt interest, the two of them were as much of a curiosity as the dead body. They weren't in Kansas City anymore, and she'd do well to remember the distinction.

What had Mrs. Stuart been saying before the disruption? Anna recognized a gossip when she saw one. Someone had gotten engaged, and the news was obviously noteworthy. She'd ask Tony about it later. Right now they were creating a spectacle.

People around here knew the McCoys, they knew Caleb. "I'm fine. I was simply surprised. One does not expect a body to fall out of a trunk. Despite the circumstances, I'm enjoying the fresh air. I've been cooped up for days."

Caleb lifted one corner of his mouth in a wry grin. "How do you like small-town life so far?"

"It's rather more exciting than I had anticipated."

"Sit tight. I'll be right back."

After circling around the trunk, he stopped dead and met Anna's eyes over the lid. "He's familiar. I think I've seen him before."

"From where?" the marshal asked.

"Kansas City. I think. Can't say for certain."

Curious, Anna pushed off from the seat and sidled toward the men, carefully keeping the trunk positioned between her and the body.

Marshal Cain looked up. "You can't think of anything more specific?"

Caleb rubbed his chin. "No, except, well, there's something familiar about him. It's right on the edge of my memory. It'll come to me."

"What about you, ma'am?" The marshal caught her gaze. "Do you know this man?"

The stern edge in his voice sent a flush of color creeping up her neck. The marshal was no fool. Someone wanted her dead, and now he had a body sprawled before him.

Anna gingerly peered over the side. The dead man stared with unseeing eyes. In his thirties with dark hair and a full beard and mustache, he might have been anyone. Judging from the position of his body, he was neither tall nor short, fat nor thin.

Her stomach lurched, and she pressed a hand against her lips. "I've never seen him before."

Anna leaned forward once more, then jerked back. "Perhaps he was a guest at the hotel."

With so many people milling about, she might have passed him on the stairs or seen him in the lobby before the accident.

The marshal hoisted an eyebrow. "We'll need to talk."

"I assumed as much."

Anna returned to the bench where Tony waited. "Can you see Jo?" she asked.

Tony stood and tented her eyes with one hand. "Nope. She must be in the telegraph office. Probably staying put since she's got the young'uns with her."

"I'm sure that's best." Though there'd been nothing gruesome about the sight, seeing a dead man was unsettling. "Can you help keep an eye out for my traveling companion? Mrs. Franklin? She's tall and slender with gray hair, midsixties or so."

The press of curious townspeople closing in around the trunk and the dead man had left the platform a confusing mess.

"I'll keep a lookout." Tony remained standing, searching the faces of the crowd. "Nothing yet."

Curious about the younger girl, Anna asked, "Do you have any brothers and sisters, Tony?"

If Tony was an example, she wanted to meet the rest of the family.

"Sort of. I live on the Elder place with my uncle. He's the wrangler there. He's the cook, as well. Kind of. I think he cooks more than he wrangles these days. The Elders have two children of their own, and then there's Hazel and Preston."

"Hazel and Preston?"

"Hazel came on the cattle drive with us. Her and Sarah

and Darcy. Sarah lives in town. She's sweet on Brahm McCoy. Darcy is Preston's mother. She's been staying with the Elders since Preston's pa died."

The names buzzed around her head like a swarm of bees. "Where did Hazel come from exactly?"

"The orphan train."

"I thought she was from the cattle drive."

"That, too."

"Tony, I might need a pen and paper to keep this all straight."

"Did you hear about the outlaw who hid his loot in a cave out by Hackberry Creek?" Tony asked.

"I heard that part of the story." At least they were once again in familiar territory.

"We live in his old homestead. John Elder is Jack's brother."

"And who is Jack?"

"Jack married the outlaw's widow," Tony said.

"Ah, yes, the infamous outlaw of Cimarron Springs. And they live in Paris."

"Texas."

A few of the confusing people in the jumbled explanation fell into place. "Then you live by Hackberry Creek."

"That's the place," Tony said. "Say, if you ever want to see the cave where he hid the loot, I can show you."

"That's a lovely offer, but I've heard the description enough I feel as though I've been there already." Anna couldn't help but think of Caleb and his fear of closed spaces. "Sounds like quite a place to live."

"Mr. Elder asked me to meet the train. He sells horses. Mostly to the cavalry. I guess word about his stock has got out. There's a fancy couple interested in starting a horse farm down South. They're looking to buy a whole passel of horses. Mr. Elder sent me on ahead to fetch them."

Tony tapped her chin and squinted at Anna. She glanced at the telegraph office and back. "Jo was exchanging letters with someone named Anna. Are you…." She searched the space around them and lowered her voice. "Are you one of them suffragists?"

By now Mrs. McCoy was probably at the haberdashery swearing the proprietor to secrecy about the recipient of her housewarming gift. Which meant that by this afternoon, the news of her identity would blanket the town like fluffy seeds from the cottonwood trees.

"I am," Anna admitted, knowing her "secret" was anything but. By tomorrow, the whole town would know. So much for remaining anonymous.

"What do you do? I mean, is it like a job being a suffragist?"

"It's more of a calling than a job."

This was precisely why coming to Cimarron Springs was not a waste. There was always an opportunity for changing someone's mind, for educating someone about the cause. She'd have another recruit, another person who spread the word. They needed all the soldiers they could muster. The cause depended upon the next generation. While her mother believed the fight was winding down, meaning they didn't need the younger generation, Anna disagreed. There was always another mountain ahead, always a need for fresh troops. Not every gesture need be grand.

"Then, how do you make money? What do you live on?"

"My mother is comfortably set, as am I."

Tony nodded sagely. "You mean she's rich."

Anna sighed. In for a penny, in for a pound. "She doesn't have to worry about money, that much is true. She gives speeches around the country and organizes other chapters. Right now she's working on a sixteenth amendment to the constitution. She's in Boston meeting with another chapter about a state amendment. Some people think we should target the states, others think we should target the federal government. Some members favor a militant approach, some members favor a peaceful approach. The chapters split over the direction of the movement after the War Between the States. It's a job all on its own keeping everyone together in a united front."

"Why didn't they put the women's vote on the fifteenth amendment?" Tony braced her hands on her knees. "You know, after the war when they gave the black man the vote? Never could figure that one out."

"The process is complicated," Anna continued more slowly. "The fifteenth amendment is another case where people didn't agree. I think most people felt that the black man deserved his day in court without anything else clouding the waters. But I was just a baby back then. I don't really know for certain. You'd have to ask one of the older members."

"Do you think Mrs. Franklin will know?"

"She might."

If someone had told Anna two weeks ago she'd be sitting on a train platform with a tomboy telling her the history of the suffrage movement while waiting for her escort to clear the crowds away from a dead body, she'd have laughed at the absurdity. Life had a way of changing in a flash.

"I'm glad we talked," Tony said. "This stuff is interesting."

"If you ever want to know more, you can stop by. We're staying in the old Stuart house."

Tony patted her knee. "I'm sure all those stories about how Mr. Stuart's mother-in-law haunts the place are false. You should be fine."

"Uh. I don't believe in ghosts."

"Neither do I. That thumping and chatter people hear at night, probably just bats or raccoons taking up residence. There's nothing a raccoon likes better than an abandoned building."

"Bats?" Anna said weakly.

Perhaps she should have been more open to Mrs. McCoy's offer of cleaning help. Small-town life was definitely more stimulating than she'd expected. The next time someone bemoaned the sluggish pace of country living, she'd tell them about her first hour in Cimarron Springs.

Word of the body had spread like wildfire. Everyone within a mile of town must have arrived by now. A string of wagons stretched down Main Street. Children fought their way past bustled skirts to get a better look, while scolding mothers held them back.

The storefronts along Main Street soon emptied, signs reading Closed had been flipped into view. A gentleman scooted past the bench, a bit of foam from the barber visible behind one ear.

The body was hoisted onto a makeshift litter, and a hastily salvaged sheet draped over the macabre sight, much to the disappointment of a group of school-aged children huddling on the fringes of the gathering.

The boys jostled for a better view, shoving one another forward and ducking back until Tony marched over, her hands on her hips. Without saying a word, her presence sent the boys scattering.

The town's deputy, Caleb's brother, David, was fetched.

With all the commotion, Anna had a clear opportunity to study the McCoy brother who'd gotten Caleb's job and his girl. They shared the distinctive McCoy coloring, dark hair and green eyes. They were both tall and broad shouldered. Yet there was something softer about David. A certain rounding of the chin and plumping of the cheeks that lent him a boyish quality, making him appear younger than his years.

He was wider around the middle, as well. It wasn't simply his physique that differentiated the brothers. David's gaze lacked the sharp inquisitiveness of his sibling's. Though she'd never met this Mary Louise, Anna found her taste lacking. Caleb was clearly the better choice of the two men.

Mrs. Franklin emerged from the depot, took in the scene, and marched toward the commotion. She glanced at the sheeted body and fought her way toward Anna.

"For goodness' sake, is there a dead body beneath that sheet?"

Anna threw her a resigned glance. "He fell out of a trunk."

"He was on the train? With us?"

"I believe so."

"I left for one moment. One moment. I'm afraid to turn my back on you. We're probably lucky the train didn't derail on the way here."

"Ma'am," the marshal said. "If you were on the train as well, would you like to take a look? See if you recognize the fellow?"

Izetta tugged on her collar. "If it will end this nonsense sooner, then absolutely."

The marshal lifted an edge of the covering and Izetta leaned closer, wrinkling her nose. "I don't know him. Although, I must say, there is something familiar about him."

Disappointment flickered across the marshal's face.

He searched the crowd milling about the platform and faced his deputy. "Let's have the passengers take a look. It'll make my job easier if we can figure out his identity."

Returning to the bench, Izetta wrapped her hand around Anna's shoulder. "This is shaping up to be a rather odd day." She leaned away, pulled a handkerchief from her reticule and pressed the embroidered fabric against her nose. "Excitement trails you, my dear."

"I don't know if *excitement* is the term I'd use." Anna indicated Tony who'd been watching the exchange with unabashed curiosity. "This is Tony. She's been filling me in on the local legends."

Not to mention ghosts, bats and raccoons. She'd save those particular tidbits for later. She hoped Izetta didn't harbor any superstitions.

Tony bobbed her head in greeting. "I didn't know suffragists were married."

"Widowed. We come in all shapes and sizes, as well as marital statuses."

"Have you ever met the president?"

"I have not had the pleasure. Although I have penned him several letters in support of the cause."

The two struck up a lively conversation, and Anna let her attention drift. The train was delayed, much to the agitation of the conductor and the grumbling passengers who streamed onto the platform. David lined them up and scratched careful notes of their names and descriptions.

At a lull in the conversation, Izetta glanced around. "Where are Jo and Mr. McCoy?"

"Jo is keeping the children away from the commotion, and Caleb is managing the crowd."

"This has turned into a spectacle."

A flash of yellow caught Anna's attention. "It's the little girl from the rally."

"Where?"

Anna pointed, and Izetta shook her head. "I don't recall seeing her."

"She was definitely there that day. She gave me a bouquet of yellow flowers. Jo and Caleb saw her, as well."

Her last chance of remaining anonymous splintered into a thousand icy fragments. They knew her.

Anna tightened Caleb's coat around her shoulders. The wind had picked up, tugging at her hair and biting her ears and cheeks. She cupped her hands over her face and blew a puff of air, warming her chilled nose.

The marshal searched the now-empty trunk and read the name inscribed on the domed surface. "Is there a Mary K. Phillips here?"

The girl from the rally tugged on her mother's hand. "That's your name, mama."

Chapter Twelve

Anna stifled a groan. The marshal wasn't going to appreciate this turn of affairs one bit. Once again the coincidences were piling up. The little girl had been at the rally the day of the shooting. Mother and daughter had been staying at the same hotel. Now a body had rolled out of their trunk.

Clearly agitated, the mother stepped forward, clenching her daughter's hand, her chin set at a defiant angle. "I am Mrs. Phillips."

The woman was young, not much older than Anna. Her dress was expensively made, though a season or two out of fashion judging by the size of her bustle, a distinction Anna doubted anyone else noticed. She'd always had an eye for fashion, a useless trait in the Bishop household.

The woman was pretty, though clearly exhausted. Dark circles surrounded her hazel eyes, and the corners of her lips tugged down as though in perpetual frown. Tendrils of chestnut hair had escaped the tight bun at the nape of her neck. Neither mother nor daughter wore a coat against the late fall chill.

The marshal nudged the trunk with one booted foot. "That's the trunk you stowed in Kansas City."

"That is my trunk." The woman's frown deepened. "But I can assure you that is not what I packed."

Someone in the growing crowd tittered.

The marshal held up a hand. "This is a man's life. Show a little respect."

Several people ducked their heads. No one left the platform. They were all transfixed by the show playing out before them. No one wanted to hear about this event secondhand.

The marshal waved Mrs. Phillips over. "Why don't we let your daughter have a seat for a moment, ma'am, while we sort this out?"

The woman offered a reluctant nod. She caught sight of Anna, but no recognition flared in her gaze. Expelling a breath, Anna caught the little girl's eye. She patted the seat beside her, and the child skipped over. The mother hadn't known her identity, which was something. Her secret was much safer with the little girl.

"My name is Anna. I remember you from the rally. Would you like to sit next to me?"

"My name is Jane. You're the prettiest lady I've ever seen. That man—" she pointed at Caleb "—he said you were the prettiest lady he'd ever seen, as well."

Anna's eyes widened. "Oh, my. That was a nice thing for him to say."

"When you were giving your speech and everyone started running and pushing, he protected me."

Why was Anna not surprised? Of course Caleb had come to the rescue. "That was very kind of him."

"He stayed behind to help someone who was hurt."

The marshal and Caleb flanked the girl's mother, parting the crowd as they approached the draped body.

Caleb knelt and pulled back the cover, revealing the man's face.

The woman's hand flew to her throat.

"Do you know this man?" the marshal asked.

"Yes and no. I saw him before. In Kansas City. At the Savoy Hotel. He was always lurking around."

"Name?"

"I don't know. I never actually met him."

The marshal gestured toward the trunk. "I assume the last time you checked your trunk was at the hotel?"

She offered another hesitant nod. "Yes. The porter took the trunk from our room and made the arrangements."

"Which hotel?"

"I told you already. The Savoy. In Kansas City."

The marshal shot another look at Caleb. Anna sighed. None of this boded well for her welcome. Not only had she brought danger, she'd come accompanied by a dead body. The marshal was clearly protective of his family. How long before he decided Anna's presence was a risk that wasn't worth taking?

She was dangerous and notorious. A lethal combination. They might have forgiven one of those offenses, but not both. She had her doubts.

"How long was the trunk out of your sight?" the marshal asked.

"Not more than hour," Mrs. Phillips said.

"Time enough for killing."

The color drained from her face, and her eyes rolled back.

"She's fainting," Caleb called, catching the woman before she hit the ground.

He gently lowered her the remaining distance. Izetta leaped up and whipped off her shawl. Caleb bunched the material and tucked it beneath the woman's head.

The marshal rubbed the back of his neck. "Well, that's a fine kettle of fish."

"She's had a shock," Caleb said. "Is Doc Johnsen here yet?"

"On his way," the marshal replied.

The little girl clutched Anna's hand. "What's wrong with mama?"

Anna wrapped her arm around Jane, carefully averting her face. "Your mother will be all right. She's had a bit of a fright."

Anna glanced around the crowded depot. All eyes were pinned on their odd tableau. Sweat beaded on her temple. She recalled the girls at Miss Spence's Academy, how they'd stared at her as though she was some exotic animal. Their curiosity an odd mixture of fascination and disgust.

Once her identity as the illegitimate daughter of the famous heiress had been exposed, the other girls had kept their distance, whispering behind her back and pointing. In the week before her expulsion, they'd tossed her shoes onto the roof and hidden her nightgown. Offences which had gone unpunished.

While she assumed her shoes were safe among adults in Cimarron Springs, it was only a matter of time before their attitudes shifted. She'd leave well before that happened. Well before the McCoys were affected by her notoriety.

Jane squeezed her hand. "Is mama sad because of that man in our trunk?"

"Yes. I know this must all seem very strange and confusing."

"I saw him before, at the hotel."

Anna narrowed her gaze. "Are you certain?"

"He was watching us."

Anna pulled back from the little girl and studied her face. "When?"

"At the hotel yesterday. He made mama sad. That's when she said we had to leave."

Anna's heart sank. Mrs. Phillips had said she didn't know the man. Her daughter just revealed they'd talked. How were those two involved? Worse yet, she'd have to disclose her suspicions to the marshal.

With every new revelation, the news grew more tangled. "Don't worry, Jane. The marshal and his brother-in-law will take good care of your mother."

What would happen to the little girl if her mother was accused of murder? Anna shoved the thought aside. Simply because the man had been watching them didn't mean Mrs. Phillips was involved. Perhaps Jane was mistaken.

Not for the first time, Anna noted that Jane was wearing the same yellow dress from the rally. Memories assaulted her senses. The pungent scent of burning fuel from the fires set against the frigid wind, the sunlight bouncing off the windows of the buildings around the square. The sound of the shot. Caleb lifting her into his arms.

Calming her ragged breathing, she focused her attention back to the present.

Already Mrs. Phillips was coming around. Jane's mother struggled upright, her hand pressed against her forehead.

The conductor approached, his watch chain swinging from his fingers. "I can't hold up this here train all day. I've got a schedule to follow. If I'm late, everyone on down the line is late."

The marshal gestured for David. "Allow everyone back on the train once you've taken down their names. Did you search the rest of the luggage car?"

"Yep. Nothing suspicious. This seems to be the only body."

"Then let 'em go. Not much more we can do."

The woman stifled a sob, and Caleb helped her into a sitting position.

She gasped and frantically searched the crowd. "Where's Jane? Where's my daughter?"

Caleb placed a hand on her shoulder and pointed. "She's with Miss Anna. Safe and sound."

The woman visibly relaxed, and Caleb assisted her to her feet.

Her face pale, she approached the marshal. "Am I under arrest? This isn't our stop. We must get back on the train."

"Where are you headed?" the marshal asked.

The woman paused. "Texas."

The hesitation was only a tick, but enough that Caleb and Garrett exchanged a glance. Anna shook her head. Whatever her involvement, the woman was only making matters worse for herself and her daughter by lying.

Mrs. Phillips must have sensed her error. She glanced at her clenched hands, her face ashen.

The marshal flipped over the tag on her trunk. "According to this, you were going to Cimarron Springs."

"There must have been a mistake. We're, uh, my daughter and I, are bound for Texas."

The marshal rocked back on his heels. "Why don't

you stick around town for a day or two instead? Until we get this all sorted out. We'll put you up in the hotel. I'll even buy you both another train ticket when everything is sorted."

Judging from her stricken expression, the woman had caught the subtle undertone in his words. The question was not *when*, but *if*. The body had been discovered in her trunk. According to her daughter, she'd spoken with the dead man the day before. She'd been afraid of him. The little girl had been at the rally. None of the pieces of the puzzle were particularly damning, but taken together, they aroused suspicion.

Anna rubbed her arms.

Jane unfurled a length of string. "Do you know Cat's Cradle?"

"No. But maybe you can teach me."

Mrs. Phillips pressed her hands against her cheeks. "Are you forcing me to stay? Do I have a choice?"

The marshal's gaze was sympathetic but unwavering. "I can arrest you and force you to stay. Or you can remain here voluntarily."

Her back stiffened. "Then I suppose we'll be staying." She whipped around and marched toward her daughter. She snatched the girl's hand. "Come along."

Jane reached for Anna. "Where are we going?"

"We're going to stay in town for a while. We're going to have a little adventure."

"Can I see Miss Anna again?"

"Maybe. I don't know."

The girl glanced over her shoulder, and her look resonated with Anna: the loneliness, the isolation. Something had gone wrong in their little family. Something that had scared her mother. While Anna didn't want to believe the woman was capable of killing a man, there was a good possibility she had.

Mrs. Phillips caught Anna staring and pursed her lips. "I don't know. We'll see."

Tears welled in the girl's eyes.

Sensing her distress, Caleb rested his hand on Anna's shoulder. "Don't worry, the marshal is a good man. He'll do what he can."

Two men lifted the litter holding the dead man's body and set off down the street. The group of boys trailed behind in an odd parade. Now that the show was over, the passengers filed back onto the train.

Another thought chilled her to the bone. Jane had been at the rally. Mrs. Phillips had been conspicuously absent.

Had Mrs. Phillips been involved in Anna's shooting? They all assumed a man had shot her. A woman was just as capable of murder as a man was.

No. Anna violently shook her head. Shooting her put Jane in danger, and Mrs. Phillips clearly loved her daughter. Besides, she'd shown no recognition of Anna.

A sharp gust whipped her skirts around her legs.

At her reassuring smile, Caleb had resumed his conversation with the marshal.

She'd left one set of worries behind, only to pick up another set.

The marshal glanced at Mrs. Phillips and her daughter and back at Caleb. "How much do you know about them?"

"Nothing. Jo and I saw the little girl at the rally. She was alone. After the shooting, Jo took her back to the hotel and found her mother."

"What about Anna? How much do you know about her?"

A flush of anger crept up his neck. "She's not involved, if that's what you're thinking. We've been with her the whole time. There was a guard at her door. There's no way she could have done this. Besides, you're better off asking Jo about Miss Bishop."

"I'm asking you."

"Why?"

"Because Jo admires her. Because I like to take care of my family."

Caleb lowered his hackles. Marshal Cain was simply protecting his wife. He'd do the same. "I only know what I've seen the past few days. She's tough. She's loyal."

The marshal hitched his fingers into his gun belt. "Jo said the same thing."

"I haven't seen anything that would make me question her loyalty. You weren't there. You didn't see what happened when she was shot. She's the victim, not the aggressor."

The challenge disappeared from the marshal's expression. "That's another thing. Jo asked me to look into the shooting. Didn't discover much. They think the shooter hid out in a building across the way. The window on the second floor was unlatched. I don't get the feeling the boys up north are putting much into the investigation. They figure it's all wrapped up with the suffragists' movement. They don't think it's personal."

"They're idiots. There were two attempts on Anna's life."

A muscle ticked along his jaw. They'd been standing mere feet away from Anna while the man had waited and watched. They'd been entranced by the speech while the killer had taken aim. He'd been one door away from her when the second attempt occurred.

The marshal squinted. "And you don't know of any other reason why someone would want Anna dead?"

"She's a suffragist, you know that much. Her mother is famous. I'm sure Jo has filled you in on the family. Anna is on her way to overtaking her mother's fame. After hearing her speak, I don't have any doubt she can lead the movement."

"Then, you think this has to do with the suffragists, as well?"

"Partly, sure, but it's personal. The man tried again. He might have succeeded the second time if there hadn't been a guard at the door."

"What a mess. But if this is about the cause, why target Anna alone?"

"She's a powerful asset. Don't know if that's worth killing over, but people get odd ideas."

The marshal made a noncommittal sound in the back of his throat. "Someone wants Anna dead. Then a body shows up in Cimarron Springs. Mrs. Phillips was staying at the hotel. You saw her daughter at the rally."

"I know Anna." Caleb glanced up sharply. "She had nothing to do with any of this."

"I didn't say she did. There's a lot of bodies piling up around your Miss Bishop. A lot of the same people are circling around, winding up in the same places. You think it's a coincidence those two women were on the train with a dead man?"

"I don't know how. We were careful. No one saw us leave the hotel."

Caleb recalled Mrs. Stuart's earlier declaration and groaned. "There's something else. Before. At the hotel.

The desk clerk registered Anna as my fiancée. Mrs. Stuart's sister lives in Kansas City. Evidently she visited the hotel, put two and two together, and made five."

The marshal adjusted his hat over his eyes. "The Stuart sisters are fond of a good piece of news. Especially if they have it first. It's not such a bad idea."

"I don't think Anna would agree."

"She might not have a choice." The marshal nodded in the direction of Mrs. Stuart. "Gossip spreads faster than maple syrup on a hot day around here."

Perhaps the discovery of the body had distracted Mrs. Stuart. There was time, time for setting the rumor to rest.

"I'll think about it."

"Think about this, as well. This town is full of good people. They'll do right by Miss Bishop, I don't doubt that. But if people think the two of you are engaged, she's part of the family. The McCoys are well respected around here."

"She's a friend of Jo's. Isn't that enough?"

"Everyone knew Jo was in town for that rally. Might be better if they think the rally was a convenient excuse for you to do a little courting. A little misdirection buys us time."

The idea made sense if there weren't so many other problems. "What happens if people discover that we've deceived them?"

"You gotta give people credit. If they feel like they've helped save someone, they'll forgive soon enough."

"Anna is the last person that needs saving," Caleb said. Mostly he was worried about his own hide. She'd made her feelings about an engagement bargain abundantly clear already. "She's smart and independent. She'd rather meet this problem head on than hide behind a lie."

The marshal lifted one shoulder in a careless shrug. "You don't have to explain to me. My wife once shot me."

"To save you."

"See. It's all about intent." The marshal flashed a grin.

Anxious to leave the conversation behind, Caleb offered a greeting as Mr. Lancaster, the blacksmith, approached them with a young woman whom Caleb assumed was his new bride. "Caleb, I wanted you to meet my wife."

She was petite and shy, her head down, her two blond braids wrapped around her head like a coronet.

"This is Helga."

She offered a few murmured words of greeting, her quiet voice heavily accented.

"We've just seen her mother off." Mr. Lancaster hid his relief well, but not well enough. "We'll be seeing you at the Harvest Festival, won't we?"

The marshal touched the brim of his hat. "Our family will be there."

"Excellent. Helga hasn't had the chance to meet too many people yet." He gazed adoringly at his new bride. "Best be getting home. Looks like it might rain."

Caleb tipped his face toward the sky. Sure enough, the horizon appeared hazy and dark. Mr. Lancaster clasped his wife's hand and led her toward their wagon.

The marshal followed their progress with a slow shake of his head. "We're going to need a new blacksmith."

"Are they moving?"

"Mr. Lancaster may not know it yet, but they're moving, all right. You should have seen the tears when his wife's mother left."

"That doesn't mean he's leaving."

"Mr. Lancaster is smitten, and his wife is unhappy.

You don't need to be a Pinkerton detective to put those two pieces together."

Caleb glanced at where Anna was sitting. She tilted toward the left, her hand braced on the bench, her lips pinched and white. Her suffering touched off a fierce protectiveness, and he understood what the marshal was saying. He'd wrestle a grizzly if his actions alleviated her suffering.

"I'd best see to Miss Bishop," Caleb said. "They're staying at the Stuart house. Is it fit for them?"

"Mr. Stuart had some of the boys over yesterday to patch the roof and fix the door on the back. Still needs a lot of work, but it'll be good for tonight if the ladies aren't too picky."

Caleb wasn't certain. After the Savoy Hotel, what would Anna think of the tiny, neglected house? It was a far cry from Kansas City.

Yep, he'd do whatever it took to make her happy. Even if that meant ensuring she was back in St. Louis, far away from Cimarron Springs.

He adjusted the brim of his hat lower over his eyes. "Can anything else go wrong today?"

"Ask and you shall receive." The marshal pointed down the street toward the man marching their way.

Caleb frantically searched for an escape.

Chapter Thirteen

Caleb backed away from the man charging toward him. He glanced at the marshal for help, but Garrett only grinned and turned his back.

Caleb groaned. If he backed up any farther he'd be sitting in Anna's lap.

Mr. Aaberg thrust a squirming bundle of bleets and hooves into his arms.

Caleb fumbled with the distraught goat. "This isn't a good time, Triple A."

They'd called Avery Aaberg Triple A for as long as Caleb could remember. The man was ornery and disagreeable, more so since his second wife had died the past winter. Most folks avoided the cantankerous farmer, but Caleb didn't mind him as much. Triple A kept his barns clean and his animals tended, he never waited until it was too late to save an animal before he came calling and he didn't expect Caleb to stay for coffee and gossip after a visit.

Caleb fumbled with the goat, and Triple A crossed his arms over his chest, then stepped out of reach.

"That one there is a runt," the man declared. "The others are going to kill it. I can't look after him all the time. You'll have to take him."

"Find someone else."

"Why?"

"Because I'm otherwise engaged. This is Miss Anna, she's—" A loud bleat interrupted his words. "We've just gotten back into town and Anna—" Another bleat drowned out his explanation. "Bring the goat around to the house later."

Triple A grinned and slapped his shoulder. "Good to hear. I thought Mrs. Stuart was just gossiping again."

Caleb gaped. He'd never seen the man smile. Not once. And he'd known him all his life. In twenty-six years he'd never seen Triple A's teeth full on. Not that he was missing much. They were yellowed and uneven with a large gap down the center two.

The farmer stuck out his hand toward Anna. "Nice to meet another *a*, Miss Anna. I'm Avery Aaberg. That's two *a*'s in Aaberg. Folks around here call me Triple A."

"It's nice to meet you, Mr., ah, Mr. Triple A."

"Just Triple A. We don't stand on ceremony in these parts. Especially now that you're one of the family."

Anna kept her head facing forward, but her eyes swiveled toward Caleb. "Family?"

Biscuits and gravy. He was too late. The rumor had started.

"And now you have a goat." Triple A clapped his hands together. "Everything is settled."

"Wait," Caleb demanded. "I do not have a goat. You have a goat."

He needed time with Anna. Surely she'd understand his explanation. How things had gotten out of hand. How he'd never intended for this to happen.

"He's got his ear bit," Triple A said. "Might be an infection. Thought you better take a look at it."

The animal was definitely a runt, about half the size of a normal goat, with light gray fur that turned darker at the tips.

One hoof dug into Caleb's side, tearing his shirt and scratching his stomach. "I can take a look at his ear, but then he's going home with you."

"Can't. Told you. He's the runt."

"Yes, but why is it my responsibility to find him a home?"

"Do you have any goats?"

"No. You know that. Three horses, a lame cow and the occasional stray cat."

"Then you have room for a goat."

"I don't want a goat."

"You're the vet. You must know someone who needs a goat. He might be a runt, but he eats well enough. He'll keep the yard cleared. Just mind you don't have any roses. He likes roses."

Triple A turned his back, and Caleb limped after him, the goat impeding his pursuit. "This isn't a good time. I told you."

"If I take him back, the others will trample him," Triple A said solemnly. "His death will be on your hands."

Triple A pinned his mournful gaze on Anna. A muscle ticked along Caleb's jaw. Triple A was doing this on purpose. The old blackmailer knew exactly what would happen.

Anna gasped. "Really? They'll kill him?"

Triple A scratched the stubble on his cheek, and Caleb shot him a scalding glare. Of course she'd hear that little tidbit.

"Happens sometimes," the farmer said. "With these little ones. The other fellows weed out the weak one. It's a shame, but that's life on the farm."

Anna stood and rested her hand on the goat's back. "That's terrible." She appealed to Caleb. "Couldn't you find him a home?"

Triple A shook his head and Caleb glared. The farmer had gone and done that on purpose. Now Anna was looking at him as though he was a black-hooded executioner sending the goat off to the gallows.

"Tomorrow," Caleb spoke through gritted teeth.

"Has to be today." Triple A was grinning again with that big annoying gap-toothed smile. Right then Caleb missed never seeing the man's teeth. He didn't appreciate his sense of humor. "I'm cutting hay first thing in the morning. I won't be around. I'd hate to come and find him trampled."

Anna sucked in a breath.

"That is blackmail." The goat kicked him in the gut. "Oomph. Could we talk about this tomorrow?"

He was stuck with the goat. No amount of arguing was changing that.

"He won't last the night."

Caleb groaned and set down the squirming animal. Triple A tipped his hat toward Anna. "Pleasure to meet you, Miss Anna." Then he stuffed his hands in his pockets and set off toward town.

Caleb angled his head. "Is he whistling?"

Anna stifled a grin. "Yes. I believe he's whistling 'The Battle Hymn of the Republic.'"

"That old coot. What am I going to do with a goat?"

Anna leaned down and cupped the goat's face in her

hand. "I think he's just precious. Why, he's smaller than a collie. Will he get much bigger?"

Caleb squinted at the goat. He was barely more than six weeks old, with that curious shade of gray that darkened at the tips of his fur. "Probably not."

The goat bleated and tipped its head. One ear hung at an odd angle, a bit of dried blood matting its gray fur.

Anna stared up at him, her gaze appealing. "Can you fix his ear?"

There was no help for it, the animal needed medical attention. At the very least, Caleb was finally back in his element. Finally taking care of something he understood.

Since this detour also gave him a reprieve from telling Anna about the engagement rumor sweeping through town, he'd forgive Triple A. For the moment.

"That ear needs tending," Caleb said. "I'll have to get him home for a better look."

Mrs. Franklin appeared again, fording her way through the crowd like a steamship through rough waters. "I have secured our baggage. I had to suffer the indignities of opening each trunk and box, proving that no additional bodies had been secreted in our baggage." She sniffed. "As though a grown man could fit in a hatbox. Perhaps they assumed he'd been chopped up and distributed equally amongst the tissue paper and bows."

Anna blanched.

Caleb fought a grin that tugged at the edges of his mouth. While there was a certain absurdity to the situation, a man had lost his life.

Mrs. Franklin pulled at her collar. "I suggest we continue on to the hotel. I could use a strong cup of coffee. This has already been an eventful day."

The goat nibbled on her skirts.

Mrs. Franklin leaped back. “Why do you have a goat?”

“He’s injured,” Anna said. “He’s the runt. The other animals have been bullying him.”

Mrs. Franklin took another cautious step back, her wary attention focused on the goat. “It appears Mr. McCoy has his hands full for the foreseeable future. We’ll save him a seat.”

“Much appreciated.”

Caleb hoisted the goat into his arms once more and nodded. “My home, I mean my office, well, my home and my office are just down the street. A block or so after the hotel.” He raised the goat a notch and pointed. “The Stuart house is a couple doors down and across the street. I’ll tend to his ear and meet you. Jo should be around here somewhere.”

“Don’t worry.” Anna scratched behind the goat’s good ear. “We’ll manage.”

Caleb offered a serene smile, pivoted on his heel and grimaced. He’d just gotten home and already there’d been a dead body, a goat and an engagement rumor. Not exactly a good first impression. What did any of that matter, anyway? She wasn’t staying long.

Only her opinion did matter. Her opinion mattered too much. He just hoped she’d forgive him once she realized everyone in town thought they were engaged.

Anna stared wistfully after Caleb. While she wanted lunch, she wasn’t quite certain if she was up to the task of meeting more people.

Izetta dusted her hands. “Dead man or no dead man, goat or no goat, I’ve a mind to see this house where we’ll be staying. I want to see what needs to be done.”

She marched toward a wagon and a man leaning

against the baseboard, and Anna realized she must be arranging for their luggage.

She glanced down and discovered Caleb's familiar battered leather satchel resting on the bench. She stuck her arms through the sleeves of his coat and stood.

Catching up to Mrs. Franklin, she hoisted the bag. "Mr. McCoy may need this. Why don't I meet you at the hotel later?"

"I'm not surprised he forgot it in all the confusion. I shall have this gentleman deliver our bags and meet you at our new home."

"Perfect." Anna blew out a relieved breath. "If you see Jo, tell her where I've gone."

The day had been too full of surprises and unexpected news. She needed quiet. The idea of making small talk with a group of strangers sounded exhausting at that moment. Any excuse for escape was welcome.

Clutching Caleb's bag against her chest, she set off down the boardwalk. Though carrying the heavy bag tugged at her wound and had her side aching, the wind on her cheeks had revived her flagging reserves of energy.

She reached the end of the boardwalk and searched the street. There were three houses on the left side, spaced well apart, each featuring a barn and an outbuilding.

A gentleman passed her, and she caught his attention. "I was looking for Mr. McCoy's home?"

The bearded man paused. "Which Mr. McCoy would that be? There's a whole passel of them around these parts."

"Caleb McCoy." Anna indicated the bag she carried. "I came with him from Kansas City. He forgot his bag."

A wide grin spread across the man's face. "Of course, of course. Second house, the one with the porch swing."

Anna smiled her thanks. My, but people were friendly around here.

She walked the distance and paused before the tidy little house. The home was a perfect square with steeply pitched pyramid roof. A wrought-iron weather vane with a stamped rooster perched on the peak. From the direction of the rooster's tail feathers, the brisk fall wind was blowing from the north.

A bricked walkway flanked by two towering elm trees bisected the yard to the front porch. Though the burnt orange leaves were already falling, the trees must have shaded the whole yard in summer. She pictured sitting on the porch swing, cooled from the dappled sunlight.

One of the crisp leaves fluttered to the ground, and she caught the papery edges in her fist. This was most definitely a bachelor's residence. Painted white, there were no feminine adornments visible anywhere. No flowers lined the area below the porch railing, no colorful curtains hung in the window. Only the porch swing smacked of anything domestic. Though plain, the home was neat and tidy, the native grasses none too tall.

Three wide steps led to the porch. The door was open, leaving only the screen door in her way. She knocked on the wooden edge.

"Come in," a voice called.

Suddenly shy, she winced at the loud creak of the hinges. Inside, the house had been portioned off into another perfect square. A parlor to her left, and on her right, an area sectioned off with double doors, she presumed to be Caleb's office, with what must have been a kitchen and a bedroom behind them. From her vantage point, the corridor stretched through the center of the house, leaving a line of sight out the back door toward the barn. The design would allow a refreshing cross breeze.

She turned toward the glass double doors on her right and cautiously pushed one open.

"Watch your feet!" Caleb shouted.

The goat had broken free of his grasp and dashed toward Anna. She scooted into the room and slammed the door behind her.

Caleb sat back on his heels. "That is an incredibly stubborn goat who does not want my assistance."

"Can I help? I brought your bag and your coat."

She extended her hand, and he took the bag from her, his knuckles brushing against her fingers. The simple touch was sweetly intimate. Anna shivered and stepped back.

"I'm sorry there's no heat," Caleb said, misinterpreting her reaction. "I haven't had time to start a fire."

"That's quite all right." She rubbed her arms.

His brief touch had caused the reaction, but there was no need to tell him that.

The air was a touch chilly. "Is there something I can do to help?"

"There's a garden patch out back. I think there's some late potatoes growing. They should distract this little guy while I'm tending him. Unless you'd rather stay with the goat."

"I'll fetch the potatoes."

While Caleb held the goat, Anna slipped out the doors once more. She navigated the corridor, pausing before the kitchen door. The space was bare, and if she didn't know better, she'd have thought the house deserted. There were no pictures on the walls, no tables holding decorative objects. The place was scrupulously clean, and she admired his efforts in that regard at least.

Except the house felt lonely. Caleb clearly preferred the simplicity, and yet he struck her as a family man. A man who wanted a wife and children.

Her heartbeat skittered. Children. They'd have green eyes and dark hair. Or blue eyes. Anna reared back. If she didn't cease thinking about Caleb in terms of the future, she'd be asking for heartache. She wasn't the sort of wife he needed, and they were both well aware of the obstructions.

After passing through the screen door at the back of the home, she imagined once again the lovely breeze that must come through the house in the spring and summer. There was something inexorably peaceful about the setting.

The two garden patches were laid out in precise rows, mirroring the tidy efficiency of the house. A path led through the center to the barn, and she followed the bricks. Each square on either side of the pathway was protected with a short mesh fence. Having never had a garden, she wasn't quite certain what she was looking for.

She tapped her front tooth with one finger. "If I were a potato, where would I be?"

"In that patch on your left."

Anna shrieked and whirled around. An identical copy, albeit a younger version, of Caleb stood behind her.

He lifted an eyebrow. "Although I don't know why you'd want to be a potato."

"You must be one of Caleb's brothers."

"Yep. Abraham. People call me Brahm."

"I'm Anna. I was just getting a potato."

"I figured that."

She mentally slapped her forehead. The poor man must think her a dolt. "For Caleb."

Oh, yes, that helped. He definitely wouldn't think of her as an imbecile anymore.

He glanced at the door behind her. "Does this mean Caleb's home?"

"Yes."

"Good. Maxwell's supposed to be doing his chores, but he went into town and left them for me today."

"I'm sure Caleb is grateful for your assistance."

He stepped over the wire mesh fencing surrounding the garden patch and stared at the tufts of green, then leaned down and dug in the dirt for a moment. He straightened, turned toward her and held out his hands.

She cupped her fingers together, and he dumped three potatoes the size of eggs into her outstretched palms.

"There's been a frost," Brahm said. "That's the best you'll get this late in the season. Hope you weren't planning on a big meal."

"This should be enough. They're for a goat."

"Yep."

Oh, dear. This was not going well at all.

"I'll just—" she jerked one shoulder toward the back door "—go back inside now."

He stepped around and grasped the handle, swinging open the screen door. Anna blushed. With her hands full, the task was impossible on her own.

"Thank you. Would you like to come in?"

"Nah. Tell Caleb I changed the dressing on the milk cow's foreleg and cleaned out the horses' stalls."

"I'll tell him." She stepped into the house and glanced over her shoulder. "It was nice meeting you."

"You, too. Hope everything turns out well with the goat."

Anna flapped her elbow in what she hoped resembled a wave. So much for making a good impression on Caleb's family. She returned to the double doors and called out.

Caleb pushed open the door a slit. She twisted sideways and scooted through the narrow opening. Her skirts brushed his pant legs, and her knuckles skimmed his white shirt, leaving a streak of dirt.

Anna glanced up into his green eyes. "Oh, no. I've ruined your shirt."

He didn't reply, only stared down at her, his gaze intense. Her mouth went dry, and she swayed forward, bracing her knuckles against his chest, the potatoes still fisted in her hands. Heat from his body spread through her fingers, and her heartbeat quickened.

He rested his hand on her waist, his touch separated by layers of clothing and bandages.

She stared at the buttons on his shirt, tension coiling in her belly. "I met your brother."

"Which one?"

"Abraham."

"Maxwell must have talked Brahm into doing his chores."

"He looks like you."

"We all look alike."

"Not really. You're much more..."

He tucked his knuckles beneath her chin and urged her head up until she met his eyes. "Yes?"

The goat tangled in her skirts and dashed through the open door into the parlor. Anna tripped forward and splayed her hands for balance. The potatoes landed on

Caleb's sock foot, and he grimaced, staggering backward. Off balance, Anna followed him, her hands fisting in his shirt. Caleb yelped.

She realized her hold on him was causing the pain and instantly released her fingers.

He sat down hard on the chair behind him and grasped her waist, keeping her upright. "Mind your side."

Anna stepped back and slipped on a potato. Caleb lunged upright and caught her around the waist.

They stared up at each for a long moment. A curious sense of anticipation filled her.

He angled his head and leaned down. The touch of his lips was featherlight, barely more than a whisper. His fingers held her waist loosely, giving her every chance for escape. She pressed closer. She slipped her hands around his neck and felt the bare skin at his nape.

Footsteps sounded from the parlor.

She leaped away from Caleb, blinking rapidly. Caleb appeared equally stunned, breathing as though he'd run a great distance.

Brahm entered the room, the goat cradled in his arms. He glanced between the two of them and lifted an eyebrow.

Caleb released Anna and fisted his hand in front of his mouth, then cleared his throat. "Hey, Brahm."

"Hey, Caleb. Figured you lost this."

As Brahm handed his brother the goat, Anna took another step back and ducked her head.

"You coming by for supper tonight?" Brahm asked.

"Yes."

"Are you bringing your friend?"

"Yes."

"You know I mean Anna and not the goat, right?"

Brahm burst into laughter, and Caleb shoved him none-too-gently out of the room, securely latching the door behind his brother.

He raked his hands through his hair. “Sorry about that.”

“I didn’t make a very good impression on your brother.”

The goat remained between them, snuffling along the floor for the lost potatoes.

Anna gestured over her shoulder. “I should go now.”

“Let me walk you. The Stuart house is just across the way. It’s white with blue shutters. You can’t miss it.”

“I’ll be fine on my own.”

She fumbled with the latch. Caleb brushed her hands away and completed the task. She raced out the front doors, down the stairs and struggled with the latch on the gate. Why were there latches everywhere? Why must they be difficult?

She’d kissed him. She’d kissed Caleb McCoy. Well, he’d kissed her. She didn’t know if there was a difference. They’d kissed and she liked kissing.

She’d liked kissing him a lot.

Chapter Fourteen

A few small improvements had made an enormous difference.

Two days following her arrival, Anna stood in an exact replica of Caleb's house. The only difference being the dining room was actually a dining room and hadn't been cordoned off with glass doors for an office. The trees outside were oak instead of elm, and the garden behind the house had obviously been used for flowers instead of vegetables. Izetta had immediately fallen on the overgrown space and attacked the suffocating vines with an almost giddy zeal.

Anna had been more interested in the interior of the house. She'd used housework as her excuse for avoiding a dinner with the McCoys. The thought of looking Caleb in the eye after what had happened had been more than she could bear.

The Stuarts had kindly donated a few old pieces of furniture. There was a square wooden table in the dining room that had seen better days flanked by two mismatched chairs. Neither of the painted chairs quite fit the table, which meant one either chose to sit slightly above the optimum table height or slightly below. Given their size differences, Anna had chosen the tall chair and Izetta had chosen the shorter chair.

The whole experience was very much like playing house. Until setting her trunk in the second bedroom, she hadn't realized she'd been living her life as a guest in her mother's home. Chairs were not there to be moved, pictures were not rearranged, rugs were left where they were placed.

One particularly memorable Christmas, Anna had been given a dollhouse. Two stories high with a vaulted attic and hinges that opened the whole house down the middle. The miniature house was fully stocked with furniture and rugs and a family with painted porcelain faces dressed in their Sunday best—a mother, father, a boy and a girl. There was even a yellow tabby cat with real fur.

In the year after receiving the gift, Anna had kept the furniture straight. The second year she'd set about moving the chairs around, then the rugs, then she painted tiny murals on the walls with her oil paint set. On her sixteenth birthday her mother had declared dollhouses childish, and since Anna was no longer a child, the dollhouse had disappeared.

Surveying the tiny, well-laid-out cottage, Anna crossed her arms and studied the plaster wall in the dining room. She pictured a mural with a babbling brook lined by trees.

Voices sounded outside, and she turned away from her musing. She opened the door, surprised to find Mrs. Phillips standing on the covered front porch. Jane stood at her mother's side wearing the same yellow dress, the hem darkened with dirt.

"Miss Bishop," the woman said. "I wondered if I might have a word with you?"

Anna waved them inside and indicated the mismatched chairs. "Have a seat. May I bring you a cup of coffee?"

"Yes. Please. I was hoping Jane might play outside while the two of us are speaking."

The circles beneath her eyes had darkened since the last time Anna had seen her, only two days before. Having reached the end of her endurance after the shooting, Anna recognized the signs in others.

"Izetta is out back pruning the roses. Follow me." Anna led the girl toward the kitchen and rummaged around for the empty tin can she'd seen earlier. "If there are any good blooms left, would you make me an arrangement?"

"Yes, ma'am." Jane spoke solemnly.

Whatever sadness gripped Jane's mother was obviously taking a toll on her daughter, as well.

Anna opened the door and found Izetta hunched over a rambling hedge rose. "We have a visitor."

The older woman caught sight of Jane and smiled.

Anna leaned against the doorjamb. "Jane's mother and I are having a chat over coffee. May Jane help you in the garden?"

"I can always use a helper."

Grateful for her easy acceptance of the situation, Anna ushered Jane outside, then poured two cups of coffee into the recently washed chipped mugs, and carried them into the dining room.

Mrs. Phillips had taken the taller seat. Anna recalled her thoughts at the train depot—that Mrs. Phillips had been involved in her shooting. Seeing the woman now, her suspicions vanished. Mrs. Phillips appeared too beaten down by life to plan a murder.

She wore a different dress this morning, and Anna

caught the faint whiff of camphor, as though the dress had been in storage.

Mrs. Phillips cupped the mug with both hands. "Thank you for speaking with me. Especially, well, especially after what happened."

"You don't look like the sort of woman who'd kill a man and stuff him in her trunk."

"Evil never appears the way we imagine."

Anna sucked in a breath at the stark sorrow in the woman's eyes. "Why don't you tell me what's troubling you?"

"It's a long story, and not very pretty."

"I have all the time in the world."

Mrs. Phillips flashed a grateful smile. "I married Jane's father when I was very young. My mother had recently passed away, and I'd barely turned seventeen. Clark was the son of one of my father's business associates. I never even questioned our marriage. That's the way I was raised."

Tears sprang in Mrs. Phillips's eyes, and she gripped her coffee mug. "He wasn't a kind man. After Jane was born, well, things took a turn for the worse. The business was failing. He couldn't accept the humiliation. My father died, and he left me a bit of money." She pursed her lips. "Not much, mind you, but enough to give Jane a good start. I wanted the money for Jane. I didn't want him to have it. He'd always spent too much money on his...hobbies...his activities outside the home."

She choked off a sob, and Anna laid her hand over the woman's trembling fingers. "You needn't go on."

"No, no. I have to finish. He was enraged after that. Cruel. I tried to take Jane and leave, but he discovered us.

He had a mistress. I asked for a divorce." She paused, her mouth working. "He had me committed to an asylum."

"Oh, my."

Anna had heard similar stories before. The practice was more common before the war, but tales of such incarcerations still abounded. Often the practice was done by men who wanted to live openly with their mistresses, or wanted control of their wives' money since divorce was taboo.

"He couldn't obtain control of the money. My father must have suspected something of his true nature. He'd left the portion in my name only. I'd hoped Clark would release me once he realized his mistake. The business improved. He didn't need the money after that. He came one day as though nothing had happened." Her jaw tightened. "He assumed we'd simply pick up where we left off. As though he'd done nothing wrong. I took Jane and we ran. I knew the family who owned the Savoy Hotel, they were friends of my parents. They offered to let me stay. But then a man came around, asking questions. I knew he'd found us."

"What did the man look like?"

"Older. Dark hair, graying. He had an unusual build. Thin arms and legs with a rounded stomach. Jane noticed him first. Children, they're more observant than adults, I think."

"Reinhart."

"What?"

"I believe the man who was following you was a Pinkerton detective named Reinhart."

Mrs. Phillips pressed her hands over her face, muffling her words. "I didn't know what to do. I didn't know where to go. I think that's how he found us. I ran out of money. I had to wire the bank. That's when that man, the Pinkerton detective, appeared."

Anna stared into her coffee cup. "What about the gentleman yesterday? The man in your trunk..."

"The dead man? I don't know. I think they knew each other, him and that other gentleman, Reinhart, you said. I saw them talking once."

Anna frowned. Reinhart had mentioned something about hiring an associate, about needing more help. Was the dead man his associate? The marshal needed that information.

Mrs. Phillips drew her hands down her face and shook her head. "I used the money for train tickets. Your fiancé was ahead of me in line. Cimarron Springs sounded like a nice name. A nice town. I figured we'd stay a while and plan something else."

Anna held up her hand. "I'll do what I can. Although I don't have the resources my mother has, I can always ask for her assistance." She cleared her throat. "Although you must be mistaken, I don't have a fiancé."

"It's all right. Everyone knows about you two. About you and Mr. McCoy."

Anna gaped. "He's not my fiancé."

"You don't have to pretend with me." Mrs. Phillips patted her hand. "I can imagine what a quandary this is for you. Jane said you were one of the suffragists. You only have to pick up a newspaper to know how suffragists view marriage. But I'm a woman, too, and I know how powerful love can be. Even though my story did not have a happy ending, I always have hope for others."

"I don't, uh, we're friends. I know Mr. McCoy's sister. That's all."

"I'm afraid your secret is out. Everyone in town is

talking about it. How you came through town last year and the two of you have been corresponding ever since. How he was so smitten, he went to Kansas City and asked you to marry him. How you were injured at the rally and he never left your side. I think it's all very romantic."

"The whole town, you say?"

"Yes. Apparently Mrs. Stuart's sister lives in Kansas City. She was quite impressed that Mr. McCoy brought his sister along as a chaperone."

"And when did you hear this?"

"At the train depot yesterday."

"I see."

"And then Mr. McCoy's brother saw you visiting his house."

"I don't know how I missed all the news."

"Because you're not staying at the hotel. Jane and I have become something of a local sensation. Everyone wants to see the trunk."

Stupefied by the turn of the conversation, Anna asked dumbly, "The trunk?"

"Yes, the trunk where the body was found." Mrs. Phillips shrugged her shoulders. "Whoever killed that man tossed out most of our clothing in order to make room for the body. Jane has been wearing the same clothing for two days now."

"I can sympathize." Anna had packed for a brief trip, and she'd lost one her outfits already. "You should speak with the marshal. Tell him what you told me. He's a good man. He'll do whatever he can to help."

As much as she craved pursuing this business of her engagement, Mrs. Phillips had a problem. A much larger problem. She'd set her own worries aside for the moment.

"No." Mrs. Phillips pushed back from the table. "Absolutely not. I saw the way the marshal looked at me yesterday. He thinks I'm guilty already. I promise you, I did not kill that man. Even if I had, why would I put the evidence in my own trunk?"

Anna took a fortifying sip of her coffee. Cases such as Mrs. Phillips's were difficult, though not impossible. "I'll do what I can. I can offer you some money."

"No. I won't take charity."

"A loan, then. It's not wise for you to use the bank. If your husband found you that way once, then he can find you again."

Mrs. Phillips offered a curt nod. "A loan. Please, believe me, I don't know how that man wound up in my trunk. I know how it looks. If he was working on a case for my husband…"

There was a chance the man in the trunk had no connection with Reinhart. Either way, Mrs. Phillips didn't strike her as a killer. And if she was, why ask Anna for help? Why not simply run again? Cimarron Springs wasn't a prison. The marshal had requested she stay, a request only. Mrs. Phillips could leave anytime she chose.

"I'll do what I can. But if the marshal—"

A shriek sounded from the back of the house. Anna pushed out of her chair and dashed out the rear door, Mrs. Phillips close behind.

Izetta stood with her hands on her hips while Jane chased a very familiar-looking goat around the hedge roses.

Anna sighed. "I know the guardian of that terrifying little beast."

Jane clapped her hands, and the goat leaped into the air. "Mama, look. He's dancing."

Mrs. Phillips held out her hand. "We must be going."

Jane appeared crestfallen, though she didn't argue with her mother. They linked hands. "I'll show myself out," Mrs. Phillips said.

Anna glared at the goat nibbling the tall grasses near the fence. "You are a troublemaker."

Plastering a serene expression on her face, she turned to her guests. "I'll visit with you tomorrow. About the subject of our earlier discussion."

Anna kept her words deliberately vague, respecting the woman's plea for privacy. Mrs. Phillips appeared quite opposed to accepting charity. And while Anna trusted Izetta, she'd also learned how quickly stories spread.

Pinching off her gloves, Izetta approached. "That poor woman looks as though she hasn't slept in a week."

"She probably hasn't." The two exchanged a glance filled with a wealth of meaning.

"I hope she confided in you," Izetta said.

"She did. Although I doubt I can help very much."

"Sometimes a shoulder to cry on is help enough." Izetta's head snapped around. "Shoo, you little beast. That animal is chewing on my roses."

Anna considered her choices. Mrs. Phillips was her chance to prove once and for all that small differences were as important as grand gestures. She'd help Mrs. Phillips and the cause at the same time.

She snapped her fingers, and the goat lifted its head. "Come with me this instant. You're going home."

Sooner or later she had to face Caleb, and the goat had forced her hand.

She circled around the house, and the goat trailed behind her. Since she and Caleb were practically neighbors, the trip didn't take long.

She reached Caleb's gate in short order and lifted the latch. "Come along, then," she ordered. "In you go."

Though reluctant, the goat followed orders. Anna stepped inside the yard and latched the gate. If Caleb was home, it was best he learned of their problem sooner than later.

The whole town thought they were engaged.

They had kissed.

She inhaled a fortifying breath, stepped onto the front porch and knocked sharply. When no one answered, she circled around the house toward the barn. She'd come all this way, after all.

She reached the double doors and heard the low timbre of his distinctive voice. Once again the day of the rally came rushing back. Anna gripped the edge of the wooden door and rested her forehead against the rough surface.

As her heart pounded, she closed her eyes and pictured the flowers behind their little cottage. She imagined the garden in spring, in full bloom, the bushes filled with roses and peonies blossoms bending their stalks. After a moment, her heartbeat slowed and her breath evened out.

Satisfied she'd gotten ahold of herself, Anna stepped into the barn and waited as her eyes adjusted in the dim light. She followed the sound of Caleb's voice and discovered him in the last stall, kneeling before a milk cow. He'd removed his coat and rolled his shirtsleeves over his corded forearms.

Anna cleared her throat, and he lifted his head. When he half rose from his seat, she held up her palm. "No need to stand."

His gaze flicked toward her and quickly away. "How is the house? How are you settling in?"

This was going quite well. Not awkward or uncomfortable at all. Well, mostly not. "The whole place needs a good scrubbing. Izetta's fallen in love with the garden."

"I forgot about that. Mr. Stuart's mother-in-law planted the flowers."

"You will be happy to know that the rumors of her hauntings are grossly exaggerated. I haven't seen a single specter."

He chuckled, and the cow glanced around at the disturbance.

Soothing the animal with a gentle pat on its neck, Caleb smiled. "You must have talked with one of the local children."

"I was warned, yes. And to answer your earlier question, the house and garden are fine, though poorly tended. There are quite a few volunteer plants still making a go of it." She indicated the tuft of fur hiding behind her skirts. "We had an unexpected visitor today. Your goat is quite fond of roses."

Caleb pinched the bridge of his nose. "Was there any damage done?"

"No, thankfully. We caught him in the nick of time. I rescued him this go-around, but I can't vouch for his safety if he storms the garden again. Izetta is quite militant."

"I'll check the fence." He wrapped a length of bandage around the cow's leg. "I haven't found the little guy a home yet. Haven't had time."

Entranced, Anna followed Caleb's nimble fingers. He accomplished his task with an economy of movement, murmuring soothing words all the while.

This was the first time she'd seen him in his element. From Jo's teasing and her own observations, his dedication had been apparent. And yet only this moment did she truly understand his calling. His actions were deft and practiced, his concentration absolute until the bandage was in place.

"How was she injured?" Anna asked.

"Barbed wire. Her name is Golden." He chuckled. "Fitting somehow. She's lucky to have survived. She'll go back home in a week or two."

"Then she was too injured for her owner to look out for her?"

He lifted one shoulder in a careless shrug. "It's harvest time. That's about all folks can handle."

"Which means you're caring for her instead."

Caleb sat back and blotted his forehead with a square of white cloth. "Farmers around here can't survive without their animals. A good milk cow can cost a season's pay for some folks. It's a small thing to do."

A small thing, and yet his simple sacrifice might save that family, should something else happen.

"There's something more," Anna blurted.

Unless she planned on standing out here and making chitchat about goats and cows and chickens and whatever other farm animals she could think of until suppertime, she'd best get this over with.

"What's that?"

"Everyone in town thinks we're engaged."

That got his attention, although not the way she expected.

Not a hint of surprise showed on his face, only a sort of weary resignation. "I know. I'm sorry. I should have told you yesterday. Mrs. Stuart's sister lives in Kansas City. She…well… It's a long story. I was hoping if I didn't say anything, the rumor would go away."

"I don't think your plan worked." The goat nibbled at her hem, and she snapped her fingers. The nibbling ceased. "How did Mrs. Stuart's sister get the idea in the first place?"

"It's my fault." He braced his fisted hand on his knee. "The desk clerk registered you as my guest to keep your identity a secret. He listed me as your fiancé. We were worried about you, after the shooting. Worried about another attempt." He scoffed. "As much good as that did."

She waited for her reaction. The outrage, the betrayal, a hint of annoyance at the very least. He had lied to her, after all. Perhaps not lied, but there was a large omission on his part.

Snippets of conversation from the past few days suddenly made sense. "That explains a lot."

He rested his forehead against the cow's rounded side. "Are you very angry?"

"No." She couldn't help a grin at his mortification, especially considering she'd felt the same way only moments before. "Not at all. I was actually more concerned about you. The jilted suitor and all that."

"Don't mind me. I'll survive." He straightened. "You do realize this will be a difficult rumor to stop. The more we deny the engagement, the more people will think it's true."

"I know. Perhaps your first idea was correct. We say nothing. Simply let the whole thing blow over on its own. Once I'm gone, none of this will matter, anyway."

"I'm not making any guarantees." He rolled his shirtsleeves down his arms. "The marshal thinks it's a good idea. The engagement. Gives people something to talk about. Makes them protective of you."

"Maybe."

This was a close community of people, and yet she wasn't one of them, no matter what he said. She was a stranger.

The goat head-butted her leg. "My goodness. You are a persistent little fellow, aren't you?"

"I think he likes you. Animals are very perceptive."

Her throat constricted. He'd paid her a great compliment.

Dust motes swirled in the shaft of light slicing through the half-open door. A combination of hay and feed and animal filled the air. As he slipped into his jacket, her gaze lingered on his broad shoulders. She longed for the warm comfort of his arms, the quiet thud of his heart against her ear, the scratch of his wool jacket against her cheek.

Did he ever sit on the porch swing and watch the setting sun, his heel braced against the floor, gently rocking?

She grimaced. Of course he didn't. He was a man, not some romantic fool. Had she become the one thing she'd been warned against? A romantic ninny with nothing but fluff in her head?

If she didn't change the subject soon, she feared she'd say something entirely inappropriate. Something along the lines of...*are you sorry you kissed me?*

She was sage enough to know that one did not ask questions if one did not want the answer.

She wasn't sure which answer she feared the most—yes or no.

Instead she asked, "How is Jo?"

"Happy to be home."

A spark of guilt dampened her mood. "I'm sorry I missed supper the other evening. I hope your mother wasn't upset."

"You were tired. Everyone understands."

She considered telling him about her visit from Mrs. Phillips, then discarded the idea. The woman had taken her into confidence, and Anna honored her trust. She'd speak with the marshal instead—pointing him in the right direction was for the best. He seemed fair and open-minded. Jo obviously adored him.

"You didn't miss much at dinner, anyway," he said. "Mostly the boys gossiped about Mrs. Phillips and the dead man. I imagine she wishes she could change her identity right now. For a little peace."

Finding peace was not easy as people supposed.

"You know, it's odd. I thought I'd like to be someone else. Even for a day. I think I miss being myself."

The visit from Mrs. Phillips had reminded her of her true purpose. This was an interlude, a brief stop along the tracks. There were greater fights ahead of her. There simply weren't enough soldiers in the battle. If she bowed out, they'd lose one more.

If anything good was to come of her injury and her subsequent absence from her scheduled speaking engagements, she'd make a difference. She'd make a difference in the life of one person, and she'd prove that small changes were just as good as grand gestures.

Caleb kept his gaze fixed on the ground. "About the other day."

The moment she'd been avoiding. Clutching her hands together, she breathed deeply. Here was the reckoning. There was no reason for either of them to linger over a lapse that had most certainly been quite out of character for both of them.

Anna held up her hands. "Don't worry, it will never happen again."

* * *

A swift kick of disappointment socked him in the gut. She'd said the words on the tip of his tongue. Then why did he suddenly feel such a crushing loss?

"I'm sorry," he said. "I don't know what came over me."

Actually, I know exactly what came over me. You're beautiful and funny and smart and kind, and every time you're near I want the seconds on the clock to tick slower.

He'd altered their easy camaraderie with his careless actions. He'd kissed her, and she'd practically run from his house. He'd ruined things between them, and he had only himself to blame.

Her face grew thoughtful. "We've been thrown together in odd circumstances. I had a lot of time for thinking in Kansas City. Because of what we went through that day, I believe we feel a false sense of intimacy."

Well, that was one way of saying it. "Yep."

"About the engagement rumors."

"What about them?"

"You're all right if they stick?"

"Like I said, the marshal thinks it's a good idea if we keep up the front. People around here look out for one another. If people think we're engaged, well, it explains a lot of things. Gives them something else to talk about besides why you're here in town."

He and his brothers had played outlaws and lawmen down by Hackberry Creek for years. This wasn't all that different. They didn't even have to lie. As long as neither of them confirmed nor denied the rumor, everyone else would fill in the pieces.

Pretending to love Anna was far easier than pretending he was a lawman.

"I think you're right."

The air whooshed out of his lungs. "Really?"

"Yes. Don't worry. You needn't be concerned about any false intimacies." Her cheeks flamed. "You needn't worry I'll misconstrue the established boundaries of our relationship."

He gave a crooked grin at her obvious discomfort. "I'm not worried."

A little flattered, but definitely not worried. Perhaps he'd read the situation all wrong. Her flustered speech had him hoping she wasn't as immune to him as she'd declared.

He allowed himself a moment to simply admire her. She should have been out of place, standing in a barn, her soft leather boots scuffing across the hay-strewn floor. Instead she appeared perfectly natural. Perhaps it was the way she approached every situation with an innate curiosity and a genuine interest that was so delightfully appealing.

"I have two conditions of our engagement bargain," she continued briskly.

Yet another interesting turn in the conversation he hadn't been expecting. "What are those?"

"First, your mother must know the truth."

"Agreed," he said.

As though he could keep the truth from his mother.

"Second, when this is all over, I want you to jilt me."

"Why is that?"

Nothing had gone the way he'd expected with this conversation—why should her second demand be any different?

"Because I don't want everyone in town feeling sorry for you. If they think you're that unlucky in love, you'll gain ten pounds during the Harvest Festival with all the free slices of pie and ice cream."

Despite her teasing smile, he fought an inexplicable burst of anger. He wasn't an object of pity. He wasn't a pathetic schoolboy with his first crush.

The cow shifted and lowed. Caleb patted the animal's side before standing.

"I'm not one of your causes, Anna," he spoke gruffly, his anger simmering just below the surface. "You don't have to rescue me."

Her expression transformed slightly. The change was so subtle, he might have missed the difference a week ago.

"I know that. But I owe you. You saved my life."

She'd sensed his anger, and the realization had hurt her.

"Anybody would have done the same."

"They didn't." Her voice was barely a whisper. "You did."

The last of his fury ebbed away. "Jo made me do it."

Anna only smiled. "Either way, I owe you. No one is going to feel sorry for you or treat you like the jilted suitor."

She hadn't been pitying him at all. Instead, she thought she was protecting him.

"You aren't going to give up until you save me, are you?"

"Nope."

His gaze drifted toward her lips. How did he tell her he was already too far gone?

A scuffle sounded, and he peered around Anna. A young boy stood in the doorway of the barn, a dripping burlap sack in his hands. The bag moved.

Anna gasped and Caleb stepped forward. "You're Jasper, aren't you?"

The boy gave a hesitant nod. Caleb stifled a sigh. He was too thin for his age, his clothing barely more than rags. Caleb had heard through his sister that Jasper wasn't allowed to attend school more than a few months a year, which put him behind the other kids. When they started teasing him for the difference, he'd stopped going to school altogether.

Jasper's dad was a great bear of a man with a fierce temper, and his mother was little more than a shadow.

Caleb motioned with his hand. "What you got there?"

"Kittens."

Anna clutched her mouth.

Caleb gently extracted the squirming bundle from the boy and crouched. He rolled back the soaking edges of the bag, revealing two tiny squirming kittens, both of them orange tabbies. The boy snuffed and wiped his nose with the back of his hand. "Pa said we had enough cats around the farm, so he figured he'd drown them. Triple A fished 'em out of the pond. He said you'd maybe help."

"I'll help." Caleb stood and crossed the barn, snatching a blanket draped over one of the stall doors.

Caleb gave each of the kittens a quick exam. They'd been weaned too early; he noticed that right off.

Anna hovered near his shoulder, offering assistance when needed, handing over a prettily embroidered handkerchief for their bedding.

The kittens would require constant attention for the first days. After drying them off as best he could, he snatched the pail of milk from outside the stall and measured a portion onto the plate he'd set over the top as a lid. The kittens lurched the distance and lapped up the treat. Once sated, their bellies full, they curled up on the blanket.

How can someone do such a cruel thing?" Anna asked Caleb, out of earshot of Jasper.

The boy had taken up vigil near the kittens and didn't show any signs of moving.

A myriad of emotions flitted across her expressive face—anger, sorrow and frustration. She held up her shaking hands as though she wasn't quite certain what to do with them.

He clutched her chilled fingers and stilled their trembling.

She blinked rapidly. "I'm furious. I have a few choice words for that man."

"Let me deal with him." The thought of her confronting Jasper's father sent a cold chill through his heart. "Stay away from him."

All that she'd been through the past few weeks had finally caught up with her. He tangled his hand in the hair at the nape of her neck, and she pressed her forehead into his shoulder. He'd seen worse, he'd seen far worse.

He'd spoken more harshly than he'd intended, and by way of an apology he added, "I'll find good homes for the two kittens."

After a moment she straightened. "I'm not usually such a watering pot."

She reached for her handkerchief and realized her error.

He gestured toward the kittens. "You've given up your embroidery for a good cause."

A fat tear rolled down her cheek. He'd deal with Jasper's father, all right. If he could fix this, he would. If he thought he could make her happy, he'd never let her go.

He retrieved his own handkerchief, a plain starched square with no lace and no embroidery. This time he realized his own hands were trembling.

She accepted his offering and swiped at her eyes, then gave a delicate sniffle. "What about that little boy's parents? He doesn't appear any healthier than those kittens."

"I don't know much. The father is a drinker. He has a bad temper. The mother is little more than a shadow. She's lost two babies to stillbirth. I think she's too worn down."

Her chin tilted into a determined set, as though she'd come to a decision about a problem he hadn't known existed. "That's who I fight for. That's who I'm trying to save. That's who I'm trying to give a voice."

Something they had in common. He stayed in Cimarron Springs because of the small differences he made each day. For Jasper. For Triple A. For the animals that provided labor and even those that simply provided companionship. Except nothing he did would ever amount to much or make a great difference. He was content with his contribution. He trusted in the Bible. He trusted that those who had faith in the small things would also have faith in the large ones.

Anna needed a much larger stage. She deserved a larger stage. He ran his thumb around the curve of her ear and cupped her neck, hair and shoulder. This was a woman who needed a fight, who needed a cause.

He'd been lying to himself, clutching onto a hope that didn't exist. He'd been lying because a part of him wanted her near. He admired her, he liked her. The feelings she invoked were a far cry from those he'd felt for Mary Louise. Those had been insignificant and childish by comparison. He finally understood love. He finally understood loss.

"You already make a difference," he said. "There's nothing you can't do."

She smiled, and the last vestiges of his doubts faded. Everyone lost their way once in a while, and Anna had lost hers. He'd be doing her a great disservice if he didn't set her back on the path she'd chosen, the path that brought her joy and gave her life meaning.

Too bad he'd done a poor job of protecting himself in the process. He'd done the one thing he'd promised himself he'd avoid. He was falling for a girl who could never love him in return.

"You make a difference to everyone you meet, whether you know it or not."

Chapter Fifteen

At the pounding on the door, Anna raised her head from the floorboard she was vigorously sanding. Her hair was piled atop her head and covered with a handkerchief. Dirt streaked her hands and arms. She'd only planned on scrubbing a stain in the corner, but the task had grown. Once one part of the floor shone, the other parts appeared even duller.

While the structure was sound and Mr. Stuart had assured them the roof didn't leak, the inside had been neglected. A family of mice had taken up residence in the kitchen cupboard, and they'd had to relocate a Lark's nest built over the back door. The evidence of the birds was a touch harder to remove.

She sat back on her heels and surveyed her work. She'd sanded the floors in the entry by hand, and they were ready for a fresh coat of lemon oil.

The pounding sounded once more, and she pushed off her knee and stood. She hoped her visitor didn't stay long because there was too much work to be done and she wasn't exactly dressed for company.

She opened the door to a beaming Mrs. McCoy.

"Thought I'd better check up on you since I'm going to be your mother-in-law."

This certainly didn't bode well for the floor waxing.

Anna gaped. She was going to strangle Caleb if this web tangled any further. "But you know the truth, right? Caleb…uh…your son promised me he'd tell you."

"Of course, dear." Mrs. McCoy leaned closer. "I'm playing along."

The woman bustled past her and set her basket on the counter, then busied herself with removing jars and wrapped parcels from its interior.

"Really," Mrs. McCoy said. "I wish I'd made up the rumor myself. It's quite romantic."

"I'm not certain *romantic* is the term I'd use."

Anna was thinking more along of the lines of *hare-brained* or *ill conceived.*

"You and Caleb and your whirlwind courtship. How you're fixing up your house so Izetta will be all settled before the two of you get married. You've gained the admiration of the whole town."

"But it's not true." How had such a simple bargain spun out of control? "Any of it."

"Well if it were true then it would be news, wouldn't it? News is boring. Filled with all sorts of facts and figures. We're talking about gossip."

Right now, Anna would much prefer a weather report. Something simple and boring and not all connected to her. "You're not even a bit alarmed by any of this? I hadn't expected such a furor."

"Don't you worry. This will all blow over soon. With any luck, there'll be another dead body off the five-fifteen train. Not that I wish ill on anyone. I mean to say that something else will take the place of this rumor.

Are you feeling better this morning? You looked a might peaked the other day. Course that was probably all the fuss at the train station and the bustle of settling into a new town. We've had our share of excitement here in Cimarron Springs, but that dead fellow was a new one. Well, mostly new."

Pressing a hand against her head to still the spinning caused by her unexpected visitor, Anna said, "I'm feeling much better. I tire more easily than I used to."

"That's to be expected, I'd imagine. Never been shot myself, though." Mrs. McCoy appeared thoughtful, as though searching her memory, ensuring she hadn't taken a bullet at some point. "This engagement gives us the excuse to get to know one another. I'm absolutely fascinated by your work, my dear. Jo has done nothing but sing your praises for the last year. You've made an admirer out of Tony, as well. She's all set for a protest during the presidential election. That's next Tuesday. Or is it a week from next Tuesday? My, but doesn't time scoot by?"

"That's very brave of Tony."

Here was another example in her arsenal. Tony had taken up the cause. After only a brief conversation, she'd set about staging a protest. Small gestures built into something bigger than all of them.

"You'll find things are different out here in the country," Mrs. McCoy stated. "Women's rights are a matter of necessity. When there are only two of you doing the work, sometimes you both wear the pants on the farm. And I mean that quite literally, my dear."

Another knock sounded.

Mrs. McCoy shooed her away. "Don't mind me. Go and answer that. I thought I saw your friend Izetta working on the lilac bush out behind the house."

"It's overtaken the roses."

"Lilacs are aggressive that way. They'd be a weed if they didn't smell so sweet in the spring. My mother always kept a tincture of lilac water on her dressing table. To this day, the smell brings back memories of her. What were we talking about?"

"Izetta," Anna prompted. Mrs. McCoy had an endearing way of sliding off topic.

"Oh, yes. I wanted to ask her about the Harvest Social. You'll be coming, won't you?"

"I don't know. When it is? I don't know how long I'll be staying."

"Next Monday. Or is it a week from next Monday? It's around the corner, anyway. Certainly you'll be here that long."

The knock at the door grew more insistent.

"Oh, and call me Edith." Mrs. McCoy hustled into the kitchen. "Don't let me keep you. Seems like I've come on visiting day."

Anna patted her scarf-covered hair. Leaving a card and observing calling hours were obviously not customs of Cimarron Springs.

She returned to the door and discovered Caleb on the porch holding a bunch of flowers. Her heart beat an odd rat-a-tat-tat in her chest.

She whipped off her scarf and smoothed her hair.

"I thought you'd like an update on my unexpected guests," he spoke cheerfully. "You'll be happy to know the two kittens are fit and feisty."

Her cheeks warmed at his thoughtfulness. "I admit I was a touch worried. They had quite a traumatic time of it."

"I believe I've found them a new home and names, as well."

"You work quickly," she said.

"I had to visit the Elder ranch, and Jasper had already told them about our heroic rescue. They were immediately adopted by Hazel and named Viola and Sebastian."

"A Shakespeare reference. I must meet this young Hazel one day."

"I hope you do."

Had she imagined the note of longing in his voice? Glancing down at her dirt-streaked apron, she sighed. Was there any chance he'd simply leave and let her freshen up?

"A job well done," she said.

"Your handkerchief played a pivotal role."

Anna rolled her eyes. "In any event, thank you for keeping me apprised."

"I brought you a housewarming gift." He handed her the bunch of purple asters. "There isn't much selection this time of year."

He doffed his hat and ducked beneath the low door, crowding into the entry. Why hadn't she considered he'd visit this morning? Why had she worn her most unbecoming dress? Why was she fretting about something so mundane, so entirely feminine and frivolous?

Anna clutched the flowers against her chest and gazed into his emerald-green eyes. My, but he had the most beautiful eyes. Even that first time she'd met him, with all the commotion, she'd been entranced by those eyes. The allure hadn't faded.

He stared at her expectantly, and she started. "Do come in. And thank you, they're quite lovely. Your timing is fortunate. Your mother is here. She's around back talking with Izetta."

Caleb grimaced. "She's probably escaping the boys. All Maxwell talks about these days is the dead body."

"Apparently he's the only one interested in something as mundane as a murder. Everyone else is discussing our engagement."

"Don't blame me." He quirked an eyebrow. "You'd think a dead man was more interesting than an engagement."

"One would suppose."

"Our plan of saying and doing nothing has been wildly successful. If we never spoke again they'd probably have us married by spring."

"I'm developing a worry over the future of mankind."

Anna stepped aside and placed the flowers in a pitcher of water on the dining room table, fanning the blooms.

She returned and accepted his hat, absently running her hand along the worry spot on the brim, then hung it on the hook near the door. "You must tell me more about this Harvest Festival. When you spoke of the social in Kansas City, I had assumed you were exaggerating."

"I never exaggerate. However, I do sometimes lie outright."

Anna laughed in spite of herself. "You are incorrigible."

Her carefully constructed walls were eroding by the moment. Why hadn't nature granted him with pale blue eyes? Or boring brown? Or dismal gray? No. He'd been given the eyes of a charmer. Worse yet, he didn't even know his own attraction. A dash of arrogance might have blunted his hold on her.

"You already know about the shucking bee and barn

dance," he said. "It's a bit of a marriage market, as well. A lot of the ranchers and farmers don't get to town very often, and it's a good chance to check out the local stock."

"The local stock? Isn't that a bit crude?"

"Sorry." He had the grace to blush. "That's what it feels like, though."

"Will you be attending?"

"Wouldn't miss it. There's a whole bevy of McCoy cousins there. If I didn't go, they'd never let me live it down. It's practically a family reunion."

"How many McCoys are there?"

"As many as the County Cork in Ireland could send."

The twinkle in his eyes sent a flutter of butterflies in her stomach. "Where are my manners? Can I get you something to drink?"

"No, thank you. I can't stay long. I need to check on the Elder's stallion again this afternoon. I thought I better check on my fiancée in the meantime."

Her cheeks flushed. "I guess Mr. Reinhart was correct. We gave the town a puzzle, and they filled in the pieces."

Caleb hesitated. "You don't mind, do you?"

Actually, she was rather enjoying the wonders of everyday living. She no longer felt as though the weight of the world rested on her shoulders. She'd stepped away from the cause, and nothing had happened. They sky hadn't fallen. The sun still set in the evenings.

She'd been infused with the wonder of everyday beauty. Oddly enough, polishing the floor had given her the same sense of accomplishment as giving a speech. There was pride in a job well done, no matter what the job.

She rested her hands on the back of her hips. "Admit

the truth. If this was happening to someone else, we'd both find the situation terribly funny."

"Especially since half of Cimarron Springs knows who you are." Caleb offered an abashed smile. "It's the worst-kept secret in town, that's for certain. All the McCoys know, the Elders know, Jo's family knows, so that's the Cains, as well."

"Is there anyone left?"

"Not a lot."

"Should we simply tell everyone the truth?"

"And ruin everyone's fun? I don't have the heart. The last excitement this town had was when Jo shot her husband."

"On purpose? I've never heard the whole story."

"Of course, on purpose," he said, as though she'd asked a silly question.

The answer didn't seem as obvious as everyone around her assumed. "Did she mean to kill him?

"Just wound him. If Jo had wanted him dead, he'd be dead."

The one part of the story she had no trouble believing. "That does sound exciting."

"Someone was holding the marshal hostage. Jo took the shot as a distraction, then John Elder killed the man."

"The same John Elder that married the widow whose husband hid his loot in a cave by Hackberry Creek?"

"That's the one."

"I'm starting to like this town more and more."

"The past few years, there's been a dry spell. Now there's a dead body and a false engagement. You can't beat that kind of excitement."

"I wouldn't want to."

"How are you settling in, anyway?"

"I've been invited to a quilting bee."

"I hope you can stitch better than Mary Louise."

Anna couldn't hide her decidedly feminine emotions. She'd yet to meet this paragon, Mary Louise, but she took an unhealthy, an uncharacteristic, pride in the fact that she could sew.

Before she could reply, yet another knock sounded on the door.

Anna fumbled with strings on her apron. There was no use fighting the tide. She was going to host everyone in Cimarron Springs with her hair mussed wearing her oldest and most worn dress. "The knocking hasn't stopped since this morning."

"Don't expect the visitors to stop anytime soon. They usually allow you a day or two to get settled. After that they release the barrage."

"Exactly how long do you think this barrage will go on?"

When her mother had moved townhouses in St. Louis, they'd received a basket of muffins from the neighbor on their right and a polite but firm note from the neighbor on their left informing them of her allergy to Russian sage, and could they please not plant any.

"The visits will continue until everyone has satisfied their curiosity," Caleb said.

She caught sight of a streak of dirt on her forehead in the oval mirror hanging on the wall. "You mean to say, indefinitely?"

"Indefinitely. Welcome to life in a small town."

The knock sounded again, and they both laughed. Caleb fanned his arm. "Please, don't let me stop you from answering that."

She opened the door and gazed upon yet another,

younger version of Caleb. The boy standing on her step was tall and gangly, his arms and legs equally proportioned. She supposed he'd eventually fill out and assume his older brother's build. She cast a sidelong glance at Caleb. Lucky boy.

"I'm Maxwell McCoy," he said. "People call me Max."

"I had a feeling you were a McCoy. You and your brother and sister are remarkably similar in appearance."

"People say we look alike. But all the McCoys look alike. Except for ma. She has blond hair." He scratched his head. "I guess it's mostly gray now."

"We'll stick with blond. Ladies don't always like to be reminded of their age. Not that age denotes ability or worth. It's simply the polite thing. Are you looking for your brother?"

He appeared a touch bemused by her speech. "Nah. I came to meet you."

"That's very nice." Anna held out her hand for a perfunctory shake. "I'm Anna. It's a pleasure to meet you."

"Maxwell McCoy." A violent blush colored his cheeks. "I said that before, didn't I?"

"Quite all right."

"Did you see the dead body? I tried asking Caleb about it, but he wouldn't tell me. Tony said she got a good look, and he was waxy and pale. Is that true?"

"Um. I suppose it must be correct. I only took a peek at his face. Mostly I only saw his hand."

"Was there any blood?"

"Not that I saw."

The enthusiasm drained from his expression like air from an overfilled balloon. "No blood, huh? That's what Tony said. I guess I'll have to take her word on the rest."

"The rest of what?"

"She said his eyes were all bugged out, like he'd been choked or something."

Max wrapped his hands around his throat and stuck out his tongue, making a strangling sound in his throat.

Caleb crossed his arms over his chest. "That's enough, Max. No more talk of dead bodies. There's a lady present. It's time you learned how to behave. No more talk of bugged eyes, or blood or strangling to death."

"Mary Louise says she's not a lady, she's a suffragist."

Anna raised her eyebrows. "A woman can be a suffragist and a lady, as well."

"I don't get it."

Caleb playfully cuffed him on the back of his head. "You don't have to understand. You simply have to use your manners."

"You're worse than Ma," Max grumbled.

"What was that, young man?" Edith McCoy's voice sounded from the kitchen.

Max blanched. "Ma is here, too?"

Anna sighed. "Pretty soon everyone will be here."

A knock sounded at the door, and Anna grinned ruefully. "See what I was saying?"

She opened the door to Jo's husband. "It's a pleasure to see you again, Marshal Cain, you'll be pleased to know several of your in-laws are here."

"Not surprised. Mind if I come in?"

"Not at all. The more the merrier. I was hoping to speak with you."

Mrs. McCoy returned to the sitting room, belaying the marshal's reply. "Hello, Garrett. Wasn't expecting to see you." She turned to Anna. "Well, it's all settled. You and Izetta are coming to the quilting bee on Friday at the church."

"If you're certain the other ladies won't mind an extra."

The thought of sharing her skill held a certain thrill. If the legendary Mary Louise didn't share that skill, than so much the better. Sewing was women's work, and strictly prohibited in the Bishop household. The only reason she embroidered was because one rebellious nanny had taught Anna the basics out of spite. Serving as Victoria Bishop's employee was never easy.

During the summer of '74, Anna's mother had traveled through England meeting with other women in the movement. Her strict instructions for Anna's care had been largely ignored by the nanny, and with no one there to oversee her, the revolt went unnoticed until her mother's return. Anna certainly hadn't confided the rules broken in any of her letters. Her mother must have suspected the rumblings of a rebellion. She'd returned unannounced and discovered Anna helping with the laundry. The poor nanny had been fired immediately. Anna still kept in touch.

Undaunted, Edith forged ahead. "What about embroidery? That's a lovely piece you're wearing now."

She indicated the stitching on Anna's collar where Anna had embroidered a trail of ivy into the linen.

"Yes." She fingered the raised stitching on the collar. "My embroidery is quite up to par."

"That'll be perfect. David's wife has been doing all the piecework, but the poor girl simply doesn't have the patience for detail. Now we have a quilt full of stems without any blossoms. She has a tendency to begin with the easy stitches first, and never quite gets around to the harder work. I've got a quilt full of stems and leaves for

Mr. Lancaster's bride. You think you can finish up the flowers?"

"I, uh, I can try."

Mrs. McCoy squinted at Anna's collar. "Judging by the work you've already done, you should be quite up to the task."

"I look forward to helping?" Anna raised the end of her sentence in a question, unsure whether she'd be asked or ordered into work.

"Excellent. The roses will finally have blooms. This day just keeps looking up. Come along, Maxwell. I hope you haven't been pestering Anna with questions about the dead body."

"He's no bother."

"That's a yes, then. I've raised five boys, and every one of them the same. Oh, and I'll expect you for supper after church on Sunday. Do you like fried chicken?"

"Yes."

"Then it's settled."

Slightly confused by the rapid-fire instructions, Anna asked, "Is there anything I can bring?"

"What is your specialty?"

Anna thought for minute. "Toast."

Edith chuckled. "Then just bring yourself and Mrs. Franklin. We'll have the rest. Mary Louise isn't much for cooking either, so I'm used to fixing extra for the family."

She patted Marshal Cain on the arm. "Tell Jo to make an extra batch of rolls."

"I will," the marshal replied, clearly accustomed to taking orders from his mother-in-law.

Edith tugged a reluctant Maxwell toward the door, leaving Anna alone with the marshal and Caleb.

The marshal patted his stomach. "That's one thing about the McCoys—you never go hungry."

She'd nearly forgotten she asked the marshal over for a reason. "I wanted to talk with you about Mrs. Phillips."

Caleb lingered by the door. "Is this conversation private? Should I go?"

"Stay," Anna spoke impulsively.

His expression softened and she knew immediately he was recalling the last time she'd asked him to stay. Already they were building a past together, sharing memories of events they had in common.

She'd been taught to view affection as a destructive force. A lightning bolt or a raging inferno. Instead this gathering fondness for Caleb was more like tree roots, branching out, seeking a foundation built over time and shared experiences.

"I can't break Mrs. Phillips's confidence, but something she saw at the hotel may shed light on the identity of the dead man."

Since the conversation looked to expand past a few polite sentences, Anna glanced around the room. "I'd offer you a seat, but we don't have much furniture yet. I can pull a chair from the kitchen."

"Don't put yourself out. I can tell by the line of people filing in and out your door it's been a busy morning."

Anna glanced at the muddy footprints marring her freshly scrubbed floor. Actually, she didn't mind so much. She'd rather have friends than a clean floor any day.

Anna rubbed her temple. The girl's words returned in a rush. *My mama says you're a hero.*

"Mrs. Phillip's daughter, Jane, was at the rally." Anna grimaced; how did she speak without revealing too much?

"Mrs. Phillips saw the man discovered in her trunk speaking with another gentleman. From her description, it sounded like Reinhart."

"Reinhart?" the marshal tilted his head.

"He's a Pinkerton detective looking into my case. He had, uh, he had some information for me."

She hadn't thought about what he'd said in days. She'd pushed the information aside. Since her father had never been in her life, losing him hadn't quite sunk in yet. He was where he'd always been, hidden away like a box of photographs she planned on looking at one day, but never quite found the time.

"Then it's possible that fellow was a Pinkerton detective, as well," the marshal said.

"He's a strange man, Mr. Reinhart. But he did say something about hiring extra help. He was working on another case. I think it's worth looking into."

Caleb remained silent, his arms crossed over his chest, his gaze intent. What was he thinking?

"Did you find out any more about the man?" she asked. "About…about what happened to him?"

"The doc thinks he was strangled. Probably happened in Kansas City. Then he was stuffed in the trunk."

The marshal considered the hat he held in his hands. "Do you have any idea what other case Reinhart was working on in Kansas City?"

"I think it's possible he was looking for Mrs. Phillips." She pictured the bunch of yellow daisies the little girl had given her. Probably Jane's father had hired the Pinkerton detective. "I can't say any more without betraying her confidence."

"I've been in this business for a while now, Miss

Bishop. I can make a few guesses. That woman is mighty scared about something."

"Her fear was there already."

"I figured that much."

"How can I help?"

"She trusts you, that's good. While she may not have killed the man in the trunk by herself, I can't rule out the possibility that she knows who did. She's hiding from someone. And while I've got a fair guess who and a fair understanding of why, I have to remain cautious. Keep the lines of communication open. She may say something else."

Caleb stepped forward and held up one hand. "I don't like this at all. You want her to talk with a woman who may or may not be a murderer? That doesn't sound wise."

"It's probably the safest place for Anna. If this Mrs. Phillips is somehow involved, then this is the best thing. She's here where we can keep an eye on her. Something is troubling that woman, and I think she'd feel better if she had someone to talk with."

Anna stood up straighter. "I know what's troubling her, and I can assure you that I'm perfectly safe."

The marshal replaced his hat. "Mrs. Phillips is as jumpy as a mouse in a room full of cats for a reason, which means we all have to watch our backs. I'll have to let her go in a day or two. In the meantime, I'll see if I can run down this detective of yours. Find out if there's a connection."

"I don't want you alone with her, Anna," Caleb said.

"I appreciate your concern, but I can take care of myself."

He assumed a mask of contrition that didn't fool her

a bit. "What sort of man would I be if I didn't protect my fiancée?"

"You two sort out the details," the marshal said, a twitch of a smile appearing at the corner of his mouth. "Let me know if you discover anything. Anything at all, even if it doesn't seem important right off. You never know what might make a difference."

As she ushered him to the door, her annoyance blossomed.

Her feelings over Caleb's protective attitude were conflicted. On the one hand, she appreciated his concern. On the other hand, she resented his interference. She was independent. Used to doing things on her own without a protector. Then again, the last thing she'd done on her own, she'd wound up shot. Maybe having a companion wasn't such a bad thing after all. Not that she wanted him to put his life at risk for her. She most definitely did not appreciate him questioning her judgment.

After the marshal left, Caleb lingered. "I'll pick you up on Sunday. For church. Just after ten. People will expect that you'll sit with my family."

The change of subject left her unsatisfied. "First, I need to set a few things straight."

He hooked his thumbs in his pockets. "All right."

"I'm perfectly capable of making decisions about whom I should and should not associate with."

He sucked in a breath, and she glared.

"I am not chattel. Do not use our engagement as an excuse."

"I wasn't going to."

"Then what were you going to say?"

"I'm sorry."

Her suspicions flared. "No one says they're sorry."

"I did. Just now."

She sidled nearer and narrowed her gaze. "Do you mean that?"

No one in the Bishop household ever apologized. Ever. An apology was a sign of weakness. Which meant he obviously had an ulterior motive. "Why are you giving up so easily?"

"I'm not giving up. I'm admitting that I was wrong. There's a difference."

"What difference?'

"This isn't a war, Anna. We're having a conversation, not a battle. I said I was sorry, and I am."

"Thank you," she said, humbled by his admission.

"You're welcome." Though a crinkle appeared between his brows, he didn't question her further, and for that she was grateful. "We're set for Sunday, then?"

As easy as that. This was not at all how she'd been taught to argue. A disagreement was absolutely a war. Battle lines were drawn, troops were mustered for the opposing sides. Words were fired like gunshots, aimed to inflict the most damage. Even the vaguest of halfhearted apologies was treated as a surrender, as an excuse to humiliate the enemy.

Anna realized the true folly of what she'd been taught all her life.

Refusing to apologize was a sign of cowardice and not a sign of strength. Caleb McCoy was no coward.

Speaking of cowards, she focused on his invitation. "Um, about that. I've never been to church."

"Ever?"

"Ever. My mother doesn't approve of organized religion."

"I don't suppose that makes any difference. But you don't have to go, if you don't want to."

Anna stared at the floor. She'd stick out like a sore thumb. "I don't know what to do. I don't know when to sit or when to stand. I don't know any of the words to the hymns."

"Nobody knows all the words." He chuckled. "That's why they give us all a hymnal."

This visit gave her the opportunity to explore new things. To expand her horizons. "I'd like to go. At least I think I would. I'm fairly certain."

"You can change your mind. I promise I don't mind either way. If you still want to go on Sunday, I will walk you there myself."

"There's no need. I'm hardly likely to get lost." She'd have found a refusal much easier had he been even the least bit judgmental. "Your mother has invited me back to the house after church. I feel as though I should bring something. Since I don't cook, I thought I'd visit the General Store. Is there anything she enjoys? Preserves or the like?"

"You don't cook?" he asked, appearing shocked. "At all?"

"No."

"Nothing?"

"When I said nothing, I meant nothing."

A hint of annoyance crept into her voice. He'd wanted to court Mary Louise and she didn't cook. Edith McCoy had said as much. What was the big deal?

"How do you get along?"

Anna heaved a fortifying breath. "My mother employs a cook and a housekeeper."

He let out a low whistle. "Does this mean Mrs. Franklin will be doing all the cooking and you'll be doing all the cleaning?"

"I suppose that's all that women are good for? Cooking and cleaning?"

"I live alone. I do both."

"Oh, fine." She'd been too long without a fight. The lull was wearing on her. "You cook and clean."

"Yes."

"Point taken." She swiped at a smudge on her sleeve. "Can you teach me how to cook?"

"Uh..."

The idea was inspired. While Izetta hadn't complained, Anna knew her lack of assistance put extra work on her.

She'd surprise Izetta with her new skill. Anna immediately warmed to the idea. "I don't need to know everything. Just a few basics to get started. Mrs. Franklin can show me the rest. What with cleaning the place, I don't want to ask any more of her."

The more things she learned, the more she strengthened her own independence.

He snatched his hat from the hook and backed toward the door. "Jo is the cook in the family. I'll talk with her."

"Perfect," she said, keeping her tone cheerful.

"She likes a schedule," he said, fumbling for the door. "She makes noodles every other Friday."

"How do you know that?"

"Because I always make certain to drop by for dinner."

With a tip of his hat he spun on his heel and strode down the stairs.

She'd gone and done it again. She'd assumed a familiarity that didn't exist. Would she ever learn? It was far too easy to slip into the fictional world they'd created and forget the real one.

She closed the door and leaned back.

A shriek sounded from the back garden and she dashed through the house. Anna emerged into the garden in time to find a red-faced Mrs. Franklin chasing a very familiar goat.

"Look what he's done!"

Gleefully unremorseful, the goat galloped toward Anna, a half-eaten red rose in his mouth.

She reached down and patted the animal on the head. "Shall I return him?"

"No," Mrs. Franklin spoke firmly. "This time I shall have the honors. I don't know what this little beast likes more—you or the rosebushes."

The goat butted Anna's leg and bleated. "He does seem awfully fond of me."

"He's positively smitten."

Watching Izetta walk the recalcitrant goat back home, an uncharacteristic bout of melancholy swept over her. She couldn't shake the feeling that this was all just a dream, that she'd wake up back in her home in St. Louis the same Anna Bishop. Which was foolish, of course.

She'd never be the same. Her injury and her stay here had eroded everything she believed about herself. Yet the process had been more enlightening than corrosive.

Leaves rustled above her head and she wrapped her arms around her middle. They'd better find the killer soon, because the more time she spent in Cimarron Springs, the harder it was going to be to leave.

Chapter Sixteen

The following days passed in relative peace. All of the leaves fell, and the first frost blanketed the prairie. She'd studiously avoided any contact with Caleb and found her new strategy had failed. With each passing day he filled a greater portion of her thoughts. Today she waited for Izetta at the door.

The older woman lifted an eyebrow but didn't say anything. The church bell clanged in the distance, heralding the service. As they stepped onto the dirt-packed street, they met the Stuarts. Then Mr. Lancaster and his wife, then a whole group of other people she'd never met before. Everyone they passed smiled a greeting or offered a friendly handshake.

The engagement bargain had worked. The people in town accepted her without question, without censure. The notion left her almost giddy.

Upon approaching the church, the crowds parted and Caleb stood there. He was wearing a suit she'd never seen before, black trousers and a close-fitting black jacket. He smiled a greeting, and her heartbeat tripped, then took up a frantic rhythm. She was drawn toward him against her better judgment, longing for just another moment more in his company.

People stepped aside and let him pass as he approached them. "Will you sit with us?"

She glanced at the McCoy clan and nodded. "Are you certain?"

He frowned and tilted his head. "What's the matter?"

Leaning closer, she whispered, "Remember what I said before."

"Remember what I said before." He spoke in an exaggerated whisper. "Follow my lead."

Silly, but she'd faced hordes of people armed with rotten fruit with less trepidation than this simple Sunday service. As though the congregation might suddenly discover her a fraud or declare her a heretic before the whole church.

His stuck out his elbow, and she hesitantly looped her hand through his arm, her fears calming.

A snuffing sounded from the bushes and she paused, certain she'd spied a glimpse of gray fur. "Did you lock the gate?"

"I don't follow."

"That goat of yours is remarkably ingenious."

"His name is Pipsqueak," Caleb said. "I needed something to shout when he escaped."

"And you're certain he hasn't escaped today?"

"Positive."

Practically the entire town was present, which meant nothing could go wrong this morning. This might be a fake engagement, not to mention absolutely the worst-kept secret in town, but she wasn't letting the McCoys down. They'd been kind and welcoming, and she wouldn't embarrass them. Or Caleb. Mostly Caleb.

He led her a few feet away and she heard the sound again.

Whipping around, she glared at the bushes. "He's here. I know it."

"I'm not saying you sound crazy—" Caleb tugged on her arm "—but others might."

She glanced around to ensure no one was watching them, then pointed at the dense green foliage lining the base of the church. "Stay out of Izetta's rosebushes."

"Now that did sound crazy."

"Crazy or not, that goat has a passion for roses. And me."

"Something we have in common." His face suffused with color. "The roses, of course."

"That's odd," she said, her voice teasing. "I don't recall any roses around your house."

"It's a recently discovered passion."

Feeling absurdly shy, she abandoned her search for the mischievous goat and let Caleb lead her up the stairs. Besides, what could possibly go wrong on such a beautiful day?

The church was delightful. The sort of picturesque building depicted on Christmas cards with smiling cherubs and seraphim. The building wasn't terribly large or ornate, a white clapboard frame with a modest steeple. Plain glass panes let in sunlight from both sides, and a stain-glassed window cast colorful patterns over the altar. The effect of such simplicity in design was charming.

They filed into the sturdy, polished pews with Anna on the aisle. The first half went well. She stood when Caleb stood, she sat when Caleb sat. He held the book and pointed out the hymns, his baritone voice reverberating beside her. He had quite a lovely singing voice. She let her eyes drift closed and simply enjoyed the sound.

When her inherent skepticism reared its head during the homily on forgiveness, lightning did not strike.

All in all her first foray into religion had not been a disaster.

Until she heard the noise.

A familiar bleating sound came from the back of the church. Her stomach knotted. Heads swiveled. She kept her attention rigidly forward. The sound of hoof beats scuffling across the wood floors neared. Someone tittered. A wave of whispered voices rippled through the church. The scuffling stopped. A snout nudged her arm.

Oh, no. That little troublemaker was not ruining her morning.

Assuming her fiercest countenance, Anna confronted Pipsqueak and snapped her fingers. "Outside. Now."

Pipsqueak ducked his head and backed away.

"I do not feel the least bit guilty. You know the rules. Outside."

The animal turned and wearily trudged toward the exit.

Anna glanced up and caught the wide-eyed stare of Reverend Miller. Her heart turned to lead and dropped into her stomach. So much for making a good impression.

Beside her, Caleb's shoulder trembled against hers. From the corner of her eye she caught his merry grin. She elbowed him in the side. The shaking only grew worse.

Reverend Miller smothered a grin and fisted his hand on the pulpit. His face grew red. He searched his breast pocket and dug out a handkerchief, then mopped his brow.

A full minute went by while the reverend composed himself and began speaking once more.

Anna clenched her teeth.

The next twenty minutes passed in agony. If she could have followed the goat out the door, she would have. Except fleeing the church now only added more fuel. As soon as the congregation was released, she shot out of her seat and collided with Triple A.

He grinned at her and winked. "The missus had some mighty fine embroidered aprons. Since she passed, they ain't doing me no good. Can I bring them by your place?"

For gracious sake what was that all about? "Of…of course."

He pivoted on his heel and melted into the swirl of people.

Anna searched behind her. The aisle soon crowded with McCoys, and Mrs. McCoy planted her hands on her hips. "Land sakes. That's more words than I've heard Triple A speak in a month of Sundays. I didn't think anyone could win that man over."

She squeezed Anna's shoulder as though she'd gained a great victory instead of embarrassing herself in front of the entire congregation.

Brahm scooted past and chucked her on the shoulder. "Will you be here next week?"

"I suppose."

"I can't wait."

"I don't…uh…that is…"

Maxwell gave her two thumbs up. "Can you teach me that?"

"What?"

"Can you teach me how to train a goat?"

"I don't, that is, I didn't…"

His father gently shoved him forward. "If you can

figure out how to turn that charm on children, you let me know."

Jo and the marshal appeared next, little Shawn perched on her hip, Cora and Jocelyn in matching pink dresses.

"I second that," Jo said. "You have a way with animals."

The marshal only grinned.

By the time they emerged into the late morning sunlight, Anna was swamped with people who wanted her attention. She received three invitations to supper and one offer of another goat, which she politely declined.

Pipsqueak spent the whole time chewing on a patch of nettles near the corner of the church, seemingly unaware of the excitement he'd stirred up.

Bemused, Anna let the conversation swirl around her. Mrs. McCoy must have realized her confusion.

"That's the thing about small towns," she said, "All newcomers to a small town need a story before they're fully accepted into the fold."

"A story?"

"Yep. I remember when Triple A came to town before he even married his first wife twenty years ago. Got himself stuck up on the roof when his ladder fell over. He was too prideful to call for help. He spent the whole afternoon sitting on that roof hollering hello until my husband, Ely, came walking by. Poor Ely couldn't figure out what kind of fool sat on his roof yelling hello. Figured the man must have gone daft. He helped him down and told him that if a man needed help, he was better off asking for it than letting his vanity stand in the way. Anyway, you see how it is."

A small seed of pride took root in her chest. Sure, she'd gone and made a fool of herself in church, but no one seemed to mind. She'd established her place in town. She had her own story. While it wasn't the story she might have chosen, it was a story nonetheless.

Reverend Miller tipped his hat and grinned. "We'll be seeing you next week."

Her pride increased tenfold. She'd gotten the approval of Reverend Miller. No one held any grudge for the untimely interruption in the church.

Her steps were lighter and heart happier on the way home. Caleb walked them down the hill and around the corner toward their street.

A carriage and two horses stood outside the house. A gentleman Anna remembered from town held their lead.

Izetta frowned. "Who can that be?"

As they reached the wagon, the blood drained from Anna's face. She recognized the trunk.

Her mother was here.

Caleb sensed Anna's reaction immediately. She'd gone deathly pale, her hands gripping her reticule, her lips devoid of color.

His stomach clenched. "What is it?"

"My mother is here."

Caleb stopped his jaw from dropping in the nick of time.

The man standing near the horses' heads flagged Caleb over. "Give me a hand with the trunk, will you?"

"Sure, Berny."

Uneasy, he kept Anna in his peripheral vision. He didn't know what reaction he expected, but he sure hadn't expected her obvious dread.

As Izetta and Anna made their way into the house, Caleb and Berny followed along behind them with the trunk. The impressive piece of luggage was an almost exact replica of the one Anna possessed with the same leather straps and the same brass fittings.

After reading about Victoria Bishop in the newspapers and hearing Anna's anecdotes, he wanted to see the woman for himself. He needed to understand the forces shaping Anna's life.

They stepped into the parlor, and he struggled with the heavy trunk. Was the lady carrying another body in there? He glanced and paused, then jerked forward since Berny was still moving. An imposing-looking woman sat in the chair, one hand braced on a walking stick.

Berny stopped in the doorway. "Where do I put this?"

"Back in the wagon," the woman declared sharply. "I shall be staying in town at the hotel."

Caleb chanced a glance at Anna. All the sparkle had left her eyes. She was a shadow of the woman he'd seen only moments before. Her mother had dimmed her spirit, and the result was visible.

"I wasn't expecting you, Mother," Anna said. "What a pleasant surprise."

"Not pleasant at all. The townhouse has burned to the ground."

"Our house?"

Anna sat down hard on one of the sturdy dining room chairs.

"Yes, our house. Whose house do you suppose I meant? The grocer?" She sniffed. "The houses on either side received significant damage, as well." She patted the side of her head. "Not that the Smith place was any great loss. I never did trust that man."

Anna gripped the arm of her chair. "Was anyone hurt?"

"I didn't ask. It didn't seem relevant."

Caleb's forearms strained against the weight of the trunk. Neither he nor Berny moved.

Anna spread her hands. "Do they know how the fire started? Were you there?"

"Arson. The fire was deliberately set. I received word in Boston. I returned home immediately."

"You returned for the fire?" Anna's voice was heartbreakingly quiet.

"I had to see what was salvageable." The elder Miss Bishop scowled. "You cannot trust the help to make those decisions."

The hurt on Anna's face cut him to the quick. Victoria Bishop hadn't come when her daughter had been shot. She'd been too busy, the work in Boston too important. He snorted softly. She'd found time enough when her precious belongings had been damaged.

Victoria glanced around and gathered her skirts closer, as though worried they might be sullied. "I had hoped to stay with you until things were settled. I can see now that won't be possible."

At Anna's crestfallen expression, a cold fist tightened around Caleb's heart.

She held up her hands then let them drop to her sides. "There's a hotel in town. Perhaps you'd be more comfortable there."

Her distress cut him to the quick.

"I can't imagine being comfortable anywhere this far west of the Mississippi." Victoria flicked at a bit of lint on her sleeve. "I told Elizabeth that Kansas City was a waste of time."

"That's enough, Mother."

With the sound of Victoria Bishop's sharp intake

of breath, he jerked his head toward Berny, who took the hint. Together they hauled the trunk back out to the wagon. Nothing about seeing Anna's mother had changed his initial impressions of her.

At least Anna had regained some of her fire. She needed it with that woman.

Berny mopped his brow. "You could store that lady in an icehouse. I've never seen the like." He braced his hand against the wooden slats of the wagon bed. "I don't think she likes our town very much either. She kept sniffing and covering her face."

"I was thinking the same thing."

Caleb had the feeling Victoria Bishop didn't like much of anything that didn't go according to her plans. She was treating all of them as though they were somehow involved in her great inconvenience. Was that how she treated Anna? As an inconvenience? She didn't appear the sort of woman who'd have a sense of humor about their engagement either. He doubted she had much of a sense of humor about anything.

The door swung open, and she marched down the bricked pathway toward the wagon. Mrs. Franklin had arrived by then and offered a friendly greeting.

Miss Victoria Bishop stared down her nose. "Pleasure," she said, though her voice remained hard.

Anna hovered behind her mother and motioned toward him. "This is Mr. McCoy. He saved my life in Kansas City."

He touched the brim of his hat. "Pleased to meet you, Miss Bishop."

"You are the veterinarian." Once again she managed to coat her words in disdain.

"I am."

Anna shot him an apologetic look and he returned what he hoped was a comforting smile.

"Then I suppose thanks are in order. My daughter appears to be in fine health."

She didn't wait for a reply, but rather circled around the wagon toward the passenger side.

Berny scooted past and rolled his eyes. "Glad it's a short way back into town. She's a scary one."

Caleb didn't doubt the assessment.

With everyone on the opposite side of the wagon, no one saw exactly what happened next. They certainly heard what happened.

Pipsqueak bleated. The horses startled and lunged forward, yanking on the wagon. The set brake held them at bay. Anna's mother shrieked.

Caleb sprang forward and snatched the horses' lead, murmuring soothing words. Anna and Mrs. Franklin dashed around the wagon.

Berny peeked around the corner and his eyes widened. "Well she ain't looking so high and mighty now, I'll say that."

Anna's mother wailed. "That infernal animal has broken my ankle."

An hour later Doc Johnsen stood next to the bed. "The ankle isn't broken," he said. "It's a bad sprain. I recommend staying put this evening."

The news did not please her mother. Anna cringed.

"Return me to the hotel this instant," Victoria demanded.

"We'd have to put you on a litter and carry you the distance. You won't be able to put weight on that foot until tomorrow at least."

Anna watched as her mother weighed the options. She clearly wasn't interested in remaining in the Stuart house along with her and Miss Franklin. The indignities of being carted down Main Street on a litter obviously held less appeal.

After a long silence, she sniffed. "Then I shall remain here and make do. I insist you slaughter that goat and serve him to the dogs."

Anna started. "Your fall was an accident. You can't blame Pipsqueak."

"I most certainly can."

"Can I get you a cup of coffee?" Mrs. Franklin interjected.

"Tea is better."

"I only have chamomile. Will that suffice?"

"I suppose it shall have to do then, won't it?"

"You are a guest, Mother." Anna heard the tremor in her voice and hated herself for the telling weakness. "I'm quite sure you'll be happy with anything Mrs. Franklin has to offer."

"I am a guest because this town is teeming with barnyard animals. That is hardly my fault."

"Neither is it the fault of Mrs. Franklin."

Anna was mortified, humiliated and downright furious. From Berny to Doc Johnsen, everyone in town had been nothing but solicitous. Her mother, on the other hand, had been absolutely insufferable. The strain of the fire had obviously shortened her temper.

Victoria Bishop glanced around the room. "I will need a sturdy side table along with my pens, papers and correspondence. Between your injury and the fire, it is time for another campaign. We must capitalize on these events before interest grows cold."

"What do you mean? Capitalize?" Anna hadn't yet recovered from the idea that her mother was here. Staying. For an extended length of time. Confined to her bed.

If Victoria Bishop loathed weakness in others, she abhorred weakness in herself. The next twenty-four hours were going to be miserable.

"This is our chance for front-page coverage. I saw nothing about your shooting in the pages of the newspapers back East. Absolutely nothing. Since two events of violence have occurred against our family, the papers will be obligated to report the story. I shall demand they do so."

"You're using this for the platform?"

"Do not be naive, dear. Passing up such an excellent opportunity is foolish. As soon as my leg heals, we shall return to St. Louis. Nothing can be done from this isolated location."

Her mother was wrong. There were plenty of ways one made a difference, even in a small town. The cause wasn't simply about making a change in Washington. If they made grand speeches and forgot the individual stories, then they gained nothing. They had traveled the country and focused on getting the vote, all the while forgetting the very people they were fighting for. That was Victoria Bishop's mistake.

Anna exhaled her pent-up breath. This was not the time to change her mother's mind. There were other, more pressing matters. Anna wasn't a child anymore, easily distracted by her mother's verbal sparring. She wanted answers. Needed answers. There were questions still hanging between them—about her past, about her father, about everything.

"Actually, Mother," Anna began, "I think this convalescence will give us the opportunity to clear the air between us."

"I wasn't aware the air had been polluted."

A knock sounded from the front parlor, and Izetta crossed the room, no doubt using the distraction as a polite way to leave them in privacy.

"I spoke with a Pinkerton detective named Reinhart," Anna said, studying her mother for even a hint of reaction. "He said someone was looking for me in St. Louis."

Victoria Bishop plucked at a loose thread in the tufting on the arm of her chair. "What on earth are you babbling on about?"

"I think you know."

Izetta interrupted Anna's next words, her gaze apologetic. "You're needed in town, Anna. It's Mrs. Phillips."

The look on Izetta's face indicated bad news. "Oh dear, what's wrong?"

"Her husband has arrived."

Why did everything always happen at once? She'd spent a week here with hardly more than a breeze to stir the leaves, now a veritable tornado of activity was brewing.

Anna snatched her shawl from the peg near the door and leaned into the parlor. "I shall return shortly." She pinned her mother with a stare. "You and I are not finished speaking."

"Of course not, dear. I need your assistance with a speech for the Boston chapter," her mother said.

Anna gritted her teeth. She'd finish this talk later, whether her mother liked it or not.

Her mother told women like Mrs. Phillips to wait for change. Mrs. Phillips didn't have the luxury of time.

Everything jumbled together in her mind. This was

her chance to prove she wasn't a child, to prove she deserved answers, to prove she was more than simply Victoria Bishop's daughter. She understood things her mother couldn't comprehend, about people, about their heartaches.

When she arrived at the hotel, Mrs. Phillips was tugging her gloves over her wrists. Jane sat solemnly beside her mother wearing a fresh pink dress with several layers of lace flounces.

Her feet swung, and Anna returned to her own youth, recalling her vigil outside Miss Spence's office all those years ago.

Mrs. Phillips didn't meet her eyes. "We're going home with Clark."

Panic gripped Anna. "But you can't. After what he's done. How can you?"

"We had a long talk. He's said he's changed."

Anna felt as though the ground beneath her feet had crumbled away. "Mrs. Phillips. This isn't a matter of leaving one's dirty clothing on the floor or working too many hours, or even of drinking too much. This man had you—" She caught sight of Jane and held back the words. "You know what he's done."

"I'm not like you. I'm not independent. Clark handled all the decisions, all the bills. Jane needs a stable home."

"Do you really think that's what your future holds? A stable home life? You must think about Jane."

"I am thinking about Jane. This is what's best. Clark can guarantee a comfortable life for her. I cannot."

Anna caught the slight change in her tone. "Has he done something? Has he threatened you? Is he blackmailing you?"

Her expression hardened. "I'm doing what's best for me. For Jane. I don't expect you to understand that."

The extent of her failure stole the breath from Anna's lungs. She'd lost the battle. She'd done nothing for Mrs. Phillips. She'd done nothing for Jane. She'd thought she'd understood but she was just as naive and self-absorbed as her mother. She'd been fighting for a personal victory, as well.

"Will you stay in touch?" Anna begged, grasping for any thread of hope. "Will you write and let me know how you're faring?"

"I don't think so. Perhaps it's best if we don't remain in contact."

Anna glanced between mother and daughter. She'd failed. There was nothing left. No more arguments. By the set of her jaw, Mrs. Phillips had made up her mind. Nothing Anna had done had made a difference.

Her anger burned unchecked and she knelt. "Goodbye, Jane," she said.

The younger girl stared. Anna wished she had more time. She wanted to tell her that she didn't have to continue the pattern. She needn't grow up and make the same mistakes as many children seemed to do. Mrs. Phillips had entered into an unhealthy marriage because she hadn't known the difference. Jane was destined to do the same. The chain of suppression continued from one generation to the next, unchecked unless someone took a stand.

She'd so hoped Mrs. Phillips had the strength. Jane deserved a better life.

As she stared into Jane's pale gray eyes, she willed her understanding.

Victoria Bishop had been right all along. The only

way of breaking the chain was from a position of power. They needed the vote. They needed a say in the politicians elected for office. They needed laws to protect women like Mrs. Phillips.

"You're the prettiest lady I've ever met," Jane said.

"There's more to being a girl than being pretty," Anna replied.

"You're pretty here," Jane said, touching her hair. "And pretty here." She touched Anna's chest over her heart.

"When you're older." Anna blinked rapidly. "You can write to me."

"Where will I find you?"

"Here," Anna said impulsively. "Write to me in Cimarron Springs."

Mrs. Phillips yanked Jane's hand and glared. "Time to go."

With helpless rage Anna watched them go. Anything she said or did now only made matters worse. For her. For Mrs. Phillips. For Jane. For all of them.

She hadn't made one bit of difference.

Caleb kept the porch swing moving with the heel of his boot, his eyes on the street. Anna had to pass by on her way home. They hadn't talked about her father once since that day in Kansas City. The subject was too private. With Anna's mother in town, he wondered if Anna was thinking about him.

He almost didn't recognize her. Always before when he'd seen her, her shoulders were back and she walked with purpose, her steps brisk. This afternoon her head was down, her back stooped, her steps lagging.

He leaned forward and rested his forearms on the whitewashed porch rails. "Penny for your thoughts."

She glanced up. "Where's Pipsqueak?"

"In the barn. Under lock and key. And chains. And whatever I could find to keep him from causing more mischief."

"My mother was hoping you'd feed him to the wolves."

"That's funny. Berny thought we should give him a medal and name him honorary mayor of the town."

Anna hid a grin behind her hand. "I would attend that ceremony."

"Ah, well. We rarely get everything we wish for, do we?"

Anna turned toward the gate, remaining just outside the fence. "No, we don't."

She was only fifteen feet away, yet he sensed the gulf separating them. "I heard Mr. Phillips arrived on the same train as your mother."

"He did."

"The marshal talked with him."

"Good."

"She's making the best choice she knows how."

"Why do we cling to things that hurt us so?"

He stood and crossed the distance, standing on the opposite side of the gate. "Animals are creatures of habit. Look at the buffalo. They followed the same trails for so long, they cut divots into the earth. Then the wagon trains came along and did the same. Because people aren't much different, I suppose. Taking chances means taking risks. Not everyone has the stomach for change."

"We all simply stay with the devil we know?"

"Rather than risk greater pain."

"What a sad state of affairs."

"Except sometimes, on very rare occasions, someone comes along who's willing to make a change," he said.

"Someone who's willing to stand on a stage in front of hundreds of people and risk everything for what they believe in."

Her smile was tinged with sadness. "I didn't make a difference, though."

"You don't know that. No one truly knows the changes we make on people. Look at Jane. She's met you. She's seen a different way of living, of thinking."

Anna had changed him. He'd been careless of the life he'd built, of the friends and family surrounding him. He'd been complacent with their love and affection. He'd even been dismissive of their relationships, rolling his eyes at Jo's fondness for her husband.

No more. He had something rare and precious, something he wasn't going to take for granted anymore. He had a family who loved him, a community who supported him and a job that fulfilled him. There were pieces missing, a wife and a family. He'd always mourn that loss. After knowing Anna, he'd never settle for anything else. Instead, he'd appreciate the things he did have.

"Maybe." Anna shook her head. "I'm not certain anymore. My mother works in grand gestures. I get caught up in the details. In the people and their stories."

The two kittens they'd rescued frolicked in a large crate near the porch. "Would you like to see the boys? They're doing well. Should be on their own in a week or two."

"No." She tilted her head toward the sky. "I don't want to grow attached."

She kept her distance, and he sensed her purpose. She was separating from him, from the town, from everything. She was going home. He'd known she'd leave, he'd always known. He just hadn't considered how soon. With her mother here, they only had a few days at best.

"I lost sight of everything," she said. "I was impatient. I wanted to see a change. I wanted to know I was making progress."

"Haven't you?"

"I don't know anymore."

He chose his words carefully. "Everyone has different gifts. You see the human side of each story, and you are moved by the individual stories. Use that strength."

"How?"

"I don't know. That's for you to discover." A deep, abiding sadness filled his heart. "Are you coming to Harvest Festival tomorrow night?"

"I shouldn't. My mother. I shouldn't leave her alone."

"You'll miss the husking bee."

"I did want to see Gus and Becky. I've been here one week already, and I've never even seen your Mary Louise."

"She isn't mine. She's simply a girl who caught my fancy a long time ago."

A thousand reasons for her to stay remained locked away. There was only one reason for her leaving. She was better off without him. The very thing that drew him toward her was the very thing that stood between them. She craved independence and reveled in the public eye. He was a man who preferred a quiet life. She defied convention. He embodied convention.

She twisted the filial atop the gate. "After we left church, I felt such a sense of peace."

"Have we made a believer out of you?"

"It's too soon to tell, but I believe you have. I hadn't expected the sense of grace. I keep thinking about what you said before, how all relationships require work, even our relationship with God. I've never put in the effort before, but I'm willing to try."

"Then I wish you peace on your journey."

They had developed a friendship, which was something. A rare gift he was grateful for. Eventually, though, they'd tear each other apart. If they tried building a life together, there was no way of avoiding a terrible rift. They were each moving in opposite directions. For a moment in time they'd crossed paths. He'd known the truth all along, only he hadn't counted on the pain.

She started to turn and he called out, "Wait. Come to the Harvest Festival. Only for an hour. Surely your mother will be fine for a short length of time? One last memory of Cimarron Springs."

"I'll come," she conceded. "But only for a short time."

He didn't know why the concession was important, but her acceptance of the invitation was vital. "I'll take you there myself. It's only a mile down the road. I'll take you and Mrs. Franklin," he added quickly.

He rested his hand over hers. Their fingers entwined. She sighed, and he pressed his mouth against her temple, the soft beat of her heart beneath his lips. They stood that way for a long time, neither willing to break the moment. There was nothing more to say, he'd spent all his words.

He swallowed thickly and stepped away, his feet crunching over fallen leaves. It seemed fitting they'd met in autumn. A fiery end before a long, cold winter.

She turned and smiled wistfully over one shoulder. "Will you save a dance for me?"

"Of course."

He wouldn't burden her with words of love. His heart, so painfully empty before, was replenished. He'd hold these feelings close through the coming years. They weren't courting. They weren't engaged. They were neighbors. They were acquaintances. Nothing more, nothing less.

He was a selfish man. He'd begged her to come not because he wanted her to remember Cimarron Springs, but because he wanted his own memory of her.

One last dance before they said goodbye forever.

Chapter Seventeen

The evening of the shucking bee arrived with a brisk wind from the north. Winter was well on its way. Any lingering fall blooms had died with the frost, and most of the leaves had fallen, leaving only the oak trees with their crown of browned leaves.

Anna had worn her shirtwaist and plaid skirt, though she'd conceded she must don her navy velvet wrap against the chill. She had nicer clothing, but she wanted to blend in with the other girls, and her fine silks set her apart. She'd never realized before, but clothing was another form of armor. Tonight she was shedding her reticence and enjoying herself.

Her mother cast a disapproving glare from the parlor. "I hope nothing happens while the two of you are gone. I shall be quite all alone."

Izetta tossed Anna a sympathetic smile before saying, "Why don't I wait for you outside?"

"I'll be right there." Anna turned toward the parlor. "I know how much you value your independence. I'll only be gone an hour or so. The solitude will help you concentrate."

Her mother grimaced and set down her quill, pushing aside the paper covering her makeshift desk. "Must you attend this provincial gathering?"

"These are good people. They've been kind to me. I don't like you speaking of them with such derision."

She'd known her mother was a snob. Of course she'd known. She hadn't realized the extent of her prejudices.

"Yes," her mother drawled. "Good people. They won't miss you any more if you attend their little social."

She thought of Caleb and those eyes. Those entrancing forest-green eyes. "I will miss them."

"Will you at least say your goodbyes this evening? I don't want a scene on the train platform tomorrow. You know I detest scenes. You always were too softhearted. Makes a woman weak."

"I'm well aware of your preferences. I will not make a scene."

Her anger took root and grew. Like a living, breathing thing it took hold of her. She wasn't weak for having feelings. She wasn't weak for growing attached to the town and the people. She wasn't weak for falling in love.

Her anger crystalized and shattered.

Her mother grasped the spectacles hanging around her neck and perched them on her nose. She studied the paper before her, effectively dismissing Anna.

Caught up in the depth of her revelation, Anna barely spared her a glance. She'd missed the signs because she'd been taught to see love as a destructive thing. A crushing force. Her love for Caleb was as light as a thistle on the breeze. As bright as a blanket of stars of a moonless night.

She was halfway through the door before her mother called, "Can you bring me my tea before you go?"

"No time," Anna called in return. "I'm already late."

She slammed the door behind her, blocking her mother's ferocious mutterings.

"That was awful," Anna said to Izetta. "I should go back."

Izetta took her elbow in a firm, though not painful grip. "You will do no such thing. You should be in the annals of sainthood by now, dealing with that woman. I don't know how you manage."

"You've been extremely patient with her, and I'm grateful."

Over the past twenty-four hours, they'd done little more than fetch and carry for her mother. With no thanks besides. The tea was never hot enough, the biscuits never light enough, their service never quick enough. Anna had an hour reprieve, and she was going to enjoy herself.

"Your help has been indispensable," Anna said, hoping her apology was enough. "I'm afraid my mother has never had much patience for the weak or the sick. Being helpless is frustrating for her. She's never been home much. This is the most time we've spent with each other. Ever."

Again that morning she'd almost broached the subject of her father, only to stop herself. He was dead, what did digging up the past matter? Curiosity lingered despite all her good intentions. Tomorrow, tomorrow on the train, when they were alone, she'd ask her. After all these years, she deserved something of an answer. Even if that answer wasn't satisfactory.

Izetta patted her hand. "There's no need for apologies. I've quite enjoyed my stay in Cimarron Springs. In fact, I believe I'll stay."

Anna started. "You're staying?"

"Why not? As I said before, I'm a widow with a pension. I make my rules."

"But what about your work in Kansas City?"

"I'll still fight, never doubt that. I'll simply find another way."

Anna held her tongue. Izetta's plans were not up for debate. A tinge of jealousy caught her by surprise. Izetta had choices. Another reason Anna must return home. In St. Louis, she made a difference.

Tonight, though, she was forgetting all about the vote. Tonight was her last night with Caleb, her last hour, her last stolen moment, and she planned on enjoying their evening.

A tingle of anticipation danced along her nerves. After hearing about the Bainum farm from Caleb, she was anxious for her first view.

When she caught sight of him, her soul filled with tenderness. Caleb halted the wagon, set the brake and hopped down.

He circled toward the front and her. His gaze caressed her, and a shiver went down her back. He wore a crisp white shirt, dark trousers and a dark close-fitting coat. His hair had been brushed till it gleamed, his face freshly shaved. As he approached, she caught the faint hint of bay rum. She leaned closer and inhaled the scent, committing the sensation to memory.

Izetta urged her forward. "You sit in the middle. I'll feel claustrophobic if I have to ride squashed between the two of you."

Anna blushed. Caleb looked her up and down, his gaze slow and lingering, his eyes showing his appreciation. She fought the urge to dash back into the house and change into her blue taffeta dress. This was the last evening they'd spend together, and she wanted to look nice. Blue always gave her courage. She wanted him to remember her fondly. But no, she didn't need courage. She just needed to be herself for once.

He slipped his hands around her waist and easily lifted her into the wagon. If his fingers lingered a bit, she didn't call him out.

When he reached for Izetta, she held up her palm. "I'm too old to be lifted into the air. Just give me a foot up."

Caleb dutifully bent and threaded his finger. Izetta stepped into his outstretched hand and hoisted herself onto the seat beside Anna. Caleb circled the wagon and swung up on her opposite.

Claustrophobic was not the word Anna would use to describe the situation. The arrangement was cozy. Caleb's body pressed against her left side, shielding her from the worst of the wind. Izetta blocked the right. Each bend and dip in the road threw her more tightly against Caleb. If she didn't know better, she'd have thought he'd aimed for a few of the divots.

With a lingering sense of disappointment she alighted at the Bainum farm. Izetta hopped out on her own, sprightly despite her age. Caleb once again wrapped his fingers around her waist.

"Are you sure this doesn't hurt?" he asked.

She doubted she'd notice if his touch exacerbated her wound. All she thought about were the gold flecks around his irises and how the setting sun behind him haloed his dark hair. Pausing a moment, she memorized his features, locking away each line in his forehead, the tiny scar near his ear, the way his hairline flared at his temples.

She forced her thoughts back to Jane. A little girl without a voice. A little girl who would grow into a woman without a voice. Jane deserved better. She deserved a champion.

Their gazes held for a long moment, each realizing this was their last evening together. He looked as though he might say something, but the moment was lost.

Another wagon had arrived. One of the boys from town dashed over and grasped the lead lines, promising he'd take good care of the team.

Caleb made a show of escorting Izetta, and Anna appreciated the courtly gesture.

The Bainum barn was a rambling succession of buildings tucked against a hill, banked by shrubs and trees. The barn had been painted red at one point, although weather had faded the siding almost pink.

Music and laughter spilled from the open barn doors. With the setting sun, the men scrambled for lanterns, turning the inside of the barn a warm yellow glow.

The shucking had already begun, with a dozen men seated on low stools, a pile of corn in the middle.

A low table held an assortment of covered dishes along with an enormous jug of cider.

Caleb fetched them both a glass. At Anna's hesitation, he said, "Don't worry, it's not hard cider. The old farmer learned his lesson."

She gratefully accepted the glass. A shout sounded from the men seated behind her, and a gentleman proudly raised his ear of red corn. The man was married, and his wife made a great show of looking put out before bussing him on the cheek. A few of the single men grumbled at the loss of a stolen kiss.

Anna spotted Jo and the children. "There's your sister. This will be the last chance I have to thank her for everything she's done."

"I'll join the others," Caleb said.

Anna met up with Jo, and they made great study of the

delectable desserts and pies lining the food table. Shawn snatched a crinkle cookie and stuffed the sugary mess into his mouth quick as a flash.

He chomped through his mother's scolding and reached for another before she finished her lecture.

Jo was faster this time and caught his arm. "No more until after supper."

Shawn blinked his reluctant agreement. Anna figured Jo better not turn her back—the little sprite looked as determined as Pipsqueak staring down a rosebush.

The marshal motioned her aside. Frowning, Anna followed him toward a quiet recess.

He glanced around. "I don't mean to bother you, but I have some information that might interest you."

"Please, I'd rather hear it now."

"Reinhart is in town. He came a few days ago. We figured it was better if his visit stayed quiet."

"I understand."

"Turns out he discovered a few things about your father." He paused. "Are you sure you're okay to hear this?"

Anna clenched her hands. "I'm certain. Just don't say his name quite yet. I'm not ready to make this personal. I only want the details."

If the marshal thought her request odd, he didn't say anything. "He was an architect. Wealthy. Married and widowed once. A pillar of the community."

Another cheer went up from the crowd, and Anna turned with a smile, wondering who'd get the next kiss. Her gaze clashed with Caleb's, and she realized he held the prize.

The marshal touched her elbow and urged her forward. "We'll talk about this more tomorrow. Come by my office at lunch. I'll make certain Reinhart is there."

She nodded and caught sight of Caleb once more. Her cheeks warmed. He made a great show of rubbing his chin and searching the room. He passed before several giggling girls, his progress leading him steadily in her direction. Her heart clattered against her ribs. He paused before her and crouched.

Anna started.

He bent and kissed Cora's forehead, then planted another kiss on Jocelyn's, then hugged them close. "My two best girls!"

Jocelyn and Cora giggled, and the crowd roared its approval.

If she hadn't loved him before, she would have fallen hard right then.

She caught his eyes; those bewitching forest-green eyes were filled with a promise of more to come.

His breath whispered against her ear and sent her whole body trembling. "I'll have my boon later."

After all the corn was husked, the ears were loaded into wheelbarrows and dumped into the enormous grain stalls at the end of the barn. The stalks were bagged for kindling, and the floor swept clean for the dance.

The men relinquished their low stools and many of the ladies claimed them. A violin began playing a low, mournful tune.

"Ah, c'mon, Berny!" Maxwell yelled. "Play something happy."

A gentlemen with a guitar joined Berny and his violin. Soon a lively rendition of the "Farmer in the Dell" had several couples on their feet.

Maxwell appeared before her, his hair slicked back, his suit pants only slightly too short. He sketched a bow and held out his hand. "Dance?"

"I don't know the steps."

One of her many nannies had taught her the waltz amidst much laughter and teasing, but she'd never danced with a gentleman before. Dancing was another one of those frivolous activities her mother deplored.

"Don't worry," Maxwell urged. "You'll catch on soon enough."

He twirled her onto the dance floor, and before she knew what was happening, she'd joined in the merry jig. After that her feet never stopped moving. First one McCoy brother, then another joined her in the dance.

She watched as Sarah joined Brahm on the dance floor, his ears a vivid shade of red, a shy smile on her face. Just when she thought she'd collapse from all the activity, the music slowed.

Caleb appeared before her. "May I have this dance?"

She rested her left hand on his shoulder, her gloved right hand clasped in his. Behind them, the small band strummed out the mournful tune of the Tennessee Waltz.

Caleb swept her around the dance floor, his expression admiring. "I wasn't sure if you waltzed. I didn't know if Victoria approved."

"I don't always listen to my mother."

"Scandalous, Miss Bishop."

"One of my nannies taught me."

"Remind me to thank her."

The soothing cadence of his voice sent a warm glow through her. "That was a very sweet thing you did, giving your kiss to Jocelyn and Cora."

"They weren't my first choice."

"Oh," said Anna coyly. "And who was your first choice?"

"Mrs. Franklin."

Anna burst out laughing. "Are you ever serious?"

The light in his eyes dimmed. "I'm going to miss you."

The music cocooned them, the dancers swirled around the floor, everyone caught up in their own conversations. He was the more sensible of the two of them. The time for kisses was over. She was leaving the following day. Weak, feminine tears welled in her eyes and she didn't care a whit.

"We can write," Anna said.

"I don't think that's a good idea."

"Why not?"

"Because I love you."

She jerked away from him and dashed toward the exit. If anyone noticed her hasty departure, no one said anything.

There were people everywhere, people in the barn, in the house, wagons lining the drive. She walked away from all the noise and commotion, seeking a moment of solitude.

Why had he gone and said he loved her? She'd just discovered her own feelings, and her emotions were too chaotic. Somehow, believing only her heart had been broken had made the whole situation more palatable. Except she'd been lying to herself. Of course she'd known his feelings were deepening, of course she'd known they were both drawn to each other. She simply hadn't wanted to acknowledge his part, as well.

Leaving was much easier when she didn't know his feelings ran as deep as her feelings for him. He was a good man, a kind man. This was his home. He wasn't going to leave, and she wasn't staying. The situation was impossible, and both of them had known the truth.

Only one of them had been brave enough to state their feelings outright. She bent her head and tugged her wrap tighter around her shoulders. The coward among them was plain. She'd rather face an angry mob than the one man who held her heart.

She was so preoccupied that she nearly ran into the gentleman. In fact, he had to reach out to stop her from colliding with him.

"Mr. Baker?" she said hesitantly.

"Mr. Bekker."

She'd been introduced some time earlier. "Yes, sorry. You're here for the horses, aren't you? Visiting with Mr. Elder."

"Actually, no."

Something in his voice had her glancing behind her. "I should be going."

"Don't you want to know why I'm really here?"

She felt a twinge of alarm. She was too far from the barn. The music was loud. People were dancing and clapping, their feet stomping on the wooden stage. Away from the light, she was vulnerable. Mr. Bekker knew it as well, she could tell. A spark of fear raced along her spine.

She spun away, and his arm snaked around her waist. With a startled cry she slammed into his chest. Summoning up all her strength, she stomped on his toe. The man yelped and released her.

She dashed toward the barn, toward the people. A heavy weight socked her from behind, knocking her onto the ground. Pain shot through her side. She sucked in a breath to scream, and his hand clamped over her mouth.

"You're a difficult woman to kill, sis."

Her world went black.

* * *

Caleb stumbled off the makeshift dance floor and into the night air. Why had he said that? He'd destroyed what little rapport remained between them. He'd destroyed any chance of maintaining even a sliver of friendship.

People milled about, talking and laughing. Triple A sat on an overturned washtub, smoking a pipe, the smell pungent and familiar. The night was crisp, the moon bright. What kind of fool ruined such a beautiful evening?

Caleb stuffed his hands in his pockets and stared into the darkness.

Triple A let out a low whistle. "How are things going with the goat? Found him a home yet?"

"Pipsqueak is staying with me."

Caleb kicked at the dirt. They had something in common, he and that goat. They both loved Anna; they might as well stick together. Beyond the circle of light glowing from the open doors, the night turned pitch. Clouds drifted over the moon, dimming the light and blocking the stars.

The patter of running feet brought him around.

Jasper dashed forward and grabbed his hand. "They took her."

Caleb crouched, and the boy grabbed his hand. Touching the boy's wrist, he felt the rapidly beating pulse. "Slow down. What's going on?"

"They got Miss Anna. Some man knocked her down. I followed him. I figured I couldn't help unless I knew where he was going. He tossed her into the back of the wagon, and that other lady joined him."

His heart twisted painfully. "What other lady? Who were they?"

"That couple from back East, the ones after Mr. Elder's horses."

Caleb had seen the couple around town, though he hadn't given them much notice. "Which way were they headed?"

"Toward town."

His blood ran hot. A sudden memory burst into his head. He'd seen the woman before, Mrs. Bekker. He'd seen her on the stairs in the hotel. He'd almost run into her, then Anna had nearly been killed. They hadn't come for the horses, they'd come to kill her.

He grasped Jasper by the shoulders. "Fetch Marshal Cain. He's inside. Tell him what you told me."

Someone had tethered their horse near a tree, and Caleb snatched the reins. He tightened the cinch on the saddle and swung into place. Kicking the horse into a gallop, he set off down the darkened road.

They were in a wagon, going slower than a man riding alone. He had the advantage; they didn't know he was following. As he reached town, ambient light from the saloon and hotel lit the street. The wagon was nowhere in sight.

His stomach churned. Whoever had taken Anna was hampered by the conveyance. He reined his horse and quickly scanned the street. The only other place they could take a wagon was near the houses on the edge of town. He kicked the horse into a lope once again and had nearly reached town when he caught sight of the wagon.

They were in his house.

He swung down and cautiously approached. Voices sounded from inside. The marshal was a smart man; if Caleb had found the wagon, Garrett wasn't far behind.

He made for the stairs, and someone grabbed his shoulder. He cocked back his arm.

"Wait!" a familiar voice grated harshly. "It's me. Reinhart."

Caleb lowered his arm. "They've got Anna."

"I know. I'll explain everything later. You'll get yourself killed if you storm in there."

At least with two of them they had a fighting chance. "How many are there?"

"Just two. A husband and wife. You got a gun?"

"Inside."

"Can you get to it?"

"If I go in around back."

"Good," Reinhart said. "You take the back. Once you're inside, I'll come in the front. We'll trap them."

Satisfied with the plan, Caleb ducked beneath the window. The voices grew louder.

"They'll think it was a crime of passion," the man said.

"You always complicated things." The woman, presumably Mrs. Bekker, spoke. "We should have shot her and dumped her body in the woods."

His fingers shook with rage and he fisted them a few times, clearing his head. Scooting on his hands and knees, he made his way toward the back door. He always left his bedroom window unlatched. If the husband and wife continued arguing, he and Reinhart had the advantage.

He eased open the window and hoisted himself over the sill. Creeping through the house, he made his way to the center corridor.

A woman blocked his view of Anna.

"Why are you doing this?" Anna asked, a quiver in her voice.

"Money. Your father left you a lot of money, and I want it."

"Then take it, there's no need to kill me. I'll do whatever you want, I'll sign over the money."

"It's too late for that now. You should have died in Kansas City. Everyone would have assumed you were killed because of your mother."

"How did you find me?" This time her voice was stronger.

"We followed your mother. The Great Victoria Bishop. Mummy must not love you very much. She didn't come until we burned down her house."

Caleb sneaked a glance and whipped back again.

"You're lying," Anna said. "Why would my father leave the money to me? He's never even met me."

"He tried, but your mother turned him away. One word—" Mrs. Bekker's voice dripped with frustration "—one word in his will shut me out. He left all his money to his *natural* heir."

"Then you're not really my sister."

"Of course not. I was three years old when my mother married your father. She died the year I married Harvey. Your father didn't think we deserved any money after that. Said he only took care of us for my mother's sake." Her tone turned shrill. "Your father owes me."

There was more to the story than what she was saying, of that Caleb was certain.

"What do you hope to accomplish by this?" Anna implored. "You'll be murderers. Living on the run."

"No one will ever know what happened here. When your lover returns, we'll kill him, too. People will think it was a lovers' quarrel." She smoothed her eyebrow with one gloved pinkie. "I am accustomed to a certain manner of living. Crime doesn't pay as well as it used to."

"You lied to Mr. Elder," Anna continued. "You were never here to buy horses."

Excellent. She was keeping them talking, keeping them distracted.

The man chuckled. "You're finally catching up. The wife here is next in line for the money, and I've a mind to settle down."

Caleb moved quietly through his bedroom. He retrieved his gun and checked the chamber, then returned to the hallway. He'd heard enough, and Reinhart should be in position by now. With the marshal on his way, so much the better.

Pulling back the hammer, he stepped into the light. "Let her go."

Mrs. Bekker spun around. "You'll have to shoot me first."

This was the same woman from Kansas City, all right. The same unnaturally blond hair and glittery cold eyes. He shifted his gun a notch to the right. "No one wins here. Turn around and go, and we'll forget all this ever happened."

He had no intention of keeping that promise, but the Bekkers didn't need to know that.

Anna sat awkwardly on the edge of her chair, her face pale. Caleb tore his gaze away from the distraction. "C'mon, Bekker, you strike me as a gambling man. You've played the odds before. You know you can't win this."

Mr. Bekker aimed the gun at Anna. "I don't have to win. I just have to eliminate the competition."

Husband and wife exchanged a glance and Mrs. Bekker lunged. Caleb fired. Another shot sounded. Then another. Gunpowder smoke filled the room.

He coughed and stumbled toward Anna.

Mr. Bekker lay on his back on the floor, his eyes sightless. Mrs. Bekker backed away from his lifeless form, her gaze skittering toward the door.

Reinhart loomed over the body. "I hope you're a good vet, because you're a terrible shot."

He jerked one thumb over his shoulder and indicated the hole in the window. "I think you hit the tree out front, if that's any consolation." The man tipped his hat at Anna. "You have my vote the next time."

Anna launched herself at Caleb, and he caught her against his chest.

Mrs. Bekker dashed for the door and collided with Marshal Cain on the porch.

He grasped her around the upper arm and guided her back into the house. "Not leaving so soon, are you?"

She shot him a look of pure loathing and flounced back to the chair Anna had abandoned, not even glancing at her husband.

The detective nudged Mr. Bekker's still body with his booted toe. "He killed my partner. I owed him one. I asked poor Owen to help me out, to ask a few questions while he was working on the Phillips case. They killed him for it."

"He knew," Mrs. Bekker snarled. "He saw us that day—the second time we tried killing that tramp. We knew he was watching Mrs. Phillips. We stuffed him in her trunk. Figured he could fail at both cases. Served him right."

The woman was clearly mad, her eyes wild and unfocused. Caleb tucked Anna against his chest and turned. "We'll be out back if you need us."

The marshal rubbed his chin. "We'll be busy for the better part of the night, that much is certain."

Caleb left Anna for a moment while he lit a lantern, then led her out the back and into the barn.

She glanced around and rubbed her shoulders. Caleb draped his coat over her and unlatched the barn door. Pipsqueak leaped out of the darkness as though he'd been shot out of a cannon.

Anna laughed and patted his head. "I missed you, too." She half turned. "How did you find me?"

"Jasper saw them take you."

"And you rode to the rescue."

"Something like that." He flashed a grin. "I have a feeling you'd have rescued yourself. I just simplified things."

She tugged her lower lip between her teeth. "I've been thinking about what you said…."

"Forget it."

"No, I won't. What if I stayed? We can…we can try. See how things are between us."

He pushed off and crossed the distance, sweeping her into his arms. "That's a nice idea. I'll tell you what—why don't you go back to St. Louis? Stay a while. Sort things out with your mother. If you still feel the same way in six months, you can come back."

She hugged him more tightly, and he prayed she never saw through his ruse. She'd never return. Once she acclimated to her own life again, she'd forget all about him.

She'd had a scare this evening. They all had. Her feelings were confused, jumbled. She was mistaking her fear and gratitude for something more. He wasn't going to take advantage of that.

"What if...what if I go for a few weeks? If you're feelings are the same..." Her voice trailed off.

He perched on a bale of hay and tucked her against his side. Pipsqueak clambered up and rested his head on her knee.

"Have you ever read *Black Beauty*?" he asked, changing the subject to something neutral, something he hoped she'd understand later.

"Everyone has."

"That story is the real reason I became a veterinarian. Anna Sewell wrote that animals do not suffer less because they have no words. That idea stuck with me. Words have power. I grew up on a farm. I never thought much about the treatment of animals beyond their general welfare. But Anna Sewell showed me empathy, and that changed me. Your words changed me."

"You've already got the vote," she scoffed. "Why would you care what I have to say?"

"Because I care about what you care about. Because your passion is infectious, because you have a way of sharing your empathy with others. Whatever you do, whatever path you choose, never forget that."

She rubbed her cheek against his shoulder and yawned. "This has been a very long day."

She hadn't understood what he was trying to say. Maybe she never would. Caleb held her away from him. "I'll walk you home. You're dead on your feet. It's been a long night, and you have a train to catch tomorrow."

"Is that tomorrow already?"

He walked her back to her home, each caught up in

their own thoughts. Izetta was waiting on the porch; she caught sight of them and quickly closed the distance.

"What happened? I turned around and you two were gone. Then the marshal dashed off, and Caleb was nowhere to be found. I feared the worst."

"It's a long story, and you'll need a strong cup of coffee."

She shrugged out of Caleb's coat and handed it to him. He fisted the material in his hands. "I'll see you tomorrow."

She kept hold of the coat and he ran his index finger down the back of her hand.

"Do you know what I remember from *Black Beauty*?" she asked, her eyes luminous in the pale moonlight.

He shook his head.

"'It is good people who make good places.'"

Izetta urged her inside, and he waited as the door closed behind them.

Six months, six weeks, six years. What did time matter? She was never coming back. She'd forget all about him soon enough.

He'd gone and done the one thing he'd promised he'd never do. He'd gone and fallen in love with a woman who could never love him in return.

He was a fool and he didn't care. His brief time with Anna was worth a lifetime of suffering.

Chapter Eighteen

After Anna had finished her tale, Izetta rose, sensing Anna and her mother needed time together.

As soon as they were alone again, Anna turned toward her mother. "Tell me. Tell me about him."

"This isn't the time. All this fuss and shooting. Things like this don't happen in St. Louis."

"Mother."

Victoria Bishop heaved a great sigh. "You don't understand. You can't. It was the war. People were dying every day. They were dying faster than we could bury them. My own brother joined up. He was only fifteen, and lied about his age. I assume the army knew full well he was too young, he was little more than a boy. By that time, no one cared. There weren't enough men, there weren't enough volunteers to replace the dead. He was killed within a month. They didn't even inform my parents. We read his name in the papers, we read his name along with all the rest."

Anna shook her head. "I never knew. You never told me."

"That's when I finally understood my purpose, that's

when I knew I had a calling. If women had the vote, there'd be no wars, there'd be no more dead bodies."

Anna had her doubts. Mrs. Bekker had seemed perfectly willing to kill without a second thought. Anna kept her views private, not wanting to interrupt her mother.

"Your father was born under a lucky star." Her mother snorted delicately. "He was one of the few who survived, and I hated him for it. He came home on leave, after I'd discovered I was pregnant. He no longer looked at me as a woman after that. I was a mother. A wife. All of our grand plans for the future were dashed. We were going to travel Europe, see the world, to have adventures. He was done with all that after the war. All that death had changed him. I gave him his freedom because I wanted my own. I wasn't going to raise a passel of brats because he'd suddenly decided to settle down."

A kick in the chest could not have hurt worse. Anna was a person, not a nuisance. And yet her mother's attitude toward her finally fell into place. Victoria Bishop would not play at domesticity. Anna was little more than an experiment for her mother, a tool for notoriety. Miss Victoria Bishop was not shackled by the conventions of motherhood.

Her mother rested her elbow on the arm of the chair and cupped her chin. "I agreed to keep his name out of the papers, and he agreed to stay out of my life."

Anna flinched from the bitterness in her mother's voice. "He simply walked away?"

"A lowering realization, isn't it? The male is a fickle species. His heart must not have been too broken. He was married within the year. Look what it got him. A stepdaughter who hated him and nearly killed his own flesh and blood."

Yet he'd left her an inheritance. He'd tried to find her. Somewhere along the way he must have questioned his choices. Anna collapsed onto a chair.

"Still, you proved useful," her mother said. "Bearing an out-of-wedlock child kept me in the news. Kept the cause in the news."

"I'm glad I was of service to you."

"Don't be peevish. You're not naive, you know how this works."

Her mother replaced her glasses and began scribbling out her correspondence, effectively dismissing Anna.

The fog that had enveloped her since the shooting cleared. She didn't want to believe that Caleb loved her because she didn't believe anyone could truly love her. Not without conditions. Not unless she brought some purpose, some value to the relationship, and she had nothing to give him.

She stepped outside and stared at the moon. A few moments later, Izetta joined her.

"How are you holding up?"

"Well enough I suppose."

"What are thinking?"

Anna studied the night sky. "I'm wondering about God. I'm wondering about forgiveness. What does it even mean, and why does any of this matter?"

Izetta walked a few paces into the garden. "I don't think I know anyone who hasn't struggled with forgiveness. After the war, we all had to forgive. There was so much pain, so much suffering. People think of forgiveness as chopping away at something, hacking at a suffocating milkweed vine until you are sweaty and exhausted and there is nothing left, not even the roots. An afternoon's work followed by a cold lemonade on the back porch.

"I always thought of forgiveness as a seed, something you plant in the best spot in the garden. A place with neither too much sun nor too much shade. A delicate seedling you fertilize and water and protect from an early frost. A plant you nurture through drought and flood, carefully guarding the first fragile blooms from encroaching weeds and voracious rabbits.

"Until one day you realize your patient labor has borne fruit, the roots have grown deep enough, and the stem is stout enough to survive the strongest wind.

"Even then you must tend forgiveness through the seasons, through harsh winters and dry springs. Like any garden, forgiveness is something you must never neglect for long."

She wasn't a legacy, she was a person. A person who had the right to choose her own future.

"Thank you," Anna said. "Thank you for everything you've done. For your friendship, for your advice. You have become very dear to me."

"And you to me." Izetta passed Anna on her way back inside and caught her shoulder in a brief embrace. "If my sons had grown and married, I hope they would have picked someone like you. I would have been honored to have you as a daughter-in-law."

Izetta stood and dusted her hands. "Don't stay up too long, you've a busy day tomorrow."

A busy day. A busy day of sitting on a train. She was returning home to a burned-out hole in the ground. All of her possessions except the ones she carried with her were gone. At the very least, she had nothing left to lose, which left her a certain freedom.

She stared at the sky and another line from *Black Beauty* drifted over her, the words resonating in her heart.

"My troubles are all over, and I am at home; and often before I am quite awake, I fancy I am still at the orchard at Birtwick, standing with my friends under the apple trees."

Where would her memories drift when her troubles were over? Anna feared she already knew the answer.

The following morning, she woke to the rain, packed to the rain and watched as two men loaded the wagon while rain sluiced off her umbrella. She'd said her good-byes to Izetta in the rain, both of them promising to write often.

Her mother had limped through the process with considerable grumbling about everything from the men's handling of the baggage to the hard bench seat.

Anna stared at the town and thought of the past few weeks. She'd been shot, nearly stabbed, she'd discovered she had a father and lost him in the same instant. She'd discovered she had a stepsibling when that woman had tried to kill her.

All in all it had been a momentous month.

She'd forgotten that is was the second Tuesday in November until she saw the bunting outside the post office. Another election gone by, and still women were denied the vote.

She was doing the right thing by leaving. A few weeks away and both of them could sort out their feelings. They'd been through a lot together. They needed space, they needed quiet. She'd test the waters in a few weeks. A letter to Jo with a few dropped hints should suffice. If Caleb wanted to see her in a few weeks, they'd see what happened from there. No need to rush things. Her mother required her assistance. This was the perfect time for them to separate. Anna would buy her own town house, and perhaps she and Caleb would strike up a correspondence.

Everything neat and tidy and devoid of the melodrama that had plagued her life these past few weeks.

One of the wheels of their carriage became stuck in the mire, forcing them out of the conveyance and into the mud. Anna assisted her mother onto the boardwalk, and they traveled the rest of the distance on foot.

She reached the train depot and found a knot of women huddled beneath the eves of the telegraph office.

One of the blurred forms broke free and dashed through the rain toward Anna. On closer inspection, she realized the woman was Jo, and she wore a Votes for Women banner across her chest.

"We're giving you a proper send-off," she said. "We're protesting as the men vote."

She grinned as though it was the Fourth of July and not a damp and drizzly November afternoon.

Tony joined her. The younger girl didn't hold an umbrella; instead she let the rain drip off her Stetson hat.

Anna did a quick head count and realized more than half the women from the town were staring at her, all of them wearing banners.

She turned to Jo. "You did this for me?"

"Mostly for you. Plus, it's good for the men around here to stand up and take notice sometimes. We can't have them taking us for granted."

"But it's raining."

Tony tipped her head forward, and a river of water

trickled from her hat. "A little rain never ruined a good parade."

Her mother took in the display with a curt nod. "How quaint. Come along, Anna. I'll catch a chill in this rain."

She trudged toward the waiting train, her walking stick splashing through the puddles.

The porter assisted her onto the train while Anna remained rooted in place.

Her mother gestured. "Come along."

"No," Anna called over the rain. "I'm staying."

"Don't be absurd." She shook her head. "Come over here this instant."

Anna walked the distance, then paused. "I'm staying here."

"Do you think that countrified veterinarian can make you happy?"

Anna blinked.

"I saw how you looked at each other. I'm not an idiot. He'll saddle you with a half dozen children and a miserable existence."

"Maybe that doesn't sound miserable to me."

"You don't know what you're saying. I groomed you for something better. I raised you for something more."

"No. You raised me to be independent. That's what I'm doing. I'm asserting my independence."

"If you choose that man over me, I will never speak to you again."

"You know what I just realized?" Anna said. "Caleb would never make me choose. That's why he asked me to leave. He wanted me to know I didn't have to choose between him and the cause. Besides, I am in charge of the flowers at the quilting bee and a Bishop does not shirk her duties."

"You're babbling now. I will not speak to you when you're in this…this emotional state." She banged her walking stick against the train deck.

"A man will ruin a woman faster than rain will ruin a parade."

"That's the difference between you and me," Anna said, turning away. "I never did mind a little rain."

The train whistle blew, and Anna didn't look back. She strode into the crowd of women, and they let up a cheer. Jo caught her around the shoulder. "You're missing your train."

"I'm not leaving!" Anna shouted. "I love your brother."

Jo whooped and did a little jump. She slipped in the mud and lost her balance, careening into Anna. Anna slid backward and bumped into Tony. They all fell into a heap in a chilly mud puddle, laughing.

For the first time in a long while, the future was rife with possibilities.

Caleb stepped into the barn and handed Pipsqueak a stem of roses. "I figure you're feeling just about as rotten as I do right now."

"I hope those roses didn't come from Izetta's garden," Anna said.

He froze. "You should be gone by now. I heard the train whistle blow."

"I decided to stay."

Pipsqueak trotted past him, the roses forgotten.

"Why?" he asked, wondering if this was all a dream.

"Because of something somebody said to me about the power of words."

He turned toward her and gaped. "What happened to you? You're covered in mud."

She smiled, her face smudged, her clothes streaked with dirt, looking a bit like the bedraggled kittens they'd rescued and more beautiful than he'd ever seen her.

"Jo and I had a slight accident."

He fished his handkerchief from his pocket and approached her. "I have a feeling this isn't the only trouble the two of you will cause."

"You're probably right."

He rubbed a smudge from her forehead. "How about I move to St. Louis? I hear it's a beautiful city."

"And why would you do that?"

A spot of dirt near her temple caught his attention and he dabbed at the mark. "To be near you."

"Then you would be terribly disappointed, because I don't have any plans to return."

"Why is that?"

"Because St. Louis is far too boring. Cimarron Springs is much livelier. There are caves for hidden treasures, and the finest Harvest Festival in the state."

"Anything else?" A bit of dirt on her ear needed tending.

"There are good people here. I read in a book once that good people make good places."

He leaned back, creating some distance between them. "You don't have to do this, Anna. I don't mind moving. Your work is important. I won't have you give that up."

She placed a finger over his lips, silencing him. "I won't be giving anything up. The cause will always be a part of my life, a part of who I am. That will never change. I don't have all the answers yet and I don't know quite how things will turn out, but I know that this is where I need to be. With you."

He remained steadfast, hardening his resolve. "You were meant for something better than this."

Her lips tightened. "I'm not a legacy. I'm a person with thoughts and feelings and hopes and dreams. All my life someone else has told me what I should do, how I should live my life. I don't know who I'm meant to be, and I need the space to find out."

A silent war raged within him. "I can't let you do this."

A shadow passed over her eyes. "Would you love me if I was ordinary?"

"Of course. How can you even ask such a thing?"

"Then let me decide my own future. Even if that future is very ordinary."

He cupped her cheek and ran his thumb along her chin, dislodging another speck of dirt. "You will never ever be ordinary."

"I've never saved a life," she said. "And that is a very extraordinary thing indeed."

His expression softened. "That's the most amazing thing I've ever done."

"Life with me will always be challenging."

"What if you grow bored here? What if you find married life unsatisfying?"

Her lips parted. "Who said anything about marriage?"

The teasing glint in her eye gave her away. "I'm very conventional. I demand you make an honest man out of me."

"I'm not very conventional at all. I still haven't learned how to cook. I can only make eggs and toast."

"I'm a very good cook."

She brushed the hair from his forehead. "I'm dazzled by your looks and enthralled by your kind heart."

"You do have a way with words, Miss Bishop. Have you ever thought of being a writer?"

"Actually, I've given that thought quite a bit of consideration. I want to write about women, about their struggles, about their pain. I want to make a very small difference in a very big way."

"I'll buy extra ink and paper."

"At least we don't have to worry about explaining our engagement to the town."

"I think they knew we were meant for each other."

"I think you're right. Even the goat knew."

Caleb grinned. "That is one smart goat."

He knelt and took her muddy hand between his own. "Anna Bishop, will you marry me?"

"Of course I will."

"Good."

"Now kiss me," she ordered.

He gladly complied. Their kiss was full of tender promise, a gentle assault on her senses.

"You don't play fair," she said.

"I know." He grinned.

She returned his smile. "Kiss me again."

Caleb decided then and there that it wasn't a bad thing to have a woman in charge, not a bad thing at all.

Epilogue

Three years later

Anna snatched her bonnet from the stand near the door. She checked her appearance in the mirror and swiftly tied the strings beneath her chin.

Caleb waited patiently, holding one-year-old Susan in his arms. "Don't worry," he said, "they can't start without you."

"Yes, but the mayor should at least be on time."

Women had won the municipal vote in Kansas that year and Anna had run for mayor the very next election.

She'd won by a landslide.

Caleb caught her gaze in the mirror. "We might even have time to stop by the new house and see what progress they've made."

"There's no time!" After Susan's birth, they'd realized their house was far too small for their growing family. "I heard Maxwell teasing you about the money. You're not annoyed, are you?"

"I rather enjoy being a kept man." Caleb grinned.

Anna rolled her eyes. Her father had left her more

money than she could possibly spend in a lifetime, especially considering their modest lifestyle. Figuring out ways to donate the surplus was a job in and of itself.

She adjusted her collar. "All right. I'm ready to cut the ribbon on Cimarron Springs' first ever salon for women only."

Caleb pecked her on the cheek. "I wonder who donated the money for the remodel of the old haberdashery."

Anna assumed an air of innocence. "I couldn't say. Although events turned out to be quite fortuitous. Since Mr. Phillips passed away last spring, Mrs. Phillips needed a source of income and a place to stay that accommodated Jane. The salon is the perfect solution."

She turned toward the door, but something in his expression stopped her. "What's wrong?"

"I wasn't going to tell you until after the ceremony, but you received a letter today."

Anna's chest tightened. "From the publisher?"

She'd spent the past two years writing letters and gathering stories, interviewing women and compiling their heroic journeys into an anthology. She'd sent off the manuscript months ago.

"I can't read it," she said. "I'll wait until this evening."

"Whatever you say."

She made it as far as the door and then stopped. "Hand it over."

Caleb complied, and she tore open the envelope, scanning the first few lines, then clutched the letter against her chest.

"They're going to publish my book."

Caleb grinned. "I never had any doubts."

She smothered him and Susan with kisses.

Caressing the back of her head, Caleb pressed his forehead against hers. "You are one extraordinary woman."

Anna smiled, her heart swelling with love, Susan squirming merrily between them. "I am one happy woman. Thank you for supporting me."

"Always," he said simply. "Always."

* * * * *

Dear Reader,

I hope you enjoyed getting to know another McCoy. There are lots more stories featuring the McCoy brothers and their cousins coming your way in the Prairie Courtship series.

It's hard to believe women in America have had the vote for fewer than 100 years. In July of 1848, the Seneca Falls Convention issued the first formal demand authored by American women for suffrage. More than seventy years later, in August of 1920, the Nineteenth Amendment to the Constitution received the necessary thirty-sixth state ratification with a narrow victory in Tennessee. The deciding vote was issued by Harry Burn, a twenty-four-year-old senator who received a letter from his mother urging him to vote in favor of the amendment.

You may also be surprised to note that although the thirty-six state ratification made the Nineteenth Amendment a federal law, the last state to formally ratify the amendment was Mississippi—in 1984. The history of the suffrage movement is fascinating, and I hope I have inspired you to learn more!

I love to hear from readers. You can email me at sherri@sherrishackelford.com, visit my website at sherrishackelford.com, or if you're feeling nostalgic, drop me a letter at PO Box 116, Elkhorn, NE 68022.

Sherri Shackelford

SPECIAL EXCERPT FROM

Love Inspired® HISTORICAL

Nurse Catherine Stanway is kidnapped by Drew Wallin's brother to help their ailing mother... but she soon realizes that she's also been chosen by Drew's family to be his bride!

Enjoy this sneak peek from WOULD-BE WILDERNESS WIFE by Regina Scott!

How could his brother have been so boneheaded? Drew glanced over his shoulder at the youth. The boy had absolutely no remorse for what he'd done. Where had Drew gone wrong?

"I'm really very sorry," Drew apologized to Catherine. "I don't know what got into him. He was raised better."

"Out in the woods, you said," she replied.

"On the lake," he told her. "My father brought us to Seattle about fifteen years ago from Wisconsin and chose a spot far out. He said a man needed something to gaze out on in the morning besides his livestock or his neighbors."

She smiled as if the idea pleased her. "And your mother?" she asked, shifting on the wooden bench. "Is she truly ill?"

"She came down with a fever nearly a fortnight ago. I hope you'll be able to help her before we return you to Seattle tomorrow."

"You did not seem so sure of my skills earlier, sir."

With Levi right behind him, he wasn't about to admit that his fear had been for his future, not the lack of her skills. "We've known Doc for years," he hedged.

"My father's patients felt the same way. There is nothing like the trusted relationship of your family doctor. But I will do whatever I can to help your mother."

Levi's smug voice floated up from behind. "I knew she'd come around."

Drew was more relieved than he'd expected at the thought of Catherine's help. "As you can see," he said to her, "my brother has a bad habit of acting or talking without thinking."

"My brother was the same way," she assured him. "He borrowed my father's carriage more than once, drove it all over the county. He joined the Union Army on his eighteenth birthday before he'd even received a draft notice."

"Sounds like my kind of fellow," Levi said, kneeling so that his head came between them. "Did he journey West with you?"

Though her smile didn't waver, her voice came out flat. "No. He was killed at the Battle of Five Forks in Virginia."

Levi looked stricken as he glanced between her and Drew. "I'm sorry, ma'am. I didn't know."

"Of course you didn't," she replied, but Drew saw that her hands were clasped tightly in her lap as if she were fighting with herself not to say more.

"I'm sorry for your loss," Drew said. "That must have been hard on you and your parents."

"My mother died when I was nine," she said. "My father served as a doctor in the army. He died within days of Nathan."

Drew wanted to reach out, clasp her hand, promise her the future would be brighter. But he couldn't control the future, and she was his to protect only until he returned her to Seattle. He had enough on his hands without taking on a woman new to the frontier.

Don't miss WOULD-BE WILDERNESS WIFE
by Regina Scott,
available March 2015 wherever
Love Inspired® Historical books and ebooks are sold!

LIHEXP0215

SPECIAL EXCERPT FROM

Love Inspired®

A young Amish woman yearns for true love.
Read on for a preview of A WIFE FOR JACOB
by Rebecca Kertz, the next book in her
***LANCASTER COUNTY WEDDINGS** series.*

Annie stood by the dessert table when she saw Jedidiah Lapp chatting with his wife, Sarah. She'd been heartbroken when Jed had broken up with her, and then married Sarah Mast.

Seeing the two of them together was a reminder of what she didn't have. Annie wanted a husband—and a family. But how could she marry when no one showed an interest in her? She blinked back tears. She'd work hard to be a wife a husband would appreciate. She wanted children, to hold a baby in her arms, a child to nurture and love.

She sniffled, looked down and straightened the dessert table. And the pitchers and jugs of iced tea and lemonade.

"May I have some lemonade?" a deep, familiar voice said.

Annie looked up. "Jacob." His expression was serious as he studied her. She glanced down and noticed the fine dusting of corn residue on his dark jacket. "Lemonade?" she echoed self-consciously.

"*Ja*. Lemonade," he said with amusement.

She quickly reached for the pitcher. She poured his lemonade into a plastic cup, only chancing a glance at him when she handed him his drink.

"How is the work going?" she asked conversationally.

LIEXP0215

"We are nearly finished with the corn. We'll be cutting hay next." He lifted the glass to his lips and took a swallow.

Warmth pooled in her stomach as she watched the movement of his throat. "How's *Dat?*" she asked. She had seen him chatting with her father earlier.

Jacob glanced toward her *dat* with a small smile. "He says he's not tired. He claims he's enjoying the view too much." His smile dissipated. "No doubt he'll be exhausted later."

Annie agreed. "I'll check on him in a while." She hesitated. "Are you hungry? I can fix you a plate—"

He gazed at her for several heartbeats with his striking golden eyes. "*Ne,* I'll fix one myself." He finished his drink and held out his glass to her. "May I?"

She hurried to refill his glass. With a crooked smile and a nod of thanks, Jacob accepted the refill and left. The warm flutter in her stomach grew stronger as she watched him walk away, stopping briefly to chat with Noah and Rachel, his brother and sister-in-law.

Annie glanced over where several men were being dished up plates of food. She then caught sight of Jacob walking along with his brother Eli. The contrast of Jacob's dark hair and Eli's light locks struck her as they disappeared into the barn. They came out a few minutes later, Eli carrying tools, Jacob leading one of her father's workhorses.

As if he sensed her regard, Jacob looked over and locked gazes with her.

Will Annie ever find the husband of her heart?
Pick up A WIFE FOR JACOB to find out.
Available March 2015,
wherever Love Inspired® books and ebooks are sold.

LIEXP0215